THE FAVOR

THE FAVOR

STEVE BADMAN

THE FAVOR

Copyright © 2024 by Steve Badman
ISBN: 978-1-944653-34-7 (HC)
ISBN: 978-1-944653-35-4 (PB 6 x 9)
ISBN: 978-1-944653-6-1 (eBook)

Cover Art and interior formatting designed by Anita Dugan-Moore of Cyber-Bytz, www.cyber-bytz.com.

Author photo provided by photobywendy llc

If you would like permission to use material from this book for any reason other than for review purposes, please contact the publisher at: imzadipublishing@outlook.com.

Published by Imzadi Publishing, LLC
"Our Only Limitation is Your Imagination"
www.imzadipublishing.com

Printed in the U.S.A.

ACKNOWLEDGMENT

It's truly amazing how much of a driving force a little encouragement, enthusiasm, and positivity can be. The impact is exponentially larger than the act itself. This sentiment applies to any endeavor but in this case, I am referring specifically to the publishing of my first novel. I would like to thank the following people for their impact on me.

Family first and I thank and truly appreciate my wife, Wendy; our daughters, Ally and Stacey; Mom and Dad and my mother-in-law, Diane. Your collective and individual support means everything to me.

The Favor was not my first attempt at writing a novel. I believe it ranks around number five or six. Those early attempts were also met with enthusiasm, encouragement, and surprise. I leaned on some people who were not family for their thoughts way back when I got the bug to write. Their feedback and positivity was and still is great appreciated. Dr. Karen Detweiler, Katie Nicholas, and the Bruce and Melissa Johnson family. Thank you for trudging through my initial writings and for concealing your surprise that I made a book that did not involve crayons!

Anne Hoskins. My Aunt Annie provided upbeat reviews and red-inked, underlined scolding over my (very infrequent) use of the F word were immensely appreciated. She knew I had finally gotten a publishing deal but passed before the book was printed. You will be missed.

Dr. Curt Herr. Thank you for your suggestions, and positivity.

Mark and Karen Bilak. Again, the positivity is so very much appreciated. Mark… your questions made me work harder. You found things nobody else did and helped add credibility to the story. Thank you for making me think just a little deeper.

Arthur Vidro. I may not agree that The Green Lantern is better than Spiderman but your wordsmithing is amazing. Thank you for the detailed critique.

Janice Grove and Anita Dugan-Moore, thank you for giving me a chance. What once was a fantasy, turned, dream, turned goal has become a reality because you gave me an opportunity.

Lastly, I'd like to thank the few, and I mean very, very few, naysayers that I have encountered. Either through complete apathetic ambivalence, or a scoffing chuckle, you challenged me to prove you wrong. While positivity and enthusiasm is so very much appreciated, strong doubt and a "You? Write a book? Yeah right" is a huge motivator as well. Thanks for suggesting I'm not good enough.

Contents

Chapter 1

Monday

Lisa Turner lay on the couch pretending to sleep as her husband, Brian, trundled through the living room carrying his scarred and stained lunch box, an equally battered clipboard with job files and notepaper, and his dented travel mug filled with black coffee out the door. He said goodbye but she ignored him. Same shit, different day.

Sadie, their younger of two daughters, was already in the truck waiting. She was a sophomore at Justin C. Smith High School and was the type of kid who loved school. A gifted student who absorbed information like a sponge, she was ranked number two in her class. She loved sports and had tons of friends. Life was good for Sadie Turner.

Life was also good for Hannah Turner, the oldest, who had graduated and was now a freshman at Gettysburg College where she played soccer on the women's team and was pulling a 3.7 GPA. Also, a very popular kid who did not succumb to peer pressure and the type of person who fit in wherever she went. She was a morning person, rare in the college culture, and had already texted **HAPPY MONDAY** to her father.

Sadie had started the truck and was rapidly air-drumming to Disturbed's *Ten Thousand Fists*. It was just getting warm inside when Brian handed his mug and clipboard to her. She set the clipboard beside her and wedged the mug into the cup holder in the grimy console then resumed her morning jam session drumming wildly yet keeping her head relatively motionless so as to not mess up what promised to be a good hair day.

Brian loaded his big yellow compound miter saw, his lunch box, and some materials into the bed of the truck, then climbed in. He grinned at Sadie, left the volume where it was, and put the job-worn Dodge 3500 work truck into gear. Ten minutes later, they were outside the school entrance. A lot of people drove their kids to school, so the line always backed up. Brian didn't mind. He enjoyed the time with Sadie.

The line crept closer to the school entrance and Sadie said goodbye. As Brian watched her walk away gathering friends with every stride, he was startled by a knock on his window. He cranked the driver-side window down with a curious look on his face. An impatient-appearing man stood outside sporting an insincere smile. He had never seen this guy before, and Brian knew just about everyone in the tight knit Upper Bucks County community.

"Hey, you Brian Turner?" the man inquired with a New York accent.

"Depends on who's asking," Brian replied with a friendly smile and a nod.

"I hear you're pretty good at fixin' old farmhouses." The man pushed an unmarked cardboard box through the open window. "I got a job for you, but I can't talk about it now. Everything's inside the box. I'll check back with you later today."

Brian looked down at the box. "Where's the job…." The man had already left. In the side-view mirror Brian could see him getting into a gray Cadillac XTS with New York plates. He stared curiously until Carla Gibbons honked for him to move along. Brian frowned at her through the rearview mirror. He put his truck in gear then eased by the meandering kids until he came to the exit. He glanced at the box again, reached to open it then heard another impatient honk from Gibbons. He had never liked that woman nor her miserable daughter. Resisting the urge to flip her off, Brian left the lot and went to work.

When Brian arrived at the job he was inundated with questions from the electrician and plumber. Their time and material meters were spinning. At eighty-five and one hundred dollars an hour respectively, he needed to stay ahead of them to keep them productive. The day turned into a full sprint so it wasn't until Brian got back into his truck to go home before he had a moment to examine the box. He sliced open the tape and peered inside. There was a wad of twenties and hundreds, a cell phone, some kind of futuristic-looking bracelet, and two legal-sized envelopes, one marked **Job** and the other marked **Reminder**.

Brian flipped through the cash. He then counted it. Five thousand dollars in hundreds and a few twenties. His spider sense was tingling. It was a reference to *The Amazing Spider-man* comics that he and other contractors would use when a potential client just didn't seem right. After more than twenty-five years as a self-employed carpenter and general contractor, Brian could sense when someone might be trouble and he either priced the job accordingly or, more often than not, refused to take the person as a client.

He picked up the cell phone and stared at it, perplexed. His spider sense was now more than a tingle. It was screaming to return the box and run away from this guy. He had dealt with control freaks before but being given his own cell phone? That was a first and more than Brian cared to deal with. The phone suddenly vibrated in his hand, causing him to jump. He stared at it as it hummed a second time, not recognizing the number then wondering why he should have. He flipped open the phone and pressed the green button.

"Hello?"

"Brian! You answered on the second ring, so I guess you've opened the box. What do you think?" The man's voice was husky with a thick Brooklyn accent making the question sound more like *waddya tink*.

"Uh, well, I think I'm pretty busy right now. I …"

"You didn't open the envelopes yet, did you?"

"No. But look, I appreciate the confidence you have in me to give me a deposit, but I am really busy. How did you hear about me anyway?"

The Voice sighed heavily. "Open the envelopes, Brian."

Brian rolled his eyes. He didn't have time for this. It was late and he wanted to get home. He doubted Lisa had even begun to cook dinner so he would have to make it or if Sadie didn't have much homework, he would stick the chore to her. Lisa was too busy with her TV shows or on the phone with her mother or any one of the myriad people she spent day after unproductive day talking to. Or she may have been drunk already. Begrudgingly he tore open the envelope marked **Job**.

The envelope contained three eight by ten color photos. One was an un-posed portrait of a very tastefully dressed man that Brian guessed was in his early sixties. Another photograph was of the same man eating at an outdoor café and the third was an overhead shot of a very large house with ostentatious grounds surrounded by a large wall. A forest surrounded three sides of the property to the point where it butted up to a large lake. There was one paper with the name Dr. Cooper Rollins, an address, his height and approximate weight, and general comments about his daily routine.

"What's this *job*?" Brian asked with poorly concealed annoyance. "All I see are pictures of some guy in…,.." he squinted to read before snatching his scratched reading glasses from the dashboard. "New Concord, Kentucky? *Kentucky*? I'm not going to Kentucky for a job and what's this have to do with carpentry?"

"Open the other envelope", said The Voice. The man's impatience was also poorly concealed.

"Look sir, I really don't see how this can apply to me. I am not interested in whatever you need done. This is getting…" Brian froze mid-sentence. He had opened the other envelope while he was talking and what he saw made his blood run cold.

More pictures. Lots of pictures. Lisa sleeping on the couch with an empty wine bottle next to her, Sadie at her friend's house, Hannah at Gettysburg College, Brian and Sadie stacking firewood, and even pictures of their three dogs. There were photos of his house, too, all of them were *taken from the inside*.

"Look asshole," Brian growled, "I'm going to the police with this. You are one messed up dude. This conversation is over."

Brian was about to click off when The Voice said, "You owe us a favor. Did you forget?"

"A favor? I don't even know who the hell you are!"

"Let me remind you then. Remember a cornfield outside of Stroudsburg? September 1986?"

Brian couldn't breathe. He opened his mouth, but nothing came out. He began sweating profusely. Trying to speak again he only managed a dry, whispered croak.

"Ah, so you do remember."

"That was over thirty years ago! I was twenty-two years old! You can't be serious. And I don't know who the hell you are, but I dealt with someone else, not you."

There was a long sigh on the phone but The Voice wasn't losing his patience this time, he seemed almost amused. "Okay, okay. I understand your point but you're wrong. Let me explain." The voice paused for effect. "Let's say your grandfather, Pop-pop Calvin not Grampa John, did…"

"You know the names of my grandfathers?" Brian screamed into the phone.

"Brian. It's my job to research the people I work with. I know everything about you. That's how I know I can *motivate* you to fulfill your obligation to my business." Brian was shocked into silence and the Voice continued. "As I was saying, let's say that Pop-pop Calvin helped you learn to ride a bike. That would be a personal favor. A gift of his time and his love for you, his only grandchild. And someday, if you were worth a shit, you might help him, I dunno, clean out his gutters or something. Another personal favor. Nobody really keeps score of personal favors. They're unofficial.

"Now, let's say Pop-pop Calvin bought stock in IBM back in the forties. And let's say he gave that stock to you. That stock would be worth something today, now, wouldn't it? You would own that stock. It's a tangible asset. IBM wouldn't tell you to get bent because they sold it to Pop-pop Calvin, right? You acquired that stock. Pop-pop Calvin gave them money to use and in turn they gave him a piece of the pie. That's like a business favor. See there's a difference because while you may not forget how he helped you ride a bike, that favor has no intrinsic value. The stock that Pop-pop Calvin *transferred* to you, well, that has value. It's a business favor which is a commodity, a *transferable* commodity.

"Back in that cornfield, the business that I took over and now operate, granted you a favor. A *business* favor, Brian. I own stock in you. It doesn't ever go away until I decide to cash it in and that is what I am doing right now."

Brian was trembling as he sat in his truck. His mind was racing in multiple directions. He could picture that night, that horrible, horrible night in the cornfield. He thought about the shocked and disappointed expressions his girls would have if they knew what he had done in his youth. And he thought about the vindicated smirk Lisa would have as he failed yet again in her eyes. Slowly he managed to ask, "What do you want me to do?"

"Atta boy," The Voice cheered into the phone. "That man in the picture? I need you to kill him."

A fresh and much stronger wave of panic slammed into Brian coursing through every nerve ending from his scalp to his toes. "Kill him?" Brian shouted, incredulous.

"Yell a little louder. Not sure if everyone around heard you the first time. Yes, kill him. Look, you're a hunter. You helped Sadie shoot that nice eight-point last year. It's no different than stalking a deer. You scout where the guy is, and I provided research on that, and you set up and you shoot him. Or whatever. I don't really care how you do it, just do it. Poison, bombs, electric, drowning. It doesn't matter, just do it." The Voice went silent for a beat then added, "By Friday."

Exasperated, Brian threw his hands in the air. He then began to get defiant. "Fly to Kentucky and kill a man by Friday. That's ridiculous. What if I don't do it?"

The Voice sighed. Brian could hear disappointment. "Well, Brian, in that case some of my men will show up at your house. We will shoot your dogs but only after we cut their legs off and let them flop around for a bit while your family watches. We will rape and torture Lisa and Sadie while you are forced to watch and the same will happen to Hannah although she is at Gettysburg so we will have to set up a web cam so you don't miss a thing. While this happens, we will also explain to them how you brought this upon them and how it could have so easily been avoided. I don't take kindly to reneging on a favor so we will use the choice that you made as an example to others. I can send you a video clip of how we set an example with someone else if you would like to watch it. I don't recommend it though. Kinda disturbing plus, Friday keeps getting closer."

Brian slumped behind the wheel. His head throbbed. This guy knew his family, their routines, even the dogs. He knew Brian's grandfathers. He thought back to the night in the cornfield and for a fleeting moment, he wished they had just shot him then.

"Look, Brian. You got a lot to process. I get that. So, you think about it and I will check in with you but let me fill you in on a few more rules. See that bracelet?"

"Yeah." Brian mumbled automatically. He was too numb to think.

"Okay, don't touch it yet until I explain how it works. It's a tracking device that my tech guys came up with. Once you click it together, it completes the circuit, and you cannot take it off until I say so. It's like a mood ring and cell phone all in one. Pretty clever if you ask me.

"The mood ring part shows body heat and pulse so I know you're still alive. And the cell phone part is like the child locator that you can get on cell phones these days. Although I noticed you don't use that function on Hannah's and Sadie's."

"I don't need to. They're good kids and I trust them to be where they say they'll be." It was another reflexive response. Stupefied, Brian was still staring blankly at the bracelet.

"Yeah, they are," agreed the voice. "They got nothing but bright futures unless you screw it up for them and no father I know would risk doing that." The voice let the barb sink deeply into Brian before going back to the bracelet. "Now, set the phone down near your wrist so I can hear you put the bracelet on. It makes a unique sound so I will know, plus you'll complete the circuit which turns it on."

Brian did as he was told and there was an audible click as the bracelet locked on.

"Hey! It works. Good job," the voice cheered. "Now the phone. I can call you as many times as I want although rest assured, it won't be often. You can only call me three times if you have a question or need guidance. Three times, Brian. The phone goes dead after the third call or if you remove the bracelet. And believe me," the voice paused then hissed a warning. "If you remove that bracelet before I tell you to, I will have men on your family faster than you can imagine. Got it?"

"Got it," Brian whispered.

"Good. Now you're a smart guy. You have a lot to figure out, so I am going to let you go. Besides, Sadie has soccer practice tonight and we both know damned well Lisa won't be taking her, so you have to get home. I tell you what, man, that travel team Sadie plays for did real good at that tournament in Bethesda last week. She's a real scrappy player. She doesn't take shit from anybody. I like that."

Brian stared at the steering wheel for several minutes before realizing The Voice had hung up. His hands were shaking too much to turn the key. His eyes welled up with tears and he broke down sobbing. He cried alone in his truck for a solid five minutes. Sadie did have practice that night. He was no longer surprised that The Voice knew that. Brian composed himself, stuffed the box under his seat, and drove home with the window down hoping the cold December air slapping his face would clear his mind.

Chapter 2

By the time he pulled into the driveway Brian had come up with a lie for Lisa. He needed to tell her he was going out of town for a few days on an emergency job for a good client. It wasn't the first time this had happened, but he usually gave her more advance notice. Her memory wasn't so good anymore, so he decided to *remind* her that he was leaving.

When he got home, Sadie had already made dinner. Lisa was on the couch holding a partially empty bottle of merlot, she only used a glass when company was around, talking to someone on the phone. Brian said hello but his greeting was ignored by Lisa. Their three Siberian huskies, Suzie, Arfie, and Murphy, however, enthusiastically welcomed him home.

Hannah had named the dog King Arfer when they first got him as a rescue eight years ago. The family agreed it was a stupid name, but it had made everyone laugh so hard that it stuck. They called him Arfie for short. As time went on, it turned out to be an appropriate name as King Arfer was a very vocal dog.

Brian dumped his lunch box and clipboard in the usual spot on the kitchen counter and gave Sadie a bigger-than-usual hug. "Da-ad," she said, making his name into two whiny syllables. She had hugged him back though. Sadie called, "Mom. Dinner." Then, without being prompted, began regaling him with the events of her school day.

They waited for a few minutes, but Lisa had continued talking, so Sadie and Brian began eating without her. Time was precious and they needed to leave for soccer practice. As they were finishing, Lisa shuffled into the kitchen, complained that her dinner was cold, and got another phone call. Brian and Sadie had eaten, cleaned up their dishes, and were out the door before Lisa had even sat down at the table.

Sadie happily talked non-stop on the fifty-minute drive to practice. Once there, she bounded from the family car and joined her travel soccer team, a group of talented under-sixteen-year-old athletes all excitedly chattering away at once yet still comprehending a myriad of unrelated topics. The U16 designation was as of a certain date and over half of the team, including Sadie, were now sixteen years old with the other half anxiously awaiting their birthday and the driver's permit that came with it.

The stream of babble never slowed as the team began their warm-ups. Brian had seen this phenomenon countless times with Hannah and never understood how eighteen girls could have eighteen unique high-speed conversations going on simultaneously and understand everything that was said along with the appropriate emotional reaction that each topic required. Now it was Sadie's turn to partake in the uniquely feminine communication. Brian smiled and shook his head in disbelief. *They both grew up too damned fast…. and now I have to make sure they continued to grow up.*

Brian climbed out of the car. It was finally feeling like winter. The week after Thanksgiving had been warm but then a cold front arrived and temperatures dropped and stayed low. Maybe reaching upper thirties by the afternoons and it felt great. Brian exhaled a cloud into the evening air and began to walk. He meandered through the parking lot and found a paved walking path that was used by runners during daylight hours. It was not well-lit, which could often be unnerving but tonight it suited Brian just fine.

He Googled New Concord, Kentucky which he had never heard of. *Oh great. The farthest point in Kentucky. Twelve hours from here.* Brian had five grand. He could fly down. He rubbed his tracking device. *They'd make me take it off to get through security*. He rubbed his head as Plan B quickly came into focus. The Bird.

For reasons even Brian couldn't explain, he had maintained his fake identities from his pot dealing days in the eighties. All the cash he had made selling weed was gone but he always renewed his driver's licenses. All three of them. He also maintained his 1973 Pontiac Firebird that was registered to one of his aliases. Lisa didn't know about the car or the aliases, but when they had been dating he had mentioned that he sold pot a few times. He kept the old car in a very secure garage on one of two rental properties in Easton. More leftovers from his weed-dealing days. Lisa didn't know about those properties. He had planned to sell them and fold the money into their joint account, but it never happened. When Lisa began drinking more and their marriage started getting shaky, he decided to keep things the way they were.

Brian had the car modified for high-speed handling in case he needed to get away from some place fast. The car passed inspection but barely. It was essentially a street-legal NASCAR machine. The turbo charged 455 cubic inch motor was professionally built and put out just under seven hundred horse power without the nitrous boost. It had a six-speed transmission geared such that the top gear could only be employed over sixty miles per hour. The suspension had been re-worked for curvy road conditions. And there was some James Bond influenced tricks added as well.

Brian had run some cables to boxes hidden in pockets next to the fuel cell. If someone was pursuing him, he could release sharp shards of twisted metal to flatten their tires. He tried it once on some asshole who was tailgating him. It worked perfectly. With the Firebird Brian could cut some major time off the drive to Kentucky.

He would pack a few things, like his deer rifle and ammo, in the truck tonight after Sadie went to bed. He would leave for Easton before Sadie woke up. He'd load the Bird then go back home for breakfast, take Sadie to school, go to work and finish his job. After work, he would say goodbye to Sadie and Lisa, telling them he was off to Ocean City, Maryland to work on a client's shore house. He'd drive through the night, maybe stopping for a nap around three. He figured he would arrive in New Concord mid-morning and have time to scout his quarry.

He was mentally trouble-shooting his plan when the burner phone buzzed. It was *him* calling just like he said he would. "Hello?" Brian's voice was emotionless.

"We good?"

"Yeah. I should be in Kentucky by Wednesday morning. That'll give me two days to scout and figure out how to do this."

"Good. Any questions?"

"Yeah. What's your name?"

The Voice snorted. "I can't tell you that."

"Well, what should I call you? Ben? Tom? Mike? Oh, I know. How 'bout Dick? That one seems appropriate."

The Voice laughed. "You got spunk. I like that. But I don't want to be called Dick. Mike works." Mike was silent for a beat then asked, "So how you gonna get down there?"

"Well, Dick…Mike, I guess I can't get on a plane very well with this electronic leash on my wrist and I just don't walk fast enough so I thought I would drive." Brian began to fantasize about putting a bullet in Mike's head after he completed The Favor.

"Hey, you can get as wise-ass as you want. I'm here to help. If you want to go over your plan, fine. If not, you're on your own. You takin' Lisa's car, right? You ain't drivin' that truck of yours down, are you?"

"I thought I'd use some of your operating cash to rent a car," Brian lied. *Mike didn't know about the Firebird.* The thought made him smile. "My truck would be too slow."

"They can still trace a rental back to you."

"What do you want me to use? My bicycle isn't on top of my list."

"I'm just sayin'. And lose the attitude, if you don't mind. Last I checked I'm the only one you can discuss this with so if this isn't gonna be a productive conversation, then quit wasting my time."

A thought came to Brian. It was a lie but still, a thought to make Mike happier. "I'm taking the rental to New Concord. Then I will get a taxi or something like that, so nobody sees me in a Pennsylvania car."

"Okay, good. You're thinking but maybe you might consider swiping someone's plates so you have what looks like a Kentucky car. You won't stand out so much."

"*Steal* a license plate?" Brian was not a thief.

Mike snarked, "Oh you're right. You are only going down there to whack a guy. You don't want to break no other laws."

Brian blushed with embarrassment. Mike had a point. "Okay, yeah. Good idea. Thanks."

They hashed over plans for another twenty minutes. Pre-arrival planning was hypothetical, but it helped Brian nonetheless and he felt that Mike's confidence in him had grown. Oddly, as the conversation continued, he began to not hate Mike. This really was just business to him. However, so was using the Turner family as an example. Brian renewed his contempt and vowed not to fall into the trap of some twisted form of Stockholm syndrome.

Brian walked back to the parking lot and watched the final minutes of team scrimmage. He felt better now that he had a plan.

Lisa was already asleep on the couch, two empty wine bottles on the floor, phone in her hand. Sadie pretended not to notice, and Brian ignored his wife. He went into his office and waited for Sadie to shower, call down a goodnight, and then he crept into the basement and unlocked the gun safe. It was time to load the truck for tomorrow.

*****

A phone vibrated alerting Dr. Cooper Rollins that he had a text. It was from his guy in New York. HEADS UP. A GUY IS COMING TO VISIT YOU. SOME DOUCHEBAG FROM DUNNING, PA NAMED BRIAN TURNER. HE WILL BE THERE THIS WEEK. IT'S A FAVOR.

Dr. Rollins pursed his lips and contemplated the text before replying. WHEN?

A minute later the phone buzzed again. NOT SURE. HE CAN'T JUST LEAVE WITHOUT A REASON FOR HIS FAMILY. I GUESS 24 HOURS.

Dr. Rollins rubbed his chin. ADDRESS?

The phone buzzed two minutes later with the Turner family's address.

Dr. Rollins smiled. He'd show those pricks not to screw with him. Brian Turner's murder would be so twisted and gruesome that it would make headline news in foreign countries. He had just the crew to do it. Dr. Rollins sent another text but this time to a different recipient. SEND TOMMY TO FIX THIS. Dr. Rollins supplied the address, directives on how to make it a grizzly scene of torture and suffering, then authorized a ridiculously generous payment.

A simple message was received in return. GOT IT.

Chapter 3

Tuesday

Brian had left the house at five-thirty and made it to Easton as the first cracks of dawn began to lighten the dark sky. He'd packed his Remington Model 700 BDL .243 with a nine power Nikon scope. The ultimate deer rifle. If Brian could see it, he could hit it. He had killed many deer over the years with this rifle and he was confident he could kill a human with it too. Just for good measure, Brian also had packed two Colt 1911s .45ACP and an old double-barreled shotgun he had bought from a friend. He wasn't even sure what make it was, but he could hit geese, rabbits, and pheasants consistently with it.

Along with more ammunition than he thought he would ever need, Brian also packed four of the five thousand in cash, a case of bottled water, some fruit, and some chocolate bars. Everything but the food and water went into the back seat of the Firebird. The food and water went on the passenger seat, so it was easy to reach as he drove. He left ample room for a suitcase that he would make sure Lisa would see him carry to the truck.

Brian returned home and had breakfast. He packed his lunch and made a sandwich for Sadie. She had showered and joined him in the kitchen. Lisa was still asleep on the couch. "Remember you need to find a ride tomorrow, Thursday, and Friday," Brian told her then he taunted, "because I will be at the shore."

"Already done, Dad. And the shore isn't too appealing in the first week of December." Sadie smiled as she scooped the last blob of oatmeal from her bowl. Brian laughed and playfully nudged her. She nudged back. Laughing, father and daughter continued to poke and push each other across the kitchen and all the way out to the truck.

The day had gone just as Brian had planned. He had made it to Easton and back in time to take Sadie to school, he finished a porch restoration job and even got paid in time to deposit the check at the bank. He rolled into his driveway about half past three and after playing with two of their three dogs for ten minutes, he packed his suitcase for the trip.

Still outside, the dogs began barking loudly. Brian and Lisa had ten acres with about three quarters of an acre of their back yard fenced in for the dogs to run unsupervised. Normally they would chase each other and occasionally bark playfully but this was a different bark. Lisa was always ordering from Amazon and Brian assumed the UPS driver was delivering yet another package of whimsical crap that would be placed on the nearest flat space and forgotten to gather dust.

The unarmed alarm systems chirped announcing that someone had come in. Maybe it wasn't the UPS guy but instead was his mother-in-law. She would show up when she could find someone to drive her. He didn't need that, but he'd been successfully ignoring her the past few visits so ignoring her one more time wouldn't be an issue. At least not in Brian's opinion.

Brian lugged his suitcase down the steps and into the kitchen where he was met with a harsh punch to the stomach. He dropped his case and fell to his knees. Immediately he was yanked back to his feet and punched again. His assailant shoved him into a chair and punched him in the nose. Brian's eyes teared up from the hit blurring his vision as the assailant quickly wrapped a rope around Brian's torso, pinning his arms to his sides and anchoring him in the chair. Zip ties were strapped around his wrists and to the legs of the chair.

As his vision cleared, Brian saw a second man holding Lisa. His tattooed hand cupped over her mouth, long cords of greasy hair hanging heavily from his scalp. He had three tear drops tattooed below his right eye. When the second man saw that Brian was secured to the chair, he let go of Lisa and pushed her back onto the couch. She began to protest, and he pulled a silenced pistol from his waistband and shot her once in the head.

"No!" Brian screamed. The blood flowing from his nose sprayed when he yelled. "I told Mike I would do the job! Why are you doing this?"

"Mike? Who the hell is Mike?" the first man laughed in a southern drawl.

"I don't know his real name. My handler, he said to call him Mike and he said nothing would happen if I did the favor. I was just leaving to do it! I told him I would! What are you doing?"

The second man smiled as he entered the kitchen. He produced more lengths of rope each about four feet long and he tied one to each of Brian's ankles. It was then that Brian noticed the bone saw, drill, and large set of pliers on the kitchen table. The second man said nothing as he opened a nondescript black case and produced a video camera and tripod.

Brian swallowed hard. "What are you doing?"

The Turners' third dog, a twelve-year old Siberian Husky named Suzie, entered the kitchen. Suzie barked twice but not particularly threateningly. The dog was old and stiff. She was basically going through the motions of defending her family but was hardly a threat.

After checking that Brian was tightly tied to the chair, the tattooed man turned his attention to Suzie. The dog growled loudly as the man approached her. She repositioned stiffly with hind legs that had lost their muscle tone. Suzie moved closer to Brian, but the tattooed man kicked her hard in the stomach dropping her to the floor.

Brian could only watch in horror as the man continued to kick Suzie. He stomped on her joints, broke her tail and when her cries grew louder, he kicked her throat until she stopped. The family pet wheezed for several minutes then went silent.

Brian felt a rage he had never experienced before. Lisa, while no longer the love of Brian's life, didn't deserve to die and the ruthless beating of Suzie before his eyes were acts of cruelty the likes of which he had never imagined.

The first man, who had hit him, smiled a wide nefarious grin displaying teeth that were stained from tobacco and apparently rarely brushed. "We need to make an example of why people shouldn't try to kill our boss." Again, he spoke with a heavy southern accent and Brian began to put the pieces together. These guys didn't work for Mike. The man explained, "First, we pull all of your teeth. Then we start removing parts. Toes and fingers first because you won't bleed out with them, but it still hurts like hell. Then we open your guts. Again, you won't bleed out, but you may pass out. Hope not but if it happens, we will keep working. Last, we start cutting bigger pieces like your feet, then lower legs, and if you still got a heartbeat, we will take off your arms. You'll probably bleed out by then though." A tinge of disappointment in his voice. "It all gets taped, and we will put it on the internet for your buddy *Mike* to see how we feel about him sending someone to kill the good doctor."

Brian was horrified at the thought of Sadie in her room. If they were going to do this to him, they would also do unspeakable things to her. They probably didn't know she was home. He had to warn her. Her only chance would be to go out her window and jump off the porch roof and run to the woods across the street. She and Brian had hunted there since she was old enough to have a license and she knew it like the back of her hand. They'd never catch her, but he also knew if he yelled, she wouldn't run, she would come down to see what was going on.

The man put a strip of duct tape over Brian's forehead knocking his ever-present hat to the floor. It ran long and he taped the ends together to form a tail, or in this case, a handle. He pulled hard and Brian's head snapped backward. It was hard to keep his mouth closed. He was about to yell to his daughter when there was an explosion from the foyer.

The man slammed into Brian knocking him and the chair over backward. The man's full weight landed on top of Brian. A second explosion erupted and there was a large thud on the floor next to Brian.

Sadie rolled the first man off of her father. Sobbing, she laid her Stevens SXS .410 shotgun on the floor next to Brian. It was an old side-by-side shotgun that his grandfather had used and had given to her when she was old enough to shoot it. Sadie ran to the utensil drawer and grabbed a large carving knife. She quickly cut Brian's bindings and he was able to tear the duct tape off his head.

Tears poured down Sadie's cheeks. "They killed Mom and Suzie!" She stared at Suzie as she sobbed. "We have to call the police."

"No!" Brian hissed. He wanted to sound more sympathetic, but his mind was racing, and he didn't have time to console his daughter.

The house alarm chimed. The Turners never actually activated their home security system, but it still beeped when a door or window was opened. It was the door from the garage.

Sadie's shotgun only held two rounds and she had used them both on the men attacking her father. Brian grabbed the silenced pistol from the man who'd shot his wife and slapped it into Sadie's hand. He then shoved her across the open doorway that led into the kitchen, back into the foyer. Brian held a finger to his lips for her to be quiet then motioned how she should ready the gun to fire. He then patted the first man's blood-soaked body until he found another pistol. Brian took up a position on the opposite side of the opening between the kitchen and living room. Anyone coming from the garage would have to pass through the living room to get to the kitchen.

Two men, weapons drawn, entered the living room. Brian held his hand up to Sadie and mouthed the words *keep shooting* to her. She shook her head no and he glared hard back at her. This was not up for debate. He then began a countdown with his fingers. Three, two, one.

Through blurry, tear-filled eyes Sadie shot first hitting one of the men square in the stomach. She kept shooting, missing twice and hitting once more, blowing a hole in the man's thigh. Brian began shooting as soon as Sadie did, peppering the second intruder three times in the chest. Brian held up his hand for Sadie to stop shooting. Through the blue haze of smoke, Brian could see the first man clutching his stomach with one hand and his leg with the other as blood flowed over his fingers. The second man lay motionless, eyes in a vacant unfocused gaze.

"I'm calling 911," Sadie announced.

Again, this time much harsher, Brian grabbed her by the arm, "No, Sadie! You cannot call the police. Not yet. Our lives and Hannah's will be over if you do."

"Dad," Sadie sobbed. "What is going on?"

Brian ignored the question and looked out back for the two remaining dogs. They were no longer barking and had run up to the deck wanting to come into the house. If someone were still in the driveway, the dogs would be barking at them. Nobody would be in the back of the house because again, the dogs would be after them. He listened intently. If someone were on the front porch, it would creak loudly. Lisa always complained that a carpenter's home was the last to be repaired. That only left one other access to the house, which was the dining room windows. The dogs could also see the dining room so most likely it was clear.

Hopeful but not entirely confident there were no more attackers, Brian turned his attention to the man softly moaning on the floor. "Move your hands where I can see them."

The man ignored him, so Brian went to the fireplace and grabbed an ash-stained poker. He repeated his request. "Move your hands so I can see them."

"Fuck you," grunted the man. He, too, had a southern accent.

Brian swung the poker hard onto the man's elbow. It made a disgusting pop and the man cried out in pain.

"Hands."

The man rolled from his side to his back in obvious pain and splayed his arms out wide. There was a bloody patch dead center in the man's stomach area and another on his thigh.

"So, Cooper Rollins sent you here. How did he find out about me?"

"Santa Claus told him," the man grunted defiantly.

Brian didn't have time for this. He wanted answers. He was also fully consumed by rage. Brian hovered over the man for a moment before plunging the fireplace tool into the center of the bloody spot in his abdomen. The tool followed the path the bullet had taken and made a dull sound as the point hit the white oak flooring of the Turner's living room. Brian repeated the question, but the man only swore at him, so Brian rotated the poker. The man grunted, his body stiffened, then he tried to grab the shaft of the tool, but Brian kicked his hands away.

Brian's mind began to clear. He turned to Sadie. "Give me your phone." She obediently handed it to him. He didn't want her calling the police. Brian pointed to a particular piece of firewood stacked on the hearth. "Hand me that."

The Turners enjoyed their big, open fireplace and it was often fueled partly by wood scraps from Brian's jobs. He had some leftover oak that was destined to be burned. Sadie handed her father the piece he had pointed to, an inch and half by inch and half square white oak baluster from an old railing job. It was about two feet long and made a perfect club.

Brian leaned on the poker and when the man tried to grab it, Brian slammed the oak piece into his wrists. Picturing the way Suzie had died, it was hard for Brian to stop. His beating had shattered the man's wrists and elbows rendering his arms useless as Sadie watched in stupefied horror.

The questioning continued with the expletive laced responses losing their gusto until finally the man could take the punishment no longer. He gasped, "Rollins was tipped off. I don't know by who, I swear." The tough guy had a tear in his eye.

"How do you check in? You know, to tell Rollins that I'm dead." Brian figured he should ask more questions, but it was the only one he could come up with. His mind was racing a mile a minute.

"It won't be Rollins. It'll be Custer. He'll check in. With a text." The man was pale. He was going into shock.

Brian didn't know Custer, but he would remember the name. "Where's your phone?"

"I don't got one. Tommy has it."

Brian left the now bloody poker protruding from the man's stomach. The man was breathing erratically. Then, without even mulling it over, Brian raised the piece of oak and swung it hard onto the man's head. Each brutal swing was a cathartic release of frustration. Brian thought of Mike, the greasy man who shot his wife, the monster who was going to cut him up, Mike again, Suzie's senseless death, and anything else that remotely represented his current situation.

What he thought most about was what the situation had done to his family. He was going to go to Kentucky by himself. He was going to honor the favor. And even then, Brian felt until he pulled that trigger, he would come up with a way out. A compromise. He had time but that was now taken away from him. Lisa was dead and Sadie had shot three men.

Sadie.

Brian's mind flashed an image he cherished dearly. Sadie was maybe three years old. It was a day in early March. One of those days when even though snow and the dreariness of a lingering winter enveloped the area, the sun was strong. It was a bright, warm promise of a forthcoming spring. Brian and little Sadie had stepped from the garage, and she'd stopped, closed her eyes and faced the sun. She smiled as the warmth bathed her face. Even as a little girl Sadie had found beauty and happiness in the little things.

And now that same little girl was spattered in blood from men who came to kill her family.

Brian hit the man over and over harder each time. The man's skull indented on the third strike, but Brian kept swinging long after the man was dead. Sadie shrieked, "Dad, stop it!" He swung the oak again. "Dad!"

Out of breath and sweating, Brian met his daughter's eyes. She looked at him as if he had just turned into a monster. And at that moment, in her eyes, he realized that he had. His lip trembled at the sight of his daughter's expression. He broke away from her stare and scanned the room. Lisa dead on the couch, mouth agape in shocked silence. Blood sprayed on the living room wall and pooled on the floor he had installed not two years ago.

Through the doorway only Suzie's hind quarters were visible. She was such a good dog. Old and feeble, she wouldn't have hurt anyone. He fell to his knees and rubbed his temples.

Sadie had slowly moved over to him. "Dad?"

He said nothing.

"Daddy?" She hadn't called him that for years. Softly, with jagged breaths, she asked, "What's going on?" Her hands had blood on them. Her shirt and face had spatters as well.

His chin trembled with guilt. He had been so stupid thirty years ago and now it had come back and bitten him in the ass. Hard. Sadie put her arm around him, and he trembled even more. He was about to tell her everything and he wringed his hands anticipating and frightened of her judgement. Suddenly a fresh wave of fear and adrenaline blasted through him. He just realized that the watch he wore had been cut off when she cut his bindings but that wasn't what scared him. The tracking band had been cut off too.

Chapter 4

Brian sprang to his feet and bolted to the kitchen. Stepping over the bodies he found his watch and the cut tracking band. Desperately he tried to put the band back together despite knowing it wouldn't work.

His mind was even clearer now. Thoughts coming rapid fire fueled by adrenaline. Sadie wasn't safe at home. She'd have to go with him to Gettysburg. Mike's men would be coming to the house but also the college for Hannah. He looked at their blood-soaked clothing and started barking orders at Sadie. "Go change into something warm yet comfortable. Jeans that you can run in. Grab sweatshirts. Hunting clothes but camo, not orange."

Sadie was confused and began to ask for clarification, but Brian shouted, "Do it, Sadie! I'll explain on the way. These guys are coming after Hannah."

Sadie followed her father, bounding up the stairs two at a time. She broke right and ran down the hallway to her room. She got rid of her blood-spattered clothes and grabbed what she was told to. Brian had also changed. He had already packed camouflaged clothing in his suitcase. The pair ran down the steps and into the kitchen where Brian told Sadie to find a cell phone and any weapons these guys might have. In less than a minute they had the sole phone, a total of four semiautomatic pistols - all were Sig Sauer .45 ACPs, two of them with silencers- and several spare clips of ammunition.

Brian shoved a bowl of food onto the deck for the dogs then he and Sadie ran outside where a black Suburban with Kentucky plates was sitting in the driveway. Keys in the ignition. Sadie followed her father's lead and approached the truck when Brian suddenly yelled, "Wait!"

Sadie froze. Brian ran to his work truck. He grabbed a sun-faded knit hat, two pairs of paint-stained work gloves, and the box with the phone, the remaining thousand dollars, and the envelopes. He tossed the cap and one set of gloves to his daughter. "Here. Put these on before you touch anything. If you have to sneeze, cough, puke, whatever, do it inside your shirt. I don't want fingerprints or any of our DNA left in here."

Sadie numbly did as she was told. Brian put on his gloves, tossed the box into the back seat, and they both climbed in. He always wore a hat, and he kept his hair cropped very short. He could still shed some DNA, but he didn't have time to look for a second knit hat.

Brian wanted to text Hannah but reconsidered. She was probably safe for a little while. It had been less than fifteen, well, maybe twenty minutes since the bracelet had been severed. Mike would have to get a guy or hit squad together along with a camera or web cam then go to Gettysburg. He didn't know where Mike was from, but he guessed it was the north Jersey area or maybe New York. Unless he was a transplant. Still, he figured he had time to get to Hannah before Mike did. He hoped. Brian turned the keys and they were on their way to Easton.

Mike.

Brian barked at his daughter, "Sadie, get the phone out of that box."

She reached back for the box, blindly felt inside until she found the phone.

"Okay," Brian said. "Find the last number and call it. It's the only number."

Sadie did as she was told but there was no service. The phone was dead. Brian's face lost its color when she reported this. His chin trembled for a flash then his face turned into a mask of resolve. It was a level of intensity that Sadie had never seen on her father before. She didn't know what to say so she just stared out the window and tried to process what had just happened.

"You okay?" Brian asked his youngest daughter. She hesitated and he clarified, "I mean physically. Any cuts or anything like that?"

"No, I'm not okay," Sadie whispered. "We need to call the police."

"NO! We CANNOT call the police!" Brian was feeling unhinged.

After about five minutes of deafening silence, Sadie, now growing irate and sounding more like her mother than Brian cared for, demanded an explanation. "Talk."

Brian felt like a softball was lodged in his esophagus. He wanted to break down and cry. Beg for his daughter's understanding and forgiveness. This wasn't the time. Not if he wanted to get to Hannah before Mike did.

"Dad!"

Brian swallowed hard. "Look in the box." As Sadie reached behind the seat and cautiously retrieved the cardboard box, he continued. "I got into a jam when I was young. I got involved in something really stupid and it caught up with me. I was given a favor to get out of the mess and…." Brian caught his breath. Tears welled up but after a deep breath he regained his composure. "I thought it had happened so long ago that my favor would never need to be honored. I got the box yesterday morning after you got out of the truck at school."

Sadie was horrified. The pictures were taken from inside her room. There was even a photo of her sleeping at her friend Becky's house. She paged through the overwhelming stack of invasive documentation before feeling so violated that she dropped the photos back into the box and shuddered.

"That other envelope is the man they want me to kill."

"Kill?" Sadie cried. "You're not a killer!" The scene of her father bludgeoning that man she had shot in the stomach replayed in her mind. "Are you?"

"No!" Brian snapped. Suddenly feeling defeated he mumbled, "At least I wasn't." His undulating resolve returned hard, and he looked her way. "NO! I am not a killer unless it means killing to protect my family and that is what I plan to do."

"What did you do that you would owe somebody such a terrible favor?"

"I sold pot, Sadie. Never smoked it but I sure could grow and distribute it."

"But pot is practically legal."

"It wasn't when I was in high school and college."

The rest of the ride to Easton was silent. Brian parked the Suburban in a gravel cut-away in a back alley behind the neighbor of his rental home. Out of survival-mode paranoia he usually parked farther away in case he was ever followed. He would then walk four or five blocks to his rental house where he would check on things and take the Bird for a spin. This time they were in a hurry. After tucking guns in his waist band, and making sure the guns Sadie carried were concealed, he motioned for Sadie to get out of the truck. They carried everything else to the heavily bolted, secure garage.

"What is this place? Why are we here?" Sadie whispered.

"It's a rental property I own. And we are getting a car that will be better equipped to get us to Hannah. It's my old Firebird from my selling days."

Sadie regarded her father as if he were a stranger. The man who had taught her to ride a bike, swim, twist Oreos in half just right so the cream wouldn't be damaged, and myriad life lessons that she treasured, had a secret.

Brian spun the combination lock and opened the door. He and Sadie stepped inside and loaded a black 1973 Firebird Formula 400 with the rest of the gear. Brian stuffed his real ID under a broken chunk of the concrete floor then opened the trunk to double check his rifle and ammo were still there. While the trunk was open, he also turned the valve on a bottle of nitrous oxide just in case he needed extra horsepower.

After closing the trunk, he opened the garage doors. Standing in front of the open door was a boy of about ten years old who was balancing on a bike that was just a touch too big. He smiled, "Hi, Mr. Breckenridge."

"Hey, Willie. How are you?" Brian replied with a nonchalant smile. He ignored the look on Sadie's face. She obviously was wondering who Mr. Breckenridge might be.

"Oh, I'm just fine. I got an A on my math test. You really helped me a lot. Thanks."

Brian gave the lad a fist bump. "I'm proud of you, Willie. Way to go!" The boy beamed with pride until Brian said, "Willie? We gotta go. I'm in a real hurry. Can you make sure this gets all locked up for me?" He motioned to the open garage doors.

"Sure thing, Mr. B," Willie replied.

Brian handed him a ten dollar bill. "Thanks. And keep up the good grades."

Willie's eyes opened wide at the money. "Wow, thanks!"

Brian didn't reply. He was already in the classic Pontiac. Sadie followed his lead, still baffled about the *Mr. Breckenridge* thing. She had to relocate the previously loaded case of water and snacks to the floor behind the seats then she slid into the high-backed bucket seat. Brian fired up the powerful motor and eased out of the building. The car thundered down the alley and out onto the main road.

"Mis-ter Breck-en-ridge?" Sadie asked over emphasizing each syllable. "What the hell is that, Dad? You *are* my dad, right?"

"You've got my toes and my nose, kiddo. I am your father, like it or not." He shifted gears and deftly merged onto the speedway called Route 22. People seemed to drive differently on Route 22 in the Lehigh Valley. Brian hated this particular stretch of road, often congested, and thus people became rude and downright nasty. Merging was usually scary. One had to get up to speed on the ramp and hope to wiggle in between cars versus most other stretches of highway where one had room to merge at a saner pace. It amazed Brian that there weren't more accidents. Brian moved into the passing lane and went as far above the speed limit as he dared in order to make time and not be pulled over. Once settled into the rhythm of the traffic, he decided to start from the beginning.

"Sadie, I love you and your sister more than anything in the world. What I did, who I was in my late teens and early twenties is not who I am today." Brian took a deep breath, dodged a car doing fifty-five in the passing lane, then started at the beginning.

"I was average. I was, and probably am, average. It bothered me. I was an okay athlete, okay looking. Okay student, I was okay at everything. But *just* okay. I was average, and I hated it.

"I never had an interest in using marijuana. I knew plenty of people who did, I'm sure you do too, and most seemed less intelligent than the kids who didn't smoke. Now I don't know if weed made them dumber or if they were dumb enough to smoke weed, but I didn't want to mess with the stuff. However, I did see an opportunity to maybe not be so average anymore.

"I asked one of the stoners who I was friendly with if he could get me some seeds. And did he ever! He showed up with the better part of a sandwich bag full of seeds. He just gave them to me at no charge. And, come springtime, I planted some in the cornfield next door. By the time school started in the fall, I had a lot of plants to harvest.

"I spent a weekend cutting and hanging the plants. I put them up in an old carriage house that Gram and Pap never used. It was even kind of dangerous to go in. Pap burned it down a few years after Mom and I got married."

The image of Lisa lying on the couch with a red blood dot on her forehead and the back half of her skull blown away was seared into Brian's mind. Their marriage had been going downhill fast but she didn't deserve that. Brian pursed his lips and passed a few more cars as he merged onto Route 78 West. The traffic wasn't as congested, and the speed limit was higher. The car purred comfortably unchallenged at seventy miles per hour.

Sadie had thought the same and began crying at the mention of her mother. Mom drank too much and didn't help out much, but she was still her mom. She thought of the weeks at the shore, a week at a lake house, and her mom yelling on the sidelines at soccer, basketball, and softball games. She remembered the four-day weekend when Dad tried to teach Mom how to ski. She sniffed and wiped tears from her eyes. Several minutes passed before Sadie said, "Then what?"

"Well, I had about twenty-three pounds of weed to sell. I contacted Bob, that stoner guy who gave me the seeds. Back then, five hundred bucks bought you a half pound. I gave some to Bob and the next day he told me it was okay. Not the best stuff he had ever smoked but not the worst either.

"I asked if he could sell it for me. We decided since it was lower grade pot, we would give more than normal. I sold it to him a pound at a time, and he divided it up into what he called 'heavy twenties. He sold what would normally be thirty dollars' worth for twenty. It was a bargain and stoners snatched it up fast. I made nine thousand dollars that summer.

"Bob got me more seeds. A couple of sandwich bags full. I also met a guy at another high school who would be my distributor. The next summer I branched out into more corn fields. I also devised a better system of growing.

"People would grow weed in fields all the time. But what they would do is tear out a rectangular patch of corn and fill it with pot. Anyone could see from the air that the plants were different. Cops would spot a pot garden easily from the sky. They wait for people to check on it and the growers got caught.

"I *blended* the pot into the cornfield. Most cornfields are rectangular or at least square. In the spring, when the corn was about six inches tall, I would always start at the southeast corner and I would pace nineteen steps west then forty-eight steps north. 1948 was the year the Eagles won their first NFL championship, so it was easy to remember. It was there that I would plant my first seeds. Three seeds to a hole, each hole was eighteen inches apart from the next. I would spell the last name of an Eagles player in cursive so it was one continuous line of plants but not in a shape such that it could be spotted from the air. I would then keep a notebook with the first name of that player and the location of each field.

"This system was easy to plant and more importantly, easy to find in the dark. I didn't need to actually see the plants to find them. I used a low-level light to harvest the leaves but navigating the fields was just a matter of knowing where to start and which Eagles player the field was named after. And with this system, I never got caught. Kids were getting caught growing all over but not me. That second growing season, I earned twenty-eight thousand dollars which was good and bad because I had no place to put it. That's where Lionel Breckenridge comes in."

Sadie snorted at the name.

Brian never took his eyes off the road, but he could imagine her expression. He was cruising the Firebird at seventy-five miles an hour now. Just enough to make good time but still occasionally being passed by a crazy driver in a hurry. Brian thought, hoped, that if a cop were looking to pull someone over, he'd pick the fastest driver.

A quick check in the rear-view mirror and then he continued. "I had stashed all that cash in a metal box up in the attic. I didn't spend it, but I also couldn't deposit it as the bank might wonder where I got it. Plus, I really didn't want to get caught. So, I decided to create an alias and Lionel James Breckenridge was it.

"I got a stoner that I knew who was really good at art to make up a fake birth certificate and social security card for me. Back then a driver's license didn't have a photo on it, so it was easy to retake the test, using my fake documents and the address of one of my dealers, and viola. Lionel Breckenridge was a driver.

"I made one dumb mistake. Lionel Breckenridge was the same age as me. I used the same birthday since I didn't want to have to remember another date. So, until Lionel and I turned eighteen there wasn't much advantage. I couldn't open a bank account without a parent's signature until I was eighteen, so I needed another ID. I went back to the forger and got another alias, Lawrence Howard Fine who was born on my birthday but one year earlier.

"I used that name as a tribute to The Three Stooges. I couldn't justify Moe, Shemp, or Curly for a name but Larry Fine was perfect. The others' last name was Howard so that became my middle name." Brian felt Sadie staring at him and shrugged.

"So, I went to another driver test place, in the Poconos this time, got my license as Larry Fine and now I had valid ID to open a bank account and get a credit card and pay taxes on my money.

"The next year I expanded even more and made over eighty thousand dollars supplying high schools and colleges with cheap weed. I set up a fictitious lawn care and handy man business for Larry. I funneled the cash through that business and soon Larry bought a rental property in Easton. I wanted to stop the business in the next two years and needed a legitimate way of investing what I made.

"The following year, Lionel was old enough to open a bank account and basically do the same as Larry with buying a rental property. I didn't expand as much and did about the same as the year before. It was the end of that growing season when I got caught."

Brian passed a few more cars and took a deep breath. The memories of that cornfield were as vivid now as they were the day after it happened. "I was dropping off a load at East Stroudsburg University. Well, I wasn't on campus, but I was meeting my distributor for that school. She paid me and left. I put the money in the car in a hidden compartment and was about to go home when two guys jumped me. Before I knew it I was duct taped and stuffed in a trunk of a big Cadillac. I rode in there for about ten minutes. When they opened the trunk and let me out, we were in a big cornfield.

"I was in the second of a parade of five cars. There were two other guys taped up like I was. My captors cut off our tape and told us to kneel. They spoke Spanish, but one guy was a translator for me. I also kind of got the gist of what they wanted when they shoved me. There was a man in the back of the last car. He was the boss, Javier Cortez. There was some kind of discussion with one of his guys and the man kneeling farthest away from me. Mr. Cortez said something and next thing I knew they cut this guy's hands off. They let him run but only so they could shoot him in the feet and legs. The poor guy was trying to get away, bleeding all over the place, and they just kept shooting in non-vital areas. They tortured that guy for ten minutes before he finally bled out.

"The next guy just got a bullet in the head. Then they came to me. The translator told me it wasn't personal, just business. He explained the first guy was stealing from them. The second guy was just an idiot who messed up one too many times. For me, it was just business. I was competition and they wanted me out. They even offered me a drink first.

"It's amazing how the mind works when there's a gun pressed against your head. I was planning on quitting anyhow and I certainly had nothing to lose so I asked permission to make an offer. I suggested that instead of killing me, I teach them my operation and give them my gardens and distributors in exchange for walking away. I told them I would set them up in the next three months and I also explained how I did it by myself and there was virtually no overhead. No shipping, no losses to customs agents, nothing like that as my product was grown locally. They were shipping their marijuana from South America and took heavy losses.

"Well, Mr. Cortez motioned for me to stand and approach him. We worked out a deal and he called it a favor. He said some day he might ask me for a favor. Well, of course I agreed. A person can be pretty agreeable when faced with having their brains blown out in a cornfield. We shook hands, I told him how to get a hold of me, and they took me back to my car. I had never been so scared in my life… until today when I thought I might lose you."

Somewhat devastated, Sadie began to process what Brian had told her. Numbly she asked, "So, if you had those fake IDs, how did you get caught?"

"Ah. Details, Sadie. Details will either save you or kill you. I had planned for being stopped by police. I could hand the cop a fake ID and leave everything behind without them knowing about my real name. A cop won't ask for your wallet, they only ask for ID, so I carried all three IDs with me.

"Drug dealers are a different story. One I had not planned on. They took my wallet. I kept the fake IDs in a slice in the cover. They never found the fake IDs, only my real one. Had they asked, I would have handed them a fake one."

Sadie just stared at her father. She tried to picture him as a drug dealer but all that she could see was the man who had coached her local travel soccer team for six years until it folded. She felt like she should hate him, but she couldn't. Not even close. It was something that happened before he had even met her mom. And like he said, it had been either the favor or certain death. Overwhelmed, she broke down crying. Brian reached over to her and squeezed her knee. Sadie wrapped her arms around his arm and buried her face in his shoulder. They stayed that way for a few long minutes when the buzz of a cell phone vibrating caught their attention.

Between the two of them, Brian and Sadie had a collection of four cell phones. The buzzing was coming from the phone belonging to one of the hit men. A simple text displayed on the screen: WELL?

"What do we do?" Sadie sounded slightly panicked.

"Can you scan any other conversations? See how this guy responded before. If he was chatty or not. I'm betting not."

Sadie looked for other messages, but everything was cleared.

"Okay," Brian said pensively. "Keep it sort and sweet. Just say it's done."

Sadie replied. IT'S DONE.

Brian glanced at it before she hit send. "Wait. Get rid of the apostrophe. I doubt these guys were big on grammar."

Sadie removed the apostrophe and hit send.

VIDEO?

"What video?" Sadie sounded worried.

"They were going to tape me getting butchered and put it on the internet. Tell him soon."

Sadie replied. A minute passed before the phone buzzed again. GOOD.

Brian checked the time. It was dark now and he could risk going a little faster. They needed to get to Gettysburg College and find Hannah before anyone else did.

Chapter 5

There hadn't been much conversation after Brian had confessed his past to his youngest daughter. It was a lot to absorb. They stopped for gas once about ten miles from campus. Sadie ran in for snacks and water while Brian fueled the car. There had been a moment when Brian got choked up with guilt, but he regained his composure quickly. Sadie, too, had had a meltdown thinking about her mother's body lying on the couch still. Brian had commented that they could not afford to have their minds clouded. They would have to postpone their grief.

"Text your sister. See what she's up to."

Sadie did. Her phone was unnervingly silent. Not that Hannah took long to respond but under the circumstances Brian and Sadie were anxious to hear back from her. They were pulling into the main campus drive when Hannah replied. UGH. She used a rolling-eyes emoji. ON THE WAY TO MEET SOME GRAD STUDENT FOR SOMETHING ABOUT CHEMISTRY. HE WANTS ME TO MEET HIM IN THE FARTHEST POINT OF CAMPUS. WTF? LIKE I HAVE TIME FOR THIS.

Sadie read the reply aloud and Brian's concern grew. He told Sadie what to type. YOU KNOW THIS GUY?

NO. HE SAID HE WAS DR GRAY'S ASSISANT. HIS NAME'S GREG. WEIRD.

Oh shit. Brian could feel his heart racing. Sadie was already sending a reply. WHERE DO YOU HAVE TO MEET HIM?

AT THE ROCK.

"The rock?" Sadie said after reading the text while Brian looked for a place to park the Firebird. He wasn't very familiar with campus, but he remembered The Rock. He tried driving closer to the rock but ended up in a dead end. It would be faster at this point to run. He backed the car into a parking space and shut off the engine.

"We saw that at orientation. They have this little area with benches and there is a big rock that kids like to sit on. It's a quiet alcove at the corner of campus." Brian thought for a minute. "We have to get there first." He rubbed his temples. "Okay. Call, don't text, but call and tell her not to go."

"Oh, like *that* will stop her. She won't listen to me." Sadie paused. "Unless…Dad, you know how some people think Hannah and I look alike?" Sadie was had already hit the call icon on her phone. "I'll tell her I need something from her computer right now. A file and I am on deadline. She goes back to her dorm, and I go meet the guy."

Brian shook his head and began to voice a protest when Sadie held up her hand. "Hey. Before you go meet that guy, I need you to send me that report you did on global warming. It's a huge paper and I need to email it in twenty minutes. I forgot all about it."

Hannah screamed at her sister loud enough for Brian to hear. "Sadie! I'm on my way to meet this guy. No. Figure it out for yourself. And you'll get an F if you plagiarize."

"I don't have time. This report must be time stamped in nineteen minutes or I get a whole grade lower. I forgot about it. Mom and Dad will kill me if I get a B in this class. Please? I'll do your chores the whole time you're home on winter break."

"You have got to be kidding me! I am …."

"Han! Not only will Mom and Dad be mad about me getting a B, it will drop my class ranking. I'm number two right now. I can be number one but not if I get a B."

"Why did you wait until now?" Hannah scolded. Brian's oldest daughter was one of the most competitive people he knew. Sadie had an angle with the class ranking point. Both girls were annoyingly competitive over-achievers, and he knew Hannah would not want her sister to fall in rank.

"Gee, Hannah, I don't know. I guess with school soccer, travel soccer, volunteering at the firehouse, and my AP classes maybe just this once something slipped my mind," Sadie snarked. "I can't be number one if I get a B."

Hannah sighed loud enough for Brian to hear. "Damn it, Sadie. You owe me big."

Sadie smiled and gave a thumbs up. Brian weakly acknowledged it. One daughter was out of danger, but she was being replaced by the other daughter. It hardly seemed like a victory.

"Thanks, sis. I love you!" Sadie said.

Hannah had already disconnected the call.

Sadie turned to her father. "Now I just take her place."

Brian began to object when Sadie dug out one of the silenced pistols. She checked the clip and swapped it for a full one. Sadie motioned for Brian's gun. He handed it to her, and she checked the clip in that as well. It too was replaced with a fuller one. Brian watched his daughter as he tried to put words to his emotions. Finally, he blurted, "I'm not comfortable with this. What if they shoot you? We've got to have a better plan." He paused for a beat. "Like sneak Hannah off campus and…"

"Run for the rest of our lives?" Sadie snapped.

"What?"

"Dad. These guys won't stop. You said so yourself. We had planned on killing this doctor guy. Once we do, it's over."

"Okay. *We* didn't plan on shooting the doctor, *I* did. And I didn't plan on having my daughters involved."

"Well, like it or not I am involved. I mean I've killed two men and honestly, Dad, you could use the help. Let's make sure Hannah is safe and then we'll go to Kentucky and do the job."

"Let's worry about tonight first. What happens if this guy grabs you?"

"Then I shoot him too," she said coldly.

Sadie spoke of killing so casually that the father in Brian wanted to have a long sit down with her. If only they had the time. He could feel threads of his morality snapping. He felt like a pimp. Did he save one daughter only to lose the other? Hardly. But putting Sadie out there as bait made him feel disgusting, whorish. Another fiber of morality snapped. He couldn't give up one daughter, he had no choice but to work with Sadie to save Hannah. Brian did not like being cornered.

Sadie picked up on his discomfort and softened her stance. "Dad, I blame these guys for killing Mom just as much as the one who actually pulled the trigger."

Brian said nothing. He felt the same way. He gave a slight nod and patted his pistol.

Sadie got out of the car and began walking in the direction she thought the rock was in. Brian got out and caught up to her. He guided her into the shadows then stopped to get his bearings. He looked at a distant light post and the building they were near. No cameras. They walked around a large brick building of unknown function and saw the rock. The area was sparsely illuminated by one pathetic overhead light. The light post wasn't even near the rock yet close enough for the ambient light to create a rock-shaped silhouette. "Text your sister and ask what's taking so long."

Sadie did and got an instant response. REALLY SADIE? I JUST GOT BACK TO THE DORM. CALM YOUR TA TAS.

Brian touched Sadie's arm and she stopped walking. He scanned the area searching for the closest vantage point while still remaining hidden. There was a hedgerow and Brian decided to follow that as far as it would take him. He turned to Sadie, "Give me three minutes then casually stroll to the rock. Be careful. And be certain this guy is not really a grad student. I love you."

Sadie smiled. She was nervous and, just like her father when he is uncomfortable, she tried to take the edge off with a dash of humor. "I love you too… Lionel." It didn't work.

Brian faked a smile then moved in a crouched run through the blackness of the shadows behind the hedgerow. His breathing became heavier as he moved, and he had to pull his sweatshirt over his mouth in an attempt to diffuse his steamy breath in the cold December air. He settled into an alcove where some dead branches had been trimmed away, readied his pistol in the direction of the rock, and waited.

Sadie had backtracked enough to use the cover of darkness to access a walking path. She bunched her jacket around her neck. Hands inside the pockets as if sheltering them from the cold instead of holding a silenced Sig Sauer .45 ACP. It was long and bulky but perfectly concealed under her heavy winter jacket. As she approached the rock a man emerged from the shadows. "Hannah?" Brian could hear the man clearly in the still night air.

"That's me. Are you Greg?"

The man didn't respond. Sadie approached him and two more men emerged from the shadows. One of them grabbed her arm and said, "You're coming with us."

Brian heard the distinctive sound of a van door sliding open. In a nearby lot, a nondescript white van was parked. A fourth man was now walking from the van toward Sadie, his head on a swivel nervously looking for any witnesses. *What the hell, do these guys always travel in groups of four?*

"I'm not going anywhere," Sadie protested. "Who the hell are you?"

"Shut up!" one of them men hissed.

Brian steadied his breathing. *It's just like hunting deer.* However, he couldn't take a shot with Sadie in the midst of the men. He tracked the group for a few more steps before Sadie decided to put a stop to their plans.

She squeezed off a round into the gut of the man to her left. With the gun under her heavy jacket combined with the silencer, Brian never even heard the shot. Evidently, the men with Sadie didn't recognize the sound either. The man to her left grunted, doubled over, and fell to the ground. Sadie spun ninety degrees and while the man who had been behind her was staring at his fallen partner gasping for breath, Sadie pumped a round into him as well.

That's when the third man in the group realized Sadie was armed. She spun to shoot him, but he was faster. He didn't have a gun drawn, instead punching her in the side of her face. Sadie dropped hard from the blow leaving the man wide open for Brian to take a shot. The bullet slammed into the man's back sending him forward landing on top of the first man down.

The fourth man, more than halfway between the group at the rock and the van, turned and bolted for the parking lot. Years of sports, hard work, and just plain age had taken a toll on Brian's knees. He sprang from the hedgerow but was too far behind and too slow to catch the man sprinting toward the van. Sadie, however, was a varsity soccer player and in top shape. She had already jumped to her feet and was in pursuit of the fourth man. Brian yelled for her to let the man go but she ignored him.

In the dim light, Brian saw one of the men on the ground was reaching for his shoulder holster. He ran closer and shot him in the chest. Brian kept running until he stood over the man. Brian looked the man square in the eyes then shot him in the head. Without hesitation he dispatched the two other wounded men laying on the ground. Brian then took up pursuit of Sadie and man number four.

Sadie had gotten close enough to take a shot. It went over the man's shoulder and slammed into the van. The man startled by the shot tripped and fell, sliding on all fours in the gravel. He rolled to his feet just as Sadie fired another shot. This one hit him between the shoulder blades, and he dropped hard.

Breathing heavily, Sadie stood over him. With her gun aimed at his head, she used her foot to push his hands to where she could see them. He didn't resist. Breathing hard almost to the point of wheezing, Brian caught up. He knelt beside the man and rolled him over. The exit wound was massive. It looked like the man's sternum had been blown out of his chest. After two gurgling gasps, the man stopped breathing.

Without saying a word Brian patted the man down. A wallet with two hundred in cash but no identification, a smaller caliber pistol, and a cell phone. Brian pocketed the cash, gun, and phone then whispered, "Help me throw him in the van."

Sadie knelt down by her father and with a heave they tossed the body into the van. The dome light had been removed so Brian felt safe to leave the door open while he and Sadie retrieved the other three bodies. Each body was patted down, and anything useful was taken from them. There was only one cell phone but all four had cash and weapons and bullets. Once all four were in the van, Brian verified for the third time that the bodies had no pulse. He grabbed the key from the van's ignition and locked all the doors then fought back tears once again as he embraced his little girl. Her face had a puffy red mark from the punch she'd taken, but she would survive. He'd seen worse from some of her soccer games.

"I don't want to leave you alone," Brian said still holding his daughter. "Let's go get the 'Bird and come back here. I think I have a plan, at least for the short term." They stole through the shadows back to the old Pontiac avoiding distant security cameras along the way. Brian fired the engine and drove a circuitous route back to the van. While the car quietly growled through campus, Brian discussed his plan with Sadie. "Check that guy's phone. What's the last number called or received?"

Sadie read the number. It was the only number the phone had in the past day, and it was used back and forth four times.

"Now check this phone." Brian indicated the burner phone he had been given the previous day. The service to the phone no longer worked. However, the call log showed the number Mike had called from. It was two digits off from the phone they took from Mike's hit man. Brian rubbed his chin pensively.

"That's too close of a coincidence," Sadie observed. "I bet they bought a bunch of phones at once. You know how your phone and Mom's phone are one digit off? You got them together, right?"

"Yup, I agree. Okay, so here's what I think. We find a place to dump the van. A lake would be great. Then, I use this phone," Brian tapped the most recently acquired burner phone, "to call Mike. Maybe he will back off Hannah. If not, we have to get her and take her with us." Brian paused at the thought of corrupting his other child. One was bad enough. "I don't want to have to do that."

Sadie grunted. She was on her phone searching Google Maps. Hannah had emailed her the file she asked for, but Sadie ignored it. Brian found the parking lot and eased the Firebird into a spot next to the van. "Look here," Sadie said handing her phone to her father. "If we take Route 116 south, we will get to Lake Heritage. It's not far."

Brian opened another tab and quickly searched Lake Heritage. "It's a gated community surrounding the lake. It says they have a security guard round the clock. That means witnesses. No way." Brian swiped the screen farther south. "What's this?" He handed the phone back to Sadie and gave a paranoid scan of the parking lot. There was movement coming from campus. He squinted through the droopy branches of a willow that was between the rock and the gravel parking lot. "Oh, shit. Here comes Hannah for her meeting."

Sadie quickly said, "Lake Mae. Its farther south but no gates and it's on the way, sort of. Look, a boat ramp."

"Perfect," Brian whispered as if Hannah would hear from inside a car at least seventy-five yards away. He reached into his pocket and handed Sadie the keys to the van. "Here. You drive the van." He regretted not having gotten her a car yet. He had mandated that her first car should be a stick shift. As of yet she had only driven Lisa's car which was an automatic.

"I only have my permit!" Sadie protested.

Brian gave her a look. "I'm sure if a cop pulls over a van full of dead bodies that he won't worry too much about your driving status. Sadie, we have to get out of here. There is a pretty obvious trail of blood and drag marks leading right to the van. Let's go. I will follow you. Move!"

Sadie slid out of the Firebird and quickly moved through the dark to the van. She started the motor and pulled out. Brian hesitated, afraid to leave Hannah alone and even more afraid not to. Again, he felt a golf ball in his throat. Only his daughters could get him choked up. He whispered, "I love you, Hannah," and started the Firebird. He caught up to Sadie and they were soon on their way south on Route 116.

Chapter 6

Twenty-five minutes later, Sadie arrived at the crossroads of Route 116 and Skylark Trail to her right and on the left was Lion Trail. Lion Trail was a dead end that had a driveway that led to a boat ramp at Lake Mae. Brian pulled in behind her, backed the Firebird around so it pointed to the exit – it was a habit he had from his pot dealing days in the event he needed to leave in a hurry- and turned the lights off but let the car idle. Sadie had already turned the lights off in the van.

Brian walked round the Ford van as a plan formed more clearly in his mind. It had back doors with tinted glass as well as a sliding side door. He whispered to Sadie, "Find a stick to jamb through the steering wheel. I want the van to drive straight." While she searched the woods nearby for a stick, Brian looked for a rock. It took a few minutes as they had no lights, but soon he found a perfect rock about twice the size of a brick.

He then scrounged a second, smaller rock which he used to break a hole in the back window. The hole was about the size of a softball. Plenty big enough for air to escape but not big enough to allow a floating corpse to pass through. He discarded the second rock. Brian opened the driver-side door and set the first rock on the floor near the gas pedal. That would weigh the pedal down when he needed to.

Unsure of exactly what her father was looking for, Sadie had returned with four sticks. One was curved and about four feet long.

It was perfect. Brian wedged the stick through the steering wheel to keep it straight. He also rolled the windows down about four inches and even tore some of the weather stripping at the bottom of the door. He wanted the van to fill fast and sink quickly.

Brian had the van, idling and with the lights off, pointed at the boat ramp on Lake Mae. There was light traffic on Route 116, so he waited for it to pass. The vehicles would have a partially obscured view of the ramp. While it was too dark to see it, they might be able to see brake lights and Brian didn't want to chance it. Three cars later, Brian stood on one foot beside the van, pushing hard through the open door on the brake with his other. He shifted into drive then pulled his leg out of the van. The van began to move forward. Brian reached in and rolled the rock onto the gas pedal. As the van lurched forward, Brian spun away slamming the door shut in one not-so-graceful maneuver.

Brian moved next to Sadie. The pair watched the van pick up speed down the driveway, onto the boat ramp, then onto the lake. Until now, neither had noticed that the lake had a rim of ice. The van skittered on the ice, tires losing traction, then after sliding about twenty yards the van crashed through the ice into the water.

Both knew they should be leaving but Brian and Sadie found themselves staring as the van floated for a minute. The drive wheel spun a momentary rooster-tail of water before it dipped below the surface. The exhaust gurgled in the icy black water until the motor drowned to a stop. The van bobbed, going deeper with each dip, until the water level hit the open windows. After that point, the van sank very quickly. Aside from a few bubbles, the van had disappeared in less than two minutes. No longer mesmerized, Brian and Sadie climbed into the Firebird and rumbled out of the small park and eventually back on to Route 116 South. Neither spoke until Sadie, working Google Maps on her Galaxy S5, told Brian the best route to New Concord, Kentucky. Eleven hours, forty-two minutes, and seven hundred seventy miles away.

Maryland was six miles away. After that, they wound through small roads for the next forty odd minutes until they hit I-70

West. Brian settled into a comfortable cruising speed and mustered the nerve to look at Sadie. The past thirty-some hours had been hell on him but the more recent seven hours had engulfed his daughter into his mess.

She had killed at least four people, her mother had been murdered, and her only sibling had almost lost her life had Sadie not been a decoy. She also found out that her father was a fallible human who had made one hell of a bad choice a long time ago. Sadie had been silent since they plunged the van into Lake Mae. She had a lot to process, and Brian let her be. He had a lot to process, too.

The ambient noise of the motor growling was the only sound until one of the cell phones buzzed. It was the one from the guy from Kentucky. VIDEO?

"What do I tell him?" Sadie asked in a tied voice. She had been so strong back at Gettysburg College. Now, to Brian, she sounded like a little girl. He wanted desperately to stop the car and hug her but there was no time for that.

"Isn't there something called a Webmaster or something like that?" he asked.

"I have no idea." Sadie gave him the look she often uses when he or Lisa would use an antiquated term. In the computer world, terms could become antiquated in a week.

Brian sighed. He was suddenly very tired. "Tell him the video got rejected and you are trying another site."

"Rejected?" Sadie asked.

"I don't know this stuff, Sadie. You know more than I do. Aren't there filters that block videos of terrorist murders?"

"Not that I know of." She stared at her father emotionlessly for a beat then said, "I'll handle it." She read aloud what she typed and sent. "VIDEO DIDN'T GO THROUGH. WENT TO INTERNET CAFÉ TO TRY AGAIN."

"Internet café?" Brian asked.

"Yeah, coffee shops have free Wi-Fi so it should be easier to load something there. I guess." Sadie shrugged.

The phone buzzed. WHERE?

QUAKERTOWN.

HURRY UP.

Sadie didn't reply.

The phone buzzed once more. HOW DID JERRY, PETE, AND JOE DO?

Sadie frowned and looked at her father. "What's that supposed to mean?"

"I guess the guy with the phone was the leader. They only had one phone, right?" He didn't wait for her answer. "Maybe they were new or something. I don't know. Say 'good'."

GOOD.

That was the final correspondence.

Brian ruminated on the texted conversation. He didn't like it but what was done was done. Time to move on. "Get the last phone we took." Sadie sorted it from the others. "What's the last number called or received?"

Sadie scrolled through the log. The past seven calls were to the same number which she read aloud.

Brian furrowed his brow in thought. "Grab the phone they gave me. What's the number in there?"

Brian's throw-away phone no longer had service but the log still worked. Sadie read that number and realized it was only two digits off from the previous number. "They probably bought, or acquired, a bunch of these throw-away phones."

"I'd bet you're right." Brian thought for a minute then felt a renewed anger. Rage even. He growled at Sadie, "Use the live phone and hit redial then hand it to me."

The phone rang twice. "Yeah."

Brian recognized the voice. "Hey *Mike*," Brian growled the man's name. "Remember me, Brian Turner? You shut my phone off you piece of shit. I told you…" Mike clicked off.

Brian had a sudden wave of panic course over him. *Hannah*! "Shit. SHIT! *SHIT*!" Each expletive grew louder and more emphasized. Feeling panicked, he frantically searched for a place to turn around and head back to Gettysburg when the phone buzzed.

CAN'T TALK. CALL YOU IN FIVE.

Brian and Sadie stared at the display until Brian slammed his hand against the steering wheel. "I don't know what to do." He sounded defeated.

It was time for Sadie to be strong again. "Pull over and stop. Just breathe for a minute and let's see what he says. If we pull over now, we aren't going farther away from Hannah if we need to go back and we aren't wasting extra time if we can keep going. Just be patient for now."

Now it was Brian's turn to look like he was on the brink of tears. Just like Sadie, he had been on an emotional rollercoaster that was exacting a heavy toll on him. Sadie hugged him and cried on his shoulder. He buried his face in her hair and wept silently until the phone buzzed. Sadie put it on speaker.

Brian cleared his throat. "Mike?"

"Yeah," said the voice on the other line. Mike's voice had a different tone. He sounded curious and possibly almost compassionate, but Brian knew better. "How'd you come by this phone?"

"Long story but I took it off one of the guys you sent to kill my daughter." Brian's words oozed venom.

"And where are those guys now?" Mike asked cautiously.

"At the bottom of a lake." The lump in Brian's throat was gone. The tears were dry. Hatred filled every fiber of his being. More threads of his morality snapped.

Mike was silent.

With a hard tone to his voice, Brian explained. "I told you I would do the favor. A crew from Kentucky came to my house before I could leave. It was a messy situation and my bracelet was cut. If you hadn't killed my phone, I could have told you that before you went after my daughter."

"A…crew…from…Kentucky?" Mike's anger became more evident with each uttered word. "How do you know?"

"Well, like I said, I agreed to do the favor so why would *you* have sent them? That didn't make sense. Plus, they had southern accents and a Suburban with Kentucky plates. Oh, and one of the gentlemen said that I shouldn't kill his boss."

"What happened to them?" Mike asked out of reflexive curiosity.

Brian wanted to leave Sadie out, so he took all the credit. "After they killed my wife, I killed them."

Brian heard Mike curse then it was silent again. After a pregnant pause, Mike asked, "How did they know you were going after Rollins?"

"How the hell should I know, Mike? They barged into my house and killed my wife, you asshole! There really wasn't much conversation in the process."

"What about Sadie?" Mike almost seemed genuinely concerned.

"They only murdered my wife and dog," was Brian's hissed reply.

There was another drawn-out silence before Mike spoke again. "So you took my guy's phone. Smart move. Did you get anything off the Kentucky guys?"

"Yeah."

Mike waited a beat before asking, "You mind telling me what?"

"Cash and a phone." Brian opted not to tell him about the guns. He and Sadie had quite the arsenal at this point.

"Shit. Did they text or call you?"

"Text."

"Get rid of that phone. And the one I got for you. Keep this one. Take the batteries out, smash the phones and throw them away. Do it now!" Mike barked.

Brian gave Sadie a nod and she tore the phones open, pulled their batteries and smashed them together but only the screen cracked. She whispered, "We can toss them piece by piece as we drive. That way the pieces aren't together." Her father agreed with a nod.

"Okay," Mike kept talking. "As long as you keep your word, I won't go after Hannah. I'm gonna guess Sadie's with you. That's good. You keep your word to me and finish the favor. Keep this phone on and you can call or text as much as you want. Something's shitty and I gotta find out what. I'll be in touch." He clicked off.

Brian studied Sadie's face for a moment before deciding he believed Mike. Brian's spider sense told him that even though Mike was operating on the other side of the law, his word was good….probably.

****

Back in New York, *Mike* sat in his car seething. *How did Rollins know about Turner?* He stared through the windshield with piercing dark eyes. First thing, first. He made a call to the Moyers, two of his most trusted associates, to meet him for a beer. He would send them to Gettysburg with strict orders to protect Hannah Turner as long as her father kept his word. Usually, transactions and jobs were done via packages and coded messages. This time Mike would give the instructions in person. He suddenly no longer trusted his email or phone.

Chapter 7

Dalton Custer was a large, tobacco-chewing, ex-cop. At six foot three inches tall with muscular arms and a barrel chest, a crew cut and his ever-present mirrored sunglasses, he was an imposing figure to say the least. The utter lack of a sense of humor complemented his appearance. He was a transplant from Tennessee to Pennsylvania then transplanted again to Kentucky.

Custer had been a cop for twenty-five years, but he never managed to work his way up the ranks. He was smart enough to be a ranking officer and he certainly had good instincts but there was something amiss that the upper brass didn't like about him. It might have been the four questionable shootings he had been investigated for. It might have been his propensity to arrest persons of the wrong skin color. It may have been his resentment of authority, his unproven reputation for accepting favors from hookers, or just his nasty disposition. Whatever the reason, Custer had spent his years on the Philadelphia Police Force as a patrol cop. His seniority allowed him the perks of picking his beat and he made more money than any other beat cop, but he was not detective material.

He was now retired and collecting a pension in Calloway County, Kentucky. He owned a very comfortable lakeside home neighboring the spacious grounds belonging to Dr. Cooper Rollins on the western shore of Kentucky Lake although he didn't spend a great deal of time in it. While Custer was retired from police work, he was not spending his golden years fly fishing or rocking on his front porch. He was employed by Dr. Rollins and his salary was more than triple what he had earned in his best years in Philly.

Kentucky Lake was a very long man-made lake that was split in part by the border of Kentucky and Tennessee. It made for an easy jaunt via ski boat from Rollins' private dock to The Wet Garage. Like many of his real estate holdings, The Wet Garage was owned by a shell company that was a subsidiary of yet another shell company. If one were determined enough, along with an undaunted forensic accountant, one could eventually trace the twisted paper trail back to Dr. Cooper Rollins.

The Wet Garage was a dockside boat repair shop. It was leased to an energetic young couple, Scott and Peggy Jones, who sold supplies for myriad aquatic activities from SCUBA to water skiing. They had fuel pumps and snack foods. They also did boat repairs much like a service station did for cars.

In the back half of one of the three side buildings used for storage was a section that was off limits to the Joneses. It was converted to an efficiency apartment that was always locked and in exchange for an extremely low rent, the Joneses had promised to never acknowledge it or anyone who may use it. This was where Dalton Custer spent the majority of his time.

There was a bedroom, full bath, small eat-in kitchen, and a compact living room. Another room which adjoined the living room had been converted to an operation center with banks of computers and several flat screen high-definition monitors. Custer sometimes slept in the small but comfortable bedroom. More often than not, Custer used the bedroom for his encounters with one of Rollins' many hookers. It was a perk that Custer often took full advantage of. Tonight, however, Custer was alone watching the computer monitors.

Dalton Custer had sent one of his up-and-coming enforcers, Tommy Kincaid, to Dunning, Pennsylvania to pay a visit to Brian Turner. Kincaid was to wipe out the family and then make a gruesome display of Brian Turner's death. Kincaid was also instructed to capture it on video and put it on the internet for not only the boys in New York, but the whole nation, to know not to mess with Dr. Cooper Rollins.

Kincaid wasn't the smartest guy Custer knew, but he was no dope either. He had good street smarts and Custer trusted him enough to let him choose the other three guys for the job. But the delay in uploading the video had concerned Custer. He texted Kincaid about the video and the response was 'good'. At the time Custer presumed that meant the video would be on the web soon.

When a couple hours had passed and there was still no video, Custer began to wonder what was going on. He texted again and Kincaid told him he had problems and was at an internet café.

A person didn't work twenty-five years in law enforcement without developing a gut feeling. Custer's gut was feeling that something wasn't right. Kincaid would never use the phrase 'internet café'. That's when Custer asked how Jerry, Pete, and Joe did. Kincaid said they did 'good'. Custer smashed his meaty fist onto the desk he was seated at and swore out loud. He didn't know the names of the other two guys Kincaid took for help, but he did know one thing: the third man Kincaid had taken was his brother and Kincaid's brother's name was Chris.

Custer pounded the desk again. Not only was Kincaid and his crew probably dead but now he had a target that either went to the cops or was on the run. *Think. Calm down and think.* Turner probably didn't go to the cops. If he were to do that, he would have done it when New York had first contacted him. No, Brian Turner is running for his life. But where?

Custer couldn't trace Kincaid's cell phone, but he could trace the Suburban. He tore open a drawer and rifled through some papers until he found a heavily worn composition book. He paged through it and found the tracking information for the Suburban. Tapping hard on the keyboard, Custer quickly pulled up the GPS locator. The Suburban was in Easton. He stared at the map on the screen for a moment before jotting down the closest street intersection.

Drumming his fingers on the desk, Custer decided he wanted this taken care of as quickly as possible. It would take a full day to get another crew together and get them up to Pennsylvania from Kentucky. No, this was a job for a more local guy. Custer called a freelancer named Seamus Finney, a man he knew from his days in Philadelphia.

Finney was of average height and weight. Maybe six feet tall if he stretched and about one hundred eighty pounds, Finney was more or less average. It was his intellect and ill-tempered demeanor that made him seem much larger.

Custer had arrested Finney when Seamus was still a juvenile. The kid had spunk and was shaking down drug dealers for money. Finney wasn't stupid either. He picked low level dealers who wouldn't have much support from their distributors but also wouldn't go to the cops. He wouldn't have gotten caught if it weren't for a bicyclist whizzing by the alley Seamus had chosen to inflict his message upon the drug dealer.

Finney made money by asking for what he called insurance money. If the dealers balked, they were beaten so ruthlessly that many left the hospital disfigured. While Finney wanted monthly fees from every dealer in his self-proclaimed territory, it was the black and Hispanic dealers that he concentrated on the most. This also appealed to Custer.

As the arresting officer, Dalton Custer got to know Seamus Finney enough to pique his interest in the young man. Eventually, along with an inexperienced and overly zealous public defender, Custer was able to lessen the charges of aggravated assault to simple assault which was the difference between a felony and a misdemeanor. The victim's jaw was wired shut so he couldn't orally dispute the public defender's hints of self-defense, not that he would have anyhow. The self-defense angle combined with a written letter of apology and the fact that it was Finney's first arrest, was enough to sentence the young man to six months of probation.

After that, Custer offered guidance to who, where, and when Finney could resume his operations and a few larger jobs that required Finney's special talents for a percentage of the take. Over the years the pair had made some nice side money from extorting dealers, pimps, and any other individuals who would not run to the police.

Finney was intelligent, ruthless, and Custer had groomed him into the perfect thug. Custer shook his head annoyed knowing that if he would have used Seamus Finney first, the job would have been done by now.

The fee was agreed to and while he was still on the phone Custer emailed photos of Brian Turner, his address which at this point was useless, and the location of the Suburban in Easton, Pennsylvania. The call ended and Custer sat back. Now all he could do was wait.

Custer was tense. It was still early in the evening and waiting on Finney would keep him up all night. He needed to relax. Take his mind off of Tommy's blunder. He made another call. This time it was to a grouchy middle-aged woman who ran one of Rollins' several brothels. He ordered the delivery of a six pack, a pizza, and a young brunette.

Chapter 8

Wednesday

It was well past midnight when Brian Turner gave in to fatigue. After dispersing phone parts along the Maryland countryside, Sadie had fallen into a fitful slumber next to him. They had stopped for gas earlier in a town called Newton, West Virginia. He had felt okay then but the drain on his body caught up to him quickly. He found a motel and pulled in.

Brian had to ring the desk bell a few times before a sleepy man stumbled out of a nearby room clearly not happy about being roused to do his job. He looked upon Sadie and Brian with disdain not only for waking him but also for being Yankees and unbeknownst to the Turners, the man padded the price by twenty-five dollars for the intrusion. Brian didn't complain, paying in cash and even tipping the man ten bucks for getting him out of bed. The man muttered something about preferring to have stayed in bed and slid the room key across the counter before shuffling indignantly back to his room.

Brian moved the Firebird to a spot two doors down from their room. He and Sadie grabbed his suitcase and her hastily packed duffle. They entered the room, which Brian found surprisingly fresh and clean, and unloaded Sadie's bag. Brian took the empty bag back to the car and filled it with all of the guns and ammunition they had taken from the hit squads. He left his hunting rifle in the car. It was in a case under a blanket in the back seat.

He flicked a switch in the car's console and locked the doors. The switch was to a motion detector that when activated would transmit an alarm to a receiver that Brian kept on his person. It was a subtle alarm system that would allow Brian to see who might be messing with the Firebird without scaring the person away. It was an older system, but it worked. Brian set the receiver on a nightstand between the two double beds in the motel room.

With the door locked and shades drawn, Brian carefully unloaded the guns he and Sadie had acquired. There were ten. Eight were .45 ACP and two of those were Sig Sauer P227s that had been outfitted with silencers. The remaining two were .38 caliber revolvers. There were twenty-six clips, mostly loaded to capacity. Brian filled the ones that were short a few rounds and began dividing the clips into two piles of thirteen. He then unloaded four of the .45s and added those clips so each pile had fifteen clips. Each clip contained fourteen bullets. That made for some serious firepower. Too much firepower as there was no practical way to carry that many clips.

Brian put the unloaded .45s into his suitcase and reduced the pile of guns down to three. He put a silenced pistol and an unmodified pistol, both loaded, with three spare clips to one side of the bed. He made an equal pile on the other side of the bed. Everything else went into his suitcase then he changed his mind again. He pulled another gun and two clips out and put them on Sadie's duffle.

"What are you doing?" Sadie asked, concerned about the odd behavior.

Brian regarded her helplessly. "I don't know." They stared at each other for a moment. "I don't want to carry all this, but I don't want to have it too far out of reach either. I want you to have protection, but I don't want you in a gun fight. I just ... I … I don't know what I am doing."

Sadie didn't say anything. She just looked sad for a minute then grabbed toothpaste from Brian's suitcase and went into the bathroom. She hadn't packed her toothbrush so she just squeez3ed a glob out and used her finger.

Brian sat on the bed next to the pile of guns and ammunition. He just stared. The toilet flushing brought him from his trance as Sadie exited the bathroom. She padded across the motel room and climbed into one of the double beds without saying a word. Her back was turned to her father.

Brian wanted to, *needed to*, say something but the words just weren't there. He put the guns in his suitcase save the two silenced ones which he set on the floor flanking the shared nightstand. He stared at his daughter for a beat then brushed his teeth and climbed into the other bed, too stressed to sleep but too fatigued to drive.

At some point in the night Brian had fallen into a deep asleep. As his subconscious sorted out the shit storm he was in, flashbacks of his life with Lisa bubbled to the surface.

He dreamt of the night at the outdoor Aerosmith concert. It had rained and they were both soaked but the band played amazingly. He relived Lisa dancing, clapping, and singing along as if he were there again by her side.

Memories of their wedding day, the birth of each of their two daughters, and their first house. So many wonderful memories of his life with Lisa before the alcohol had become a problem. The alcohol. It had driven them apart to the point that he was not sure if he missed her now that she was dead. Sure, he missed the pre-wine Lisa, but that Lisa had died four years ago. The dreamt memories ceased abruptly.

Brian opened his eyes shortly after nine Wednesday morning. At some point during the night Sadie had crawled into bed with him just like she did when she was a little girl and had a bad dream. He watched his sixteen-year-old daughter sound asleep and could picture her as she was ten years ago, a knobby-kneed little girl toting her well-worn teddy bear and fighting back the tears from a scary dream as she climbed between him and Lisa. She was too stubborn to cry but still needed Mommy and Daddy. He closed his eyes and savored the decade-old memory. Sadie was sixteen years old and on the brink of womanhood now, but she would *always* be his little girl.

The sleep did him a world of good. His thoughts were clearer. They made more sense. As Sadie lay sleeping, Brian began to review the series of events that had led them to a motel somewhere in West Virginia and tried to form a plan for the next twenty-four hours. He slowly slid out of bed only enough to reach the envelope marked **JOB** then eased back under the covers.

Brian looked at the photo of the property that Rollins owned. It was surrounded by trees on three sides and the back bordered a lake. He wanted to stay away from the lake. Brian was not a strong swimmer plus being slightly more than three weeks before Christmas, hypothermia was a concern. However, it was a concern for anyone. Brian began to view the picture like he would a hunt. The lay of the land would often dictate how deer or bear would travel. In this case the lake actually formed a buffer that eliminated close to one hundred eighty degrees of potential escape. It was a barrier that the good doctor could not use without being seen. It restricted travel to watercraft and if Rollins took a boat, Brian was confident enough with his rifle that it would be the last boat ride Rollins would ever have. Now all Brian had to do was find the most efficient shooting lanes. Just like hunting a deer.

And also, just like a deer needed to leave cover to browse or drink, Dr. Cooper Rollins would have to leave his home sometime too. All Brian needed to do was wait. His Remington Model 700 .243 was a flat-shooting hunting rifle. Brian knew if he could see it, he could hit it. At least it was that way with deer where the shots were at most two hundred yards. He wasn't sure yet how close he would need to be to Rollins. He had never hunted a human before.

Brian's thoughts returned to the more immediate future. He needed a shower and food.

Sadie's steady breathing had grown quieter. She was awake and staring at him. "I hated you last night," she croaked in a sleepy voice. She rubbed her eyes and before Brian said anything she hugged him. "I didn't like that. I blamed you for Mom's murder and for Hannah being in danger but if I were in that cornfield, I would have done the same thing you did. Agree to anything to save myself. Of course, I wouldn't have sold pot to begin with but that's beside the point. It was thirty years ago. Different times than now."

Her chin trembled a bit before Sadie resumed talking. "I hear some kids talk about their parents. Not so much my group, I mean Grace, Sarah, Karen… they have great parents, but others, like *a lot* of other kids, well, their parents are divorced or don't get too involved with them, whatever. Or they drink, like Mom does…. did. But not you."

Tears welled up in Sadie's eyes, but she stubbornly refused to let them flow. "You are the best dad a girl could hope for. These people, Mike or whatever, they could have just picked a person at random and threatened their family to make them go kill some guy in Kentucky. I mean what you did was thirty years ago. It shouldn't count anymore." Sadie paused again. "But they are forcing you, forcing us, to go do their dirty work." She hugged Brian. "I love you, Dad."

Brian couldn't hold back anymore. His tears flowed over his cheeks as he held his little girl tightly. "I love you too, Peanut."

Sadie kept her face on Brian's chest. "How come you still have the house and the Firebird? I mean, it's cool and all, but why is it in Lionel Breckenridge's name?"

Brian took a moment to compose himself. While he knew the answer, putting it into words for his daughter was a bit daunting. "It's a lot harder to get rid of an alias than it is to create one," Brian laughed uncomfortably. He ruminated upon the question some more. That wasn't all of the answer. "Sadie, I am so average it's ridiculous. I worry about taxes, cholesterol, you and Hannah, retirement. You name it, I worry about it. I make just enough to almost get by, and every day is a battle. For the most part, we are comfortable and that is huge, but it is also all I've got. No vacations, no fancy cars. I have to make payments for your soccer fees. I am and for the most part, always have been, average. I have an average job, drive an average truck, in an average, well… maybe slightly larger than average house but I can barely afford the damned thing. Even before I met Mom, I was an average student with average athletic ability and average looks who dated average girls and had average friends.

"And don't get me wrong. I'm not complaining. It may sound that way, but I am not. There are a lot worse things in life than being average. I love being your dad and the time I coached soccer and going to all of your and Hannah's events. I love my life, but… I am still average." Brian paused. A mischievous, prideful grin spread across his lips. He lowered his voice. "But, for five years, this ordinary, average, run-of-the-mill dad was not so average. I was an outlaw. I was a criminal for five years, Sadie. Not too many dads can say that."

Brian smiled as he reminisced. "It's not that I'm proud of what I did, but honestly, I'm not really ashamed either. I would never want to do it again, but I still can feel the rush. Sneaking around after dark, loading the Bird with twenty, thirty, fifty pounds of weed and making deliveries. I'd make my drops, pick up gobs of cash then blast Black Sabbath, Iron Maiden, Def Leppard, and AC/DC to stay awake as I drove back to my secret garage and back to my normal, average, everyday life.

"As corny as it may sound, I had a secret identity and it felt great. I couldn't tell anyone, but it was a dark secret that was all my own. I was average Brian Turner to everyone who knew me but the real me, for five years anyhow, the real me was an outlaw. And it was a rush!

"Yeah, it would be very difficult to make Lionel Breckenridge disappear now, but I guess… deep down inside, I don't really want him to go. I know at some time, I will have to, but that time hasn't come yet, and I can still *feel* the adrenaline rush."

His smile faded abruptly. "Even the rush isn't worth what it has gotten me into now, though." A tsunami of guilt swelled inside him. "Not just me, us."

Sadie didn't say anything. She just listened, holding her father tightly as he spoke. Eventually the moment passed, and their embrace ended. When Sadie stood, she seemed hardened, cold. "So, let's get this done and over with. I blame Dr. Rollins for Mom's death. Let's return *the favor*."

Two hunters were always better than one. Sadie's help improved chances of success. Brian still had difficulty with the idea of involving her, but it was far too late for that now. Sadie was in. She had killed as many men as he had. She was as involved now as he was. He also couldn't help but wonder what this was doing to her mentally, emotionally. She should be in chemistry class right now but instead she was part of a father/daughter hit squad. He would have to deal with that after they completed The Favor… if they survived. Like it or not, he had a partner. More threads of Brian's decency snapped. He could feel it. Once Brian admitted that he had a partner whether he liked it or not, his plan began to grow firmer. "First, let's get cleaned up and find something to eat. After that, I think it's time you learned how to drive a real car."

Chapter 9

Seamus Finney woke up at four am. He had made some mental notes and packed his gear immediately after Dalton Custer's call. He trusted Custer but out of good business practice, Finney opened his laptop and checked his bank account. *Good man.* Custer had made the deposit of half of the fee. Finney finished his breakfast and tossed his gear into his 2015 Porsche 911.

Finney made a good living. He was always busy. He had a few clients like Custer who paid well for particularly nasty jobs, but Finney also had a surprisingly large list of clients who were in legitimate business such as contractors and mechanics. In fact, most of his business came from legitimate business owners.

While a businessperson would never pay for a murder, they eagerly paid for debt collection. In the long run, Finney was far less expensive than hiring an attorney and he added his fees to the debt whereas collecting within the restrictions of state law, collection fees would come out of the recovered payment. And on top of all that, Finney was far more efficient than a lawyer or debt collection agency. He often got payment faster than what the legal system would.

Finney was smart with his money. He paid taxes on enough to justify his lifestyle. He wasn't a glamorous man. He lived alone with his cats, Alice and Speedy, in a nicer-than-average home in Warminster, Pennsylvania. The house had solar panels and a comfortable deck where he enjoyed reading during his downtime. Finney had two rental properties and a decent stock portfolio which was self-managed. His only big indulgence was the Porsche.

He also donated his time and some money to the local SPCA. That's where Alice and Speedy had come from. Seamus Finney made a living being ruthless toward humans, but animals were a different story. He had always had a soft spot for them and would have owned dogs too, but his work schedule prohibited it. The rescued cats were good company and with a large feeder and waterer, they could go a week or two without Finney being home. With any luck, the trip to find Brian Turner would only take a day or two.

Seamus Finney drove north up Route 611 into bucolic upper Bucks County. He turned onto Route 212 and wound his way into Dunning. It was a small but important deviation on the way to Easton and he wanted a feel for how Turner lived. He doubted Turner would be home. If he were, then Finney's job would be far easier than anticipated.

The trip had taken a little less than an hour. Sunrise was still over an hour away when Finney shut off the Porsche. He had parked it in a cutout by the roadside and walked to Turner's house. No lights were on but there were two dogs out back in a large fenced-in yard. One of them barked once before Finney reached over the fence and petted it. Once each of the dogs met Finney, they happily wandered off to look for mice or whatever else might be in the yard. Some watchdogs they were.

Finney quietly walked around the house. There were no immediate neighbors and he doubted anyone would be up at this time of the morning anyhow. He tested the front door and it was locked. A side door and the garage were also locked. Finney entered the backyard through a gate in the fence and was greeted by the dogs again. One brought him a stick. "Not now, buddy", he whispered as he stepped onto a weathered deck. He checked a side door that was locked but a back door leading into a large eat-in kitchen was not. Finney eased the door open and was immediately greeted with the metallic scent of blood.

Using a small Maglite, Finney surveyed the kitchen. Two bodies lay motionless and cold on the tile floor. Dark pools of congealed blood surrounded each corpse. A chair was tipped over and severed straps of duct tape were beside it. The drywall had some damage to it and Finney deduced it was caused by a few stray pellets from a shotgun blast.

Stepping over the bodies in the kitchen, Finney swept his beam of light into the foyer. Clean. Same with the formal dining room. The living room was a different story. A woman lay on the couch, mouth agape, and her eyes wide and unfocused. A brownish dot was on her forehead. The back of her head was a matted glob of crusted blood and chunks of skin and bone entwined in her long hair.

Two more bodies lay on the floor of the living room. One was riddled with bullets and the other had a shot to the leg and abdomen. The second body piqued Finney's interest. The shots were not vital kill shots. If left unattended they would have killed the victim eventually, but he didn't die from them. His head was caved in, and a bloody fireplace poker was shoved into the stomach wound. Turner was angry. Rightfully so but Finney suspected Brian Turner may have conversed with this man before bludgeoning him to death. Finney rubbed his goatee. Most people would cower, panic, or try to flee a scene like this. Turner stayed and took the time to use a fireplace poker on this man. *Exactly what I would do if I were surprised at home and got the upper hand.*

Finney walked the rest of the house. There was a master bedroom that was neat and tidy. The bed unslept in. There were two bathrooms and two other bedrooms clearly belonging to teenaged girls. One, fairly neat with a made bed. A Justin C. Smith High School diploma lay on the dresser along with some Gettysburg College miscellanea. There were photos of groups of kids, mostly girls, with one common girl in them. It didn't take much deduction to figure out she was a Turner. Finney plucked one of the photos from the wall and slid it in his coat pocket. Custer had mentioned the older daughter was at college. Looking at the diploma, he noted her name was Hannah.

The other bedroom was more disrupted. The bed neatly made but the closet was left open, and some clothes were strewn on the floor. This person had left in a hurry. There were several photos in this room also. As with the other daughter, it didn't take Finney much time to discern which girl was a Turner. He swiped one of the photos from this girl's wall as well.

Finney went back to the kitchen and exited the same way he entered. The dogs met him and he petted them once more. Noticing they had several empty bowls, Finney checked his watch then the eastern sky. He had time. He went back into the kitchen and found a large bag of dog food. He filled the bowls with food and fresh water, then left the Turner property for Easton.

According to his iPad, the Suburban was still parked in the same spot in Easton that Custer had said it was. Finney drove the winding Route 611 along the Delaware River into the City of Easton. He soon found the Suburban parked exactly where it had been since Custer had called him about the job. Finney drove past the street where the truck was parked and parked his Porsche half a block away. He climbed out of his car, felt his .40 caliber Glock 22 nestled in the small of his back, and walked to inspect the Suburban.

Easton was beginning to wake up for the school and work day ahead. Some holiday lights were left on overnight, others on timers or just unplugged, gave a festive atmosphere to the working-class neighborhood. Bedroom and kitchen lights glowed in increasing number as residents woke and began their morning routine. Nobody was outside yet but Finney quickened his pace to be safe. He didn't want to be seen inspecting the Suburban.

Finney approached with practiced caution. The truck was spotless. No wrappers or any signs of use other than the keys were left in the ignition. Finney used a gloved hand to gently open the door. He pocketed the keys. After giving the truck a quick but thorough once-over, Finney locked it and moved to the corner of the alley and the road his Porsche was parked on. He leaned against a privacy fence and waited for something to happen.

Seamus Finney wore a black coat that fell just below his waist. It was comfortable and capable of adequately concealing an array of personal weaponry if he chose to carry it. On this day he only had his Glock, two spare clips, and his seven-inch KA-BAR combat knife. The Glock was nice as a backup but by far his weapon of choice was the knife. Quiet and personal so his victims knew they had messed up. Neither weapon was visible under his jacket.

About forty-five minutes had passed when a skinny kid appeared lugging a battered old trash can to the alley. The boy stared at the Suburban and shook his head. He glanced at a garage that had a heavy steel door with a thick lock on it. Again, the boy seemed almost perplexed. He knew something.

"Hey. Kid. Got a minute?" Seamus Finney walked quickly toward the boy. "Can I ask you a question?"

The boy immediately backed away from the stranger. He looked panicked. "Sorry mister. I don't want any candy and I'm not helping you look for some lost puppy. I gotta get to school."

Stranger danger. Shit. "Hey, no. None of that stuff. Look, I'll keep my distance." Finney stopped walking and the boy warily stopped his retreat. He was close enough to his house that he could yell for his mom if Finney made the slightest aggressive move.

Finney held his hands up for the kid to see. "Look, I'm looking for a man who parked that truck there." Finney pointed to the Suburban. "Do you know him or did you see him?"

The boy was wary. "Who wants to know?"

"My client does. He needs a kidney and this guy I am trying to find is a relative. He could be a donor that would save a life." Finney reached into his coat for Turner's picture.

The boy jumped and started to run. He yelled, "Mom!"

"No! Wait! Kid, it's real important. Stop. I'll leave this picture hear and you can walk to it. I will step back." Finney set the photo on the flagstone walkway and quickly backed up twenty feet, but the kid kept running.

The back door opened, and a woman stepped out holding a baseball bat. "Willie! What's wrong?" Willie ran to her side, and she quickly assessed the situation. "What are you doing with my boy?"

Finney clenched his teeth then relaxed. "I am looking for this man. May I show you his picture?" He didn't wait for a response.

Approaching as quickly as he could without being any more threatening, he picked up the photo and held it in front of him. Finney slowed his gate until he was within range for the woman and boy to see the photo.

The woman squinted muttering something about glasses. The boy, however, announced, "That's Mr. Breckenridge, Mom."

Finney double checked the photo. *Breckenridge*? He held it out for the woman again.

Leaning closer she agreed. "Oh, yes. I'm sorry. That's Lionel Breckenridge. He's our landlord. Do you know him?"

Lionel Breckenridge. What the hell is that about? "No. I need to find him to help my client. As I tried to tell your boy here, my client needs a kidney and I'm trying to track down Mr. Breckenridge. He's a distant relative and a probable donor."

"He was here yesterday but he hasn't come back," the woman offered. "Real nice guy. He stops in once a month to check on the house and to go for a ride in his Camaro."

Willie gave his mom a disgusted look. "It's a Firebird, Mom." He turned to Finney. "Mr. B has a 1973 Pontiac Firebird Formula 400 and it's awesome! He's taken me for a ride in it. It's real fast."

Finney nodded thoughtfully. "Do you have an address for, uh, Mr. Breckenridge?"

"Yes," the woman said. Letting her guard down she invited Finney into her home. "I have it right here. Would you like a cup of coffee?"

Finney declined but followed the woman and her son into the home. He closed the door behind him and deftly locked the knob, unnoticed by Willie or his mom.

Willie grabbed a battered old laptop and began typing something into the search engine while his mother found a scrap paper. She wrote Lionel Breckenridge's address, a post office box in Liethsville, and handed it to Finney. Willie proudly pointed to the computer. "Look. This is what Mr. B's car looks like."

Finney first studied the address then the image on the computer screen. "Nice car. I had a friend in high school who drove one like that," Finney lied. He turned to the woman. "So, you don't know where Mr. Breckenridge lives?"

Willie's mother shook her head.

Finney surveyed the kitchen. Just two plates in the sink. "So, I guess you're the man of the house?" he asked Willie.

"I try," he said sheepishly.

Growing a little uncomfortable, Willie's mother said, "I'm sorry we couldn't be of more help. I have to get to work, and the man of the house needs to get to school." She lovingly patted Willie on the shoulder and tousled his hair. "Is that all?"

Finney gave a grim nod and eased his hand inside his coat. He hadn't put the silencer on his Glock. His hand rested it on the KA-BAR. He didn't like witnesses. He also didn't like leaving a trail. He paused, then moved his hand past the knife and grabbed his wallet. "Look, you've been real helpful." He pulled a fifty, a twenty, and two ones from his wallet. "Thank you." He handed the fifty to Willie's mom who refused the bill initially, but Finney insisted she accept it.

Finney then knelt by Willie. He handed him the remaining bills. "The twenty is for you to save. Put your money away, as much as you can. Money won't buy happiness, but it makes being miserable a hell of a lot easier." He smiled at the boy. "The two dollars is to buy a chocolate bar but only if Mom says it's okay. It's easier to save your money if you treat yourself to a little something once in a while." Finney stood quickly and walked to the door. He unlocked it and walked out as the boy and his mother thanked him profusely.

Once back to the Porsche, Finney checked his iPad. Google Maps showed Liethsville as being only a few miles from Dunning. *Well, well. Brian Turner has a secret life.* He then placed a call to Custer. "Hey. I need you to look up a guy named Lionel Breckenridge."

Chapter 10

The ride through the rest of West Virginia was uneventful. Sadie had been practicing on a stick shift prior to their interstate drive and while she could hardly be considered proficient, she didn't do too badly with the old Pontiac. She even let the horses roar a bit on a wide-open stretch of highway hitting eighty-five miles per hour before getting nervous and easing off the throttle. The entire time Brian hadn't said a word. He just let Sadie enjoy the ride of a classic automobile.

At one point he had texted Hannah. HOW ARE YOU DOING? Five minutes later his phone buzzed. OK.

GOOD. JUST CHECKING UP ON YOU. LOVE YOU.

LOVE YOU TOO.

The pair crossed the Kanawha River into Kentucky. Brian tensed as he read the sign at the bridge that welcomed them to Catlettsburg. While they still had a long drive to New Concord, the fact that they had arrived in the final state of the trip drove a cold spike of reality into him. No longer being able to afford the luxury of watching Sadie enjoy driving, Brian opened the Job envelope and pulled out the overhead photo of Dr. Rollins' homestead.

Compound was more like it. Brian adjusted his reading glasses and noticed what appeared to be a thick wall surrounding the property. It was still tough to see, and he decided he wanted a magnifying glass. They were below a half tank of gas, and he needed to pee. "Hey, let's pull over and stretch our legs." Sadie just nodded.

Their first stop was for fuel. The Firebird had a fuel cell instead of the conventional gas tank. At thirty gallons, it was a larger capacity than most. The fuel cell had been custom fit to hang as low as what the factory gas tank would have but it was still too bulky to fit entirely under the trunk floor. So, in order to fuel the Firebird, one had to open the trunk lid. This was perfect as Brian needed to access the trunk anyhow. There was a small tool kit bolted to the sheet metal next to the fuel cell. As Brian filled the cell with high grade gas, he also removed a screwdriver from the tool kit and slid it into his pocket.

After topping the tank, they parked the car in a corner of a public parking lot and walked across the street to a CVS. He noted the lack of security cameras. Brian got a magnifying glass, some gum, a highlighter, and a Daily Independent newspaper. After leaving, they walked behind the store where the employees parked. Still no cameras and the lot was bordered by large arborvitae.

Both were carrying pistols and Brian reluctantly told Sadie to keep walking and he'd meet her back at the Bird. She continued at a normal gait as Brian ducked behind a Subaru. He quickly unscrewed the license plate, slid it into the folded newspaper then strode out of the lot to catch up with his daughter. He gestured for the keys and took over driving. They cleared Catlettsburg and got back onto Interstate Route 64 West for the next one hundred seventy miles.

"What did you do?" Sadie asked.

"I borrowed a Kentucky license plate. Once we get a little farther from the crime scene, I want to swap plates. Notice anything different with the Kentucky cars?" Sadie shook her head. "No inspection sticker. The Firebird is registered as an antique so there is no sticker on it either. With the PA tags, we stand out even more. Local plates will help us blend a little. That way we look like we're driving an old car from Kentucky."

"Wow, Dad. Being a little paranoid?"

"Yes and no. Instead of paranoid, I call it detail oriented. I know an antique Firebird stands out on its own, but the PA tags will only draw more attention. And that is something we don't need. The tiniest detail might save our lives."

"Have…" Sadie stopped. She wanted to ask but was afraid of the answer. "Have you done this before?"

"If 'this' means plot someone's murder, no. If 'this' means use the Firebird for selling pot and evading police detection, or anyone else's detection, then the answer is yes."

Sadie breathed a deep sigh of relief. Knowing her father sold weed thirty years ago paled in comparison to what she was helping him do now. It seemed less than benign. That hurdle being cleared, Sadie began to look ahead. "So, what do we do when we get there? How do we pull this off?"

Brian frowned. "Not sure. I kinda wish we had brought a second rifle. Two snipers would be better than one. We may have to just wait him out until he comes outside."

"What if Rollins is as detail oriented as you are?"

"How so?"

"Well," Sadie was thinking out loud, "I'm not sure what this guy did to Mike, but I would think he is in the same business. Therefore, he probably already knows that somebody might want him dead. So, if I were him, and my home was as easy to find, I wouldn't give anyone a clear shot."

Brian hadn't really considered that.

"And that is probably why Mike uses people like us." She wagged her index finger as she thought aloud. "Rollins wouldn't recognize us and if we get caught, there is no trail back to Mike's real identity. We are like pawns in chess, Dad."

Brian took his eyes from the road and regarded his daughter for as long as he dared. Pretty insightful for a sixteen-year-old. He returned his focus to the highway. "Know any rocket launcher stores in Kentucky?"

Sadie pondered her father's remark. It was made in jest, however, the idea had merit. She tapped her phone. "No, but according to Google, we have a couple hundred miles to go yet. I bet there are a lot of hobby shops between here and Rollins' house. And fireworks are legal in Kentucky."

"Um, not sure where you think you are going with this, but a military rocket launcher is going to be a little more accurate than a model rocket."

"Well, duh. We don't have that option though, do we? So, we hit the house with a ton of model rockets hoping to put some through the windows. If we set the house on fire, he would have to come out."

"So would all of his bodyguards. I'm not liking it."

Sadie rustled through the envelope. "Even if all of his bodyguards," she paused as she read the notes on Rollins, "and there will be anywhere from two to six on any given day, if all of them come out, we can still take out Rollins."

Brian still wasn't convinced. "Even so, I'd bet they would treat the guy like the Secret Service treats a president. If we don't have a guaranteed clear shot, he will go somewhere safe, and we lose him."

Sadie fired back, "So we take out the cars first. And his big wall keeps intruders out, but it also keeps him in."

"Okay. Hmm. I like where you're going with this." Brian glanced at the photo again trying to commit it to memory as he drove. Sadie was making sense. A thought occurred to him. "How much money do we have? About forty-five hundred, right?" He fidgeted in his seat, pulled his wallet from his back pocket and handed it to Sadie.

She counted the bills. "Seven hundred eighty plus the four thousand in the trunk. Fifty-seven eighty."

"And how much do drones cost?" Brian asked pensively.

Sadie smiled and she tapped and swiped at her phone. "Prices are all over the place but this one at Walmart is five hundred and it has a camera that connects to a phone."

"What do you think that camera weighs? Maybe eight ounces?"

"I dunno. I guess"

Brian had teased Sadie when she wanted to join the Cybersonics team at school. They were some of the nerdier kids in school however being a nerd wasn't quite the stigma as it was when he was in school. Sadie was far from nerd status, and she loved technology and science. The Cybersonics team built robots for competition and often won. Sadie loved being part of that.

"Do you think you can adapt the camera control to carry and release a payload of the same weight as the camera?"

"You mean we don't want the camera, but we have the drone deliver something else?" She shrugged. "Sure, if I had the right tools. It's a no-brainer."

Brian smiled as a solid plan formed. "Perfect. Let's go shopping."

Chapter 11

Seamus Finney had watched his phone for about fifteen minutes before deciding to grab a cup of coffee. Coffee then turned into breakfast. Eggs over easy, two pancakes, and a slab of ham. Finney read the Easton Express as he ate, occasionally studying the foot traffic outside of the diner window.

Finney liked to people watch. He hated people in general, but he liked to watch strangers in order to hone his skills. He could tell a lot about a person by the way they carried themselves. A woman had walked by earlier who Finney would have bet money that she was facing a nasty divorce and most likely her husband had violated her trust. Either by cheating with another woman or by mismanaging finances. He would have bet it was another woman.

A man walked by in a hurry. Expensive coat and shoes. He bumped two people and never acknowledged them. He was a narcissistic asshole. He was probably pretty far up the corporate ladder to feel quite good about himself yet still having a few rungs to climb. If he were in a relationship, it was probably a shallow one. He viewed women as eye candy. A status symbol to show off when rubbing elbows with the right people. Finney smiled. It was people like that man who he most enjoyed visiting. They were so tough to their underlings, but that toughness went down the drain when confronted with Finney's brand of business.

Some teenagers passed by. Jocks mostly but there was a token nerd in the group.

An hour passed. Then two. The diner wasn't busy, and Finney had already tipped the waitress once. He read the entire newspaper, completed the crossword puzzle and the Sudoku challenge, and studied at least a hundred faces when his email chimed.

Not much on Lionel Breckenridge. He was a landscaper at one time. He owned property in Easton and lived just above the poverty level. His taxes and utilities were paid and up to date. He had a 1973 Pontiac Firebird registered in his name since 1983. It was the only car he had ever owned and the registration and insurance was paid and up to date. Just like the kid said, Breckenridge drove an old car.

Brian Turner was a different story. Finney had information on him already, but it pertained mostly to him and his home. The email delved a little deeper into Turner's life. It confirmed that Turner had a wife, who Finney knew was now irrelevant, and two daughters, Hannah and Sadie. Hannah was the one at Gettysburg.

Finney had already surmised that Sadie had bolted along with her father. Hannah, however, was an unknown. He requested Hannah's class schedule. A response came back stating that it would take some time to crack the student passcodes and ID numbers. Finney didn't respond. He knew the tech understood to hurry. He left another hefty tip for the waitress. Seamus Finney thanked her for letting him stay so long then departed for Gettysburg.

The drive had taken almost three hours. Traffic had been brutal. Some information on Hannah Turner had been emailed while Finney was driving but her class schedule was not on it. The dorm and room number was, and after investing some time in cruising the perimeter of the campus and its parking lots in search of a 1973 Firebird, that was where Finney started.

Finney parked his Porsche near the faculty lot in hopes it would be less conspicuous. He then strolled through campus until he found Hannah Turner's dorm. He hadn't waited long before seeing her. She was among a group of five students walking on a path worn through the grass. Finney followed from a distance as the group went to the dining hall for a late lunch.

Forty minutes later, Hannah Turner left the dining hall with another cluster of students and went to a class. After class, it was the gym, then a run on the track and a loosely organized soccer practice. The entire time she was surrounded by at least four friends. Back to the dorm for a quick shower then studying in her dorm room. The room was located at ground level and Finney could see into it easily as the shades were wide open. There were six kids in her room all poring over open books and laptop computers.

Presumably, the only time this kid was alone was in the ten minutes when she took a shower. Even then, Finney couldn't be sure. He watched her gather toiletries and fresh clothes then reappear ten minutes later with wet hair and clean sweats. She may have been alone, but dorms often had multiple shower stalls. From what he had already seen, she probably had several other women in the showers next to her. They always went to the bathroom together, why not the showers? He watched from a distance through the open-shaded window as Hannah Turner settled into a study session among the other kids in her room.

Two pizzas were delivered, and the kids ate while they studied. Two more kids showed up, books in hand. Five of the students were men who wore various garb with the Gettysburg Wrestling logo on it. Bursting in and grabbing Turner was not an option. He would be overpowered in an instant. Shooting everyone in the room would be fine with Finney but he didn't want the attention that would be associated with such a crime. He shook his head. Out of all the freshmen at Gettysburg, his target seemed to be the most popular kid on campus. She was never alone! But, he reasoned, she had to sleep sometime.

He checked his watch and walked back to his Porsche. Finney had been up since four that morning and decided to take a two-hour nap. He settled into the leather seat, set an alarm on his watch, and closed his eyes.

*****

Custer had confidence in Finney, but he had also learned that having a solid back-up plan was always good. This Lionel Breckenridge was interesting. Turner had a secret life. It was of no real consequence yet still merited thought. Custer had the license number of Breckenridge's Firebird and he made sure everyone on Rollins' payroll knew what a 1973 Pontiac Firebird Formula 400 looked like. Turner/Breckenridge wouldn't get close to New Concord in a car that stood out like that one.

There were well over a dozen state and county cops on Rollins' payroll. Soon Brian Turner was officially a suspect in the murder of Tommy Kincaid and kidnapping of a sixteen-year-old girl from Pennsylvania. A be-on-the-lookout was issued for Turner and his antique car. The information was sent to every police department in Kentucky.

The Turners would be easy to find. They would be brought in for questioning and there would be a statement to all of the police that they were in custody. It would be discovered that they were father and daughter. It would be a simple mistake and they would be released with gracious apologies from the police department. Then, one of Custer's cops would escort them from the building and the Turners would never be heard from again. It was a slam-dunk in Custer's mind. It was only a matter of time.

Custer was amazed at the stupidity of not only Turner in using a vehicle that stood out so much but also in New York for sending someone like Turner. He knew New York had a propensity for sending amateurs that they had something on, but it was a tactic Custer didn't understand and thought foolish. Amateurs were expendable and cheap, but a professional was much safer. And a pro would not drive a car that attracted attention.

Chapter 12

Brian and Sadie began their shopping. They had picked up two drones but needed more. They had also stopped at a hobby supply store for electronic soldering equipment. There was still plenty to purchase on their trek across Kentucky and one of the items on their list was a pair of plastic two-gallon gas cans. The firebird's gas gauge was under a quarter tank and Brian was hungry, so it was fortuitous timing when they found a gas station located across from a shopping center with a Kroger grocery store in it.

Sadie pulled into the gas station. Of the two of them it was she that had been buying the drones thus she had the bulk of the money. "Filler 'er up and get two gas cans." Brian held out his hand as he spoke. "Give me a fifty and, no, make it a hundred, and I'll grab some grub. Any requests?"

"Oreos," Sadie said with a grin.

"How about something healthy?" Brian replied in a paternal tone.

Sadie rolled her eyes. "Dad. We're going to go wage a mini war on some guy's compound. I think an Oreo or two is called for."

"Fine," Brian smiled as she plopped a few bills in his hand. "Get the ninety-two octane." He climbed out of the car and walked across the street.

Sadie went inside to prepay. She had not been paying attention during previous fill-ups and had no idea what the tank would hold. There were three twenty-something men in the store that the clerk was watching with obvious distrust. The purchase of the two cans along with filling them up and a full tank was more calculating than the clerk wanted to do so she just told Sadie to pay when she finished getting gas.

Sadie filled the cans first and put them in the trunk. She put a trash bag over them in an effort to contain the fumes and then proceeded to fill the fuel cell. Sadie was not comfortable with the gas in the trunk but had no other way to transport it. There really was no other choice. The gas had to go in the trunk. She also had her mind on alterations to the drones and the overwhelming weight of what she and her father were planning to do.

When she returned to the clerk to settle her debt the clerk was arguing with one of the young men for smoking inside the building. They stopped bickering when Sadie impatiently asked for the total due. The clerk tapped the register and told her it would be seventy-six dollars and thirty cents. Sadie pulled the folded cash from her pocket and handed the clerk a one-hundred-dollar bill. The clerk made change and Sadie was on her way.

One of the young men had gone outside. The other two were about to when one paused. "Where are my manners? Allow me." He held the door for Sadie. "After you, Miss."

Sadie smiled politely. The man was dirty and smelled like tobacco, sweat, and something else she did not recognize but the thick southern drawl and his attempt at manners was pleasant. "Thank you." Distracted by the man holding the door, she never saw the blow coming.

The man who had already gone outside leveled a fist to Sadie's mouth knocking her backward into the greasy arms of the gentleman. He dropped her hard on her back and knelt over her neck pinning her to the ground. Sadie tried to push him off, but he pressed hard on her face. One of the men kicked her in the ribs then tore open her pocket spilling the folded bills onto the ground. "Jackpot!" he said in a thick drawl.

The man lifted his unwashed leg from Sadie's face. She began to get up only to receive another kick to the gut. "Stay down you stupid Yankee bitch."

The three men ran across the parking lot to a battered Ford F150. The truck roared to life in a cloud of blue haze and sped out of the lot spraying gravel until the tires caught purchase on the asphalt road. They were out of sight in seconds.

The clerk knelt beside Sadie. "Oh, mah gawd! Are you okay?"

With the clerk's assistance Sadie got to her feet. Her abs hurt from being kicked and she tasted blood from a small split in her lower lip which was beginning to swell. She was sore but the pain was dulled by rage and panic. They took the money she and her father needed to complete the job. The clerk said something to her. Her mind was clouded but Sadie tried to focus on the clerk. "What?"

"Just sit down. I'm gonna call the cops." The clerk handed her a napkin from a stack near the hot dog machine then grabbed her cell phone.

"No," Sadie mumbled. *Where's Dad? I need Dad here.* "No. Don't call the cops. Not yet anyhow. Let me get my dad."

"Oh, honey, you need to report this. Them scum do this shit all the time and nobody presses charges so they just keep doin' it an' doin' it. Plus, it's my job on the line here. I need to call the cops."

Sadie wiped her lip. It was tender but not bleeding so much anymore. Her ribs hurt but they too were unbroken, just bruised. "You know them?"

The clerk was pressing numbers on her phone. Sadie gently put her hand on the phone. "Please don't." She pushed cancel and the clerk looked at her bewildered. "I can't have the cops here. Not right now."

The clerk still looked confused.

Outside Brian was loading groceries into the Firebird. He looked impatiently at the gas station store and decided to find out what was taking so long.

Sadie saw her father coming to the store. "Look, my dad is here. Just hold off on the phone call until he comes in."

Brian entered and his body language changed instantly upon seeing his battered daughter. "How bad are you hurt? What happened?"

"I'm okay, Dad. Three guys mugged me. They took the money."

Brian said nothing. He approached Sadie and gently examined her lip. The clerk mumbled something about calling for help and Brian shot her a look that told her to put the phone down. He turned his attention back to Sadie. "Just your face?"

She shook her head. "No, they kicked me too, but I'm just bruised. Really, I'm okay."

Brian turned his attention to the clerk. He guessed she was maybe ten years his junior. It was obvious that he intimidated her. *Good.* He scanned the counter and saw a monitor. "Is that a camera rolling?"

The clerk swallowed hard. "Yes."

"Would the muggers be on that?"

The woman nodded.

"Let's take a look then." Brian moved toward the monitor.

"Oh, I can't do that. I ain't allowed. My boss would have a fit."

Brian paused. Once again, he could feel his moral compass eroding. It wasn't just threads of morality this time but bundles. Chunks of his scruples were falling into an abyss like a coastal precipice succumbing to a storm surge. He moved slowly and deliberately to the glass door and flipped the sign from open to closed. He then moved the clerk's cell phone from her hand to a shelf out of her reach. "I am going to look at the video footage. You can show me, or I can shoot you and do it myself."

The clerk smiled nervously for a beat before realizing Brian was serious. She remembered the young woman not wanting to call the police and was now understanding that the father and daughter were not to be trifled with. She began to tremble.

Brian clarified his position. "If I shoot you, I will review the video then destroy the computer and burn down the store with your corpse in it. If you show me, I will only destroy the computer. By my way of thinking, this is an easy decision on your part, but I am not going to waste much time before I make the choice for you." He brushed his jacket open just for her to glimpse the handle of his pistol.

With trembling hands, the woman keyed the computer. "Them boys was Bankers. Real assholes, if y'all asked me." The video flashed onto the monitor. Brian memorized their faces and when he saw Sadie get punched, he no longer cared about his rapidly changing moral compass.

"The car." Brian growled. "Show me their car."

"It's a truck," the clerk said. She keyed another view. This one was the parking lot. She froze the frame on the truck. The license plate was clearly seen, and Brian jotted it down on a scrap piece of paper.

"What do you mean they were bankers?"

"River Bank Village. It's a community of low-cost housing next to a trailer park. Lots of shady stuff goes on down there. It's about five miles down the road." The woman's confidence seemed to be growing. "The one that held the door was Calvin Miller. They called the other one Cooter, but I don't know his real name. Never seen the third guy. Prolly a cousin. Them people's got cousins out the ying yang."

Brian stared at the woman. She shrunk away and he decided that she had given him all the information that she could. Scanning the store, he saw a display of baseball bats strangely mixed with an outdated selection of touristy items. Louisville Sluggers.

He'd had to play enforcer twice when he was dealing weed. He was much stronger and more agile then. He didn't need a baseball bat. Brian didn't like beating people, in fact he hated it, but like all shameful acts, it got easier the second time around. "How much for the bats?"

"They twenty-five each. I mean, Louisville, right? Bat capital of the world?" The clerk shrugged. "We ain't that far away. Same state an' all."

Brian opened his wallet. He removed two hundred fifty dollars and handed the money to the clerk. "That's fifty for the bats and two hundred for you to forget you ever saw us." He nodded to the computer. "Does that run your cash register or any other business stuff?"

The lady nodded.

"Better close it out then."

She didn't catch what Brian was suggesting and he didn't offer an explanation. He ripped the computer from the counter and onto the floor. Without hesitation he smashed it into a multitude of pieces with his bat. Sorting through the wreckage, Brian found the hard drive and shook it away from the rest of the parts. Not readily seeing a way to destroy it, Brian held onto the hard drive and turned to Sadie. "You okay?"

"Yeah."

Brian turned to the clerk. "Thanks for your help." He opened the door and followed Sadie out to the car.

They drove about one mile in the direction the truck had gone before Brian pulled over. Sadie was expecting him to say something, but he didn't. He just fished the appropriate cell phone from the console and began texting. I NEED A NAME AND ADDRESS FOR THIS LICENSE PLATE. He typed the plate number then added, NOW and hit send.

To his surprise, Brian got a reply almost immediately. WHY? LET'S JUST SAY WE HAVE A SMALL DETOUR.

A minute passed before the phone buzzed. IT'LL TAKE SOME TIME. MAYBE TWO HOURS.

Brian could feel his pulse in his chest, neck, and hands. YOU GOT TEN MINUTES.

Sadie looked at her father like he was crazy. She knew they had no time to mess around but now he was giving their handler orders. She wasn't sure how that would work out.

The phone was silent as Brian drummed his fingers on the steering wheel. He stopped only to ask how Sadie felt. She said she was fine, and he went back to thrumming the wheel. Nine minutes passed then the phone buzzed. It was an address in the River Bank Village. Brian nodded once and fired up the powerful Pontiac.

Chapter 13

About a half mile outside of the entrance to River Bank Village was an old barn with two dilapidated carriage houses barely standing in its shadow. Reluctantly succumbing to the years of punishment from the weather, they listed to the east. They were filled with several tractors, but one had a space between the rusted tractors large enough to park a Firebird.

Brian pulled into the gravel driveway overgrown with scrub. He backed into the space between the tractors and shut the car off. Sadie watched her father. He just stared out the windshield. He looked angry and she felt compelled to say something. "I'm sorry."

"Huh?" He turned to her looking annoyed.

"I'm sorry."

Brian studied her for a moment. His features softened and he put his hand on her shoulder. "Don't be. I flashed some cash in the Kroger. Granted, it wasn't the wad you had but I still did it. I didn't even consider the possibility of some scumbag grabbing the money. The only difference is that there was a scumbag where you were. I'm thankful you aren't hurt any more than a few bruises.

"We both made the same mistake. We both will learn from it. From now on, we only remove what we think we will need when we go shopping." Brian smiled and rubbed Sadie's shoulders reassuringly. His features hardened again. "Now we have to

get our money back." Brian sighed. "At that's probably going to involve bloodshed."

Sadie nodded agreement. "They'll come after us it we don't use force."

Brian was silent again. He didn't like having his sense of ethics being destroyed. He hated knowing that his daughter's moral standards were being deconstructed as well.

He studied the inside of the dilapidated structure. To the left was an old International Harvester tractor in such a state of disrepair that Brian assumed it was for parts. It looked like someone had been working on it then stopped about five years ago. Next to it was another tractor with a thick canvas tarp draped over it. To the right stood a John Deere. Its unique green hue was faded but it looked like it was still in running order. Brian turned back to the tarp.

The Turners checked their weapons and packed three extra clips each. They used a blanket to cover the drones and other paraphernalia that was in the back seat and then they locked the car. Brian snatched the greasy tarp from the tractor it was covering and was dragging it toward the Firebird when a young boy of maybe twelve years old approached them.

The boy had torn clothes and a dirty face. His nose looked thicker than it should and had an odd color to it. Brian was pretty sure it was a faded bruise and maybe his nose had been broken. He had a much fresher bruise on his cheek. He looked cold but he also appeared as if he were used to it. "Who are you and what're y'all doin' with my daddy's tractors?"

Brian forced a smile. "We aren't touching the tractors. We would just like to park here for a few hours if that's okay with you. Is your dad around?"

"No."

"Will he be back soon?"

"He won't be back until I'm sixteen. He's in jail."

Sadie took over the questioning in a softer tone. "What about your mom? Is she around?"

The boy just shook his head. "She might be home tomorrow... or not."

That wasn't an answer Sadie had expected. How could a parent leave their kid alone that long? She looked at Brian for help.

"What's your name son?"

"Jarrod Thomas Belcher."

"Pleased to meet you. My name's Lionel." It may have been rude, but Brian opted not to introduce Sadie. He wanted to protect her as much as possible although she had already been in life and death situations twice now.

Brian fished in his pocket and pulled out a twenty-dollar bill. Jarrod's eyes went wide.

"Jarrod, let's make a deal. I will give you this twenty as a deposit. You don't let anyone go near this car until we come back, okay? When we get back and if nobody snooped around the car, I will give you another eighty dollars. That's a hundred bucks to protect our car. How's that sound?"

The boy was blown away by such an astronomical number. He nodded eagerly and accepted the twenty.

"Now, once our business is done, you have to forget you ever saw us. Agreed?" Brian extended his hand. Jarrod shook his hand to seal the deal.

"Okay," Brian said. "We'll be back in a few hours."

Without looking back, he and Sadie began walking toward River Bank Village. They both had their baseball bats resting on their right shoulders. Like father, like daughter. It conjured an image in Brian's mind of Andy and Opie carrying their fishing poles down a dirt road on the outskirts of Mayberry. He doubted that Andy and Opie would ever be partnered assassins. Brian sensed another large portion of his decency decay into nothingness. He envied Andy and Opie for a moment then slid his hand behind his back to verify that his Sig was within easy reach.

The pair walked in silence until they heard a car approaching. The Turners slipped into a copse of roadside trees and hunkered down low as to not be seen. The car passed and once out of earshot, Brian and Sadie stepped back onto the road. It would have been more favorable to travel through the woods, but the brush was too thick.

Soon a foul, chemical smell permeated the air. The Turners kept walking and rounding a bend they saw a faded sign announcing their arrival to River Bank Village. They tucked back into the scrub brush and using Google Maps, they got their bearings in relation to the village.

The pickup truck used to leave the scene of Sadie's mugging was licensed to a Darren Stancavage. The address Mike had provided was located near the rear perimeter of the village. Brian and Sadie opted to fight the remaining thicket of trees over approaching the home in broad daylight. It was a battle but after twenty minutes they found themselves in a secluded vantage point where they could see the back of the home.

It was a small house, probably mediocre in status in its heyday. The paint that had not already flaked away was faded, windows had clear plastic taped over them and there was a burn barrel in the backyard with the bottom rusted through in spots. A pile of trash bags was stacked near a broken fence. Stancavage's house matched the house next to it and the one next to that in each direction. Cookie-cutter homes differentiated only by color and style of outbuildings. The neighboring home had a pole building behind it. Other homes had small sheds, most likely built out of whatever scrap lumber could be found or stolen. The neighbor's pole building stood out mostly by its size but also because it was not encased in tar paper.

The front yard of the home served as a parking lot and catch-all for unwanted junk. There were the rusted husks of two cars of indeterminate make or model sitting on cinder blocks, broken lawn chairs, a pile of junk the Brian assumed was destined for a scrap yard, and a tire swing suspended from a rope that looked like it would give out at any moment. Parked between a pile of over-stuffed trash bags and a deteriorated doghouse with no dog was the old F150 that Brian and Sadie had seen on the video from the gas station.

A skinny man emerged from the back door. He walked about ten steps from the house and lit a cigarette. His flannel shirt flapped open in the front revealing a formerly white undershirt covering a bloated stomach. He stood unsteadily for a moment then unzipped his pants and urinated in the dirt. He finished and spat a thick wad of phlegm before returning to the house. Some form of heavy metal scream music blared when the man entered. Brian loved bands like Metallica, Iron Maiden, and Black Sabbath but the stuff these guys were listening to was totally foreign and lacking talent. It was horrible.

Brian sat back against a tree trunk and rubbed his chin. He felt a bit foolish. He had been so intent on finding the house that he had not planned what to do once they arrived. "Now what?" he whispered more to himself than Sadie.

"Well, I've been thinking about this, and I have an idea," Sadie replied.

Brian raised an eyebrow and listened.

"Well, we need to get them all together, right?"

Brian shrugged. "We need to get the money. I don't think it matters if we get them together or not."

Sadie frowned. It was obvious that she wanted to deliver a payback for being punched and kicked. Brian couldn't blame her, but the bigger picture was to get back on task to save themselves and Hannah from Mike's ultimatum.

"I can only think of one way to do this. I'm going to knock on the door and tell them I need the money back." Brian snorted before Sadie got to finish. She glowered at him then continued. "I will tell them I need the money back and will do anything to get it. That will…"

"No." Brian was repulsed by what his daughter was suggesting. "No, no, no. Even just thinking about that… no. There has to be another way."

"I'm not going to actually screw them, Dad!" Sadie scolded. Brian recoiled from her bluntness. "That would be disgusting. But they don't need to know that and if it gets me in the back door then I can distract them while you go in the front door."

Brian shook his head. He was appalled by the idea.

"Okay," Sadie said sounding exactly like her mother. "What's *your* idea?"

Brian narrowed his eyes and stared at her. He had nothing. He wanted to burst in with guns blazing but they needed the people to be able to tell them where the money was. He wracked his brain trying to come up with a viable alternative to Sadie's vile plan.

As she waited for his reply, a dirty old mid-seventies Oldsmobile Vista Cruiser crunched down the gravel road in a cloud of dust. The station wagon slid to a stop and the driver mercilessly slammed it into reverse. The car backed into the yard of the home and parked. Two of the men who attacked Sadie sprang from the old car and opened the back. They each grabbed two cases of beer and carried them to the house. The door opened blaring more guttural scream metal and they entered.

Sadie cocked her head as she resumed waiting for an answer from her father.

Disgusted, he said, "Wait here. I want to look at the front door."

Refusing to sit and wait, Sadie shook her head and followed her father. *Just like her mother*. Brian glowered at her once more before they left their hiding spot and stole through the neighboring yard. As they made their way to the front of the house, they saw enough silhouettes in the side window to presume that most of the activity was in a back room. That would bode well for Sadie's plan.

The front door had an aluminum storm door that swayed gently on its hinges. It revealed a sliver of light that indicated the front door was not only unlocked but it wasn't even latched. Sadie's plan began to make more sense although Brian loathed to admit it.

"Shit," Brian muttered. "Give me your bat." He paused, hating what he was about to suggest then forced himself to say it. "And you'd better give me your gun and clips. If they pat you down and find it, well, there could be problems. Once we get inside, I will get them back to you. And for the record, this idea sucks."

"Well, I can't argue with that." Sadie handed over her gun, spare clips, and the baseball bat. "How will you know when I am in?"

"I won't for sure. I'm guessing that an uninvited guest will make the party stop for a bit while they check you out. That's when I'll slip in. After that, the shit's gonna hit the fan." Brian stared hard at his daughter. "And if I can't easily open the door,

I'm coming in hot. I will shoot anyone that moves until there are two left. I'm not happy about using you as bait…again."

This time it was Sadie's turn to put a reassuring hand on her father's shoulder. "It'll be okay. We got this."

Brian begrudgingly nodded once. *Do I even have any decency left*? He doubted it. Then Sadie asked another question that confirmed his reflective suspicion. "Do we leave witnesses?"

Brian bristled at the thought. Between the two of them they had already killed eight people. Granted, the deaths were more or less in self-defense. Definitely the first four; however, they could have called the police for the second group. No, they were in too deep by then. Eight people. At this point a couple more wouldn't make a difference. Besides, they had mugged Sadie.

They were criminals.

Human trash.

And, he had a deadline.

The pieces of shit who mugged Sadie were screwing up the timeline and therefore putting Hannah, Sadie, and himself in danger.

"Dad?" Sadie leaned toward him waiting. Cautiously she opined, "I don't think we should. It might come back to haunt us later." She looked at him waiting for an answer that she already knew was there.

Brian felt hollow inside. He was disappointed in himself for bringing Sadie down with him, yet the way circumstances had played out, there was no other alternative. As disgusted as he was, he noticed that there was another feeling surfacing in the recesses of his consciousness. It was a feeling that he didn't want to admit to yet, shamefully, he couldn't ignore. Power.

Father and daughter locked eyes for a moment. Her lip was swollen and had begun to turn purple. She had a red mark on her cheek from the night before, too. Anger began to swell to the surface of Brian's thoughts. Resolutely, Brian shook his head and whispered, "No witnesses."

Chapter 14

Sadie slipped from the cover of the woods and ran into the neighbor's yard. She glanced over her shoulder but could not see where her father was. She took a deep breath to compose herself and lowered the zipper on her jacket. She had a T-shirt and a sweatshirt on. It would have to do. She wasn't about to tear her clothes to flash cleavage.

Nervously, Sadie entered the backyard. The ground was hard as pavement and devoid of grass. Thankfully there were only two steps leading to the back door. The steps consisted of cinder blocks with a warped two by twelve on top to serve as a tread.

Sadie rapped on the door loudly. A moment later a bleary-eyed man opened it and peered at her.

"Who the hell are you?"

Sadie looked down for a moment then met his eyes. "I believe your friends have something of mine. I need it back and… and I will do anything to get it."

The man made to shut the door then clued in on what she had said. "Anything?"

"I need the money back so yeah, whatever it takes."

The man smiled. His teeth were not just stained but eroded and brown. His gums were dark, and his nose was running. Sadie resisted the urge to gag. He opened the door and let her in. "Hey, Cooter! We got someone here lookin' to earn some money." The man eyed Sadie from head to toe, smirking with excitement.

As the filthy, drug-addled man called his friends to see Sadie, she leaned against the back door and inconspicuously locked it.

****

Once Sadie was out of sight, Brian snuck through the opposite neighbor's yard and crouch-ran to the house. He squeezed between the house and a large plastic bag of trash and waited.

Finally, he could hear someone calling to someone else followed by the sound of movement inside the house. The god-awful music was lowered and through the cheap walls Brian could hear voices. A couple of the men whooped loudly causing Brian to taste bile. He slid along the front of the house until he reached the front door.

The door was latched with a chain. It was one of those locking mechanisms that is often seen in apartment buildings. The beauty of it was that it was anchored to the casement trim. Being a carpenter, Brian knew there was a pretty good chance that only thin trim nails held the casement to the doorjamb and he doubted the person who installed the chain had thought to use long anchors that would reach into the rough framing of the house. Brian leaned gently on the door increasing his force until the trim nails pulled away. He grabbed the casement before it made any noise and eased into the house.

Nobody was in the front room and from the sound of it, they were all in the back with Sadie. The stench in the house was as bad as the music. Brian smelled cigarette smoke, marijuana, alcohol, and body-odor but there was a sharp chemical smell that he didn't recognize. A partition wall with a large opening segmented the front room from the main room. Another wall separated the main room from the back room where Sadie was. Brian moved to the wall and leaned Sadie's bat against the battered, finger-stained trim. He set her Sig Sauer on the crusty carpet and covered it with a stained, greasy pillow from an equally stained and greasy couch.

Brian leaned against the sticky wall and listened. Since the music had been turned down, he could hear the conversation.

"You the girl from the gas station!" The man slurred his words as he spoke.

"I need the money back. It belongs to someone else, and I have to give it to him. You have no idea what you got yourselves into."

"And you here to… earn it back?" Snickers from more than one person. "You bring knee pads?" More snickers, louder this time. Brian clenched his teeth.

"You have the money, right?" Sadie asked.

"Oh yeah, little lady. I gots it."

"Can I see it?"

"You gotta earn the right to see it." More snickers.

Brian clenched his bat so tightly that his fingers lost color. *How low have I sunken*? He fought the urge to charge the room shooting and swinging.

Sadie sighed. "You got a couch?"

Some of the men made excited sounds. Someone even let out a whoop. "Right over there," one of the men said.

Brian saw shadows and much to his relief it was Sadie leading the way to the couch. The men followed preoccupied with arguing who would get to go first. One of them said, "I got the money she wants, so I go first. Y'all can argue over seconds and thirds and whatever."

When Sadie entered the room, Brian grabbed her arm and tugged her to the side so she would see where he had stowed her bat. He deliberately kicked the pillow covering her Sig at the same time that he stepped in front of the men and lowered his own pistol. With a slight wave of the silenced gun, Brian motioned for the men to move toward a wall. "Line up."

The men were confused. In their inebriated state it took a second before they recognized that a man was pointing a gun at them. They stopped following Sadie and just blinked at Brian as if trying to decide if they were hallucinating or if he was real. Each man swayed as they processed the situation.

Brian had no patience for them. "Move!"

The six drug-addicted men scurried to the wall. One of the more stoned ones said, "Wait, we still getting' laid right?"

Brian said, "Absolutely! You first."

The man smiled stupidly and stumbled toward Sadie who was now pointing her own pistol toward the group. Clearly the guy was so high he had not grasped the severity of the situation. That was fine by Brian. He needed an example. Any reservations he had felt were long gone after seeing the men leering at his daughter. The junkie was halfway across the room when Brian tucked his pistol into his waistband and took his first swing.

The Louisville Slugger slammed into the man's knee. The addict dropped to the floor, grabbed his knee and howled wildly. Brian didn't stop there. He smashed the bat onto the man's pelvis, ankles, elbows, wrists, and any other body joint availed to him. The man extended his arms to fend the blows from the bat and Brian adjusted his swing. One after the other, both skinny arms folded over the bat.

The beating came to a point where most if not all of the man's joints were crushed and he simply could not move. He lay shrieking in pain until the final blow was levied. It left a concave impression in his forehead that perfectly fit the barrel of the bat. The sound of bone splintering was followed by a lingering silence.

The wall that the group was backed up to was under a staircase. A railing with several missing balusters made up the upper left corner of the wall. While the group absorbed the fact that one of their own was now a bloody corpse, movement at the top of the stairs caught Sadie's attention.

The scratchy voice of a woman broke the silence. She sounded like she had been a chain smoker for fifty years. "What the hell is goin' on down there?"

From his vantage point, Brian saw a pair of skinny, blistered legs begin to unsteadily descend the stairs. Behind the legs was another pair of pasty white legs belonging to a man. Brian trusted Sadie to watch the two come down the steps and returned his attention to the group against the wall.

Aside from the creak of the steps under the weight of the malnourished junkies, the room was silent. It was then that Brian heard the distinctly unique click of a gun being cocked. Sadie heard it too. Without hesitation she fired a single shot. The round passed through the woman's chest and into the man behind her. Both tumbled down the stairs landing in a grotesquely tangled pile of arms and legs.

Sadie kicked the gun from the man's grip. He looked at her with glazed eyes. Calmly she pointed her pistol at his forehead and squeezed the trigger.

Brian knew Sadie was right in doing what she had just done. The father in him was devastated by seeing his daughter kill… again. And with such ease. Of course, she had just witnessed her father bludgeon someone to death, so she was just following his lead. *What am I doing to her*? He couldn't afford to think like a father, though. Not now. He had to think like a hunter. A hunter who would not leave witnesses. More fibers snapped.

Still slightly winded from the beating he delivered, Brian regarded the rest of the group. They were stunned into silence. One had even wet his pants. They were finally coming to terms with the gravity of their situation. Brian pointed the bloodied baseball bat toward one of the men. "You stole money from us today. We will be taking it back now."

The man swallowed hard. "I, um, here." He quickly reached into his pocket. The jerky motion caused Sadie to swing her pistol at him and he froze.

"Nice and slow," Sadie told the man.

He eased his hand into his pocket and removed a wad of crumpled bills. Brian motioned for him to place it on the floor toward Sadie.

Sadie smoothed the bills and counted them. "Where's the rest of it?"

"I had expenses."

"Thirteen hundred in expenses? You stole this from me like an hour ago."

"I owed my guy a thousand and I figured while I was there, I'd stock up. Here. You can have it." He slowly reached into his other pocket and retrieved a baggie filled with what looked like large salt crystals. "We didn't use much. You could get maybe two-fifty for it." He tossed the baggie on the floor at her feet.

Sadie didn't want to touch the baggie. She looked at her father. Neither were entirely sure of what it was.

"It's glass." The man watched Sadie and Brian exchange another bewildered look. He then watched as the bewilderment began to morph into fury. In a panicked voice he attempted to explain his thinking. "It's meth. Look you could cut it up and sell it to anyone up the road, man. Cut it into teenths. You'll make at least two-fifty, probably more."

Through clenched teeth Brian replied, "We aren't selling your shit. You will get back the money you took from us, and you will do it *now*."

There was no holding back. Brian was desperate and beyond pissed-off at being delayed. He had a deadline and if he didn't meet it, it could cost him Hannah. He fired a round through the foot of the man last in line. The man toppled forward, and Brian grabbed him by the back of his sweat-stained shirt and dragged him to the center of the room. Brian returned his Sig to his waist-band and gripped his bloody bat.

The man on the floor rolled to face his friends. "Cal! Take them to Bernie's! We can get the money back!"

Cal, the one who had the money, hesitated. "You know Bernie ain't gonna give it up."

The man on the floor screamed, "We can deal with Bernie later. This guy's gonna kill me now!"

Brian made a show of gripping his bat.

Cal held up his hand. "Okay. Wait. I can call Bernie and get the money back. You can have him meet you somewhere."

Both Turners looked at Cal. Their expressions were a mixture of anger and insult. Sadie spoke first. "Oh, okay. Good. Call him up and have him meet us. Make sure it is a secluded area and give him some time to set up snipers along the way. Maybe he'll want to get a truck to haul our bodies away or do you think he'll just leave us to rot?"

Cal stammered, "No. No, wait. It won't be like that. Just…" He never finished his sentence. Brian had run out of patience and took out his frustration on the man on the floor.

After the echoes of the begging and screaming had faded, Brian stood over the bloodied corpse of the second man and glared at Cal. "Take us to Bernie. Now."

Cal began to argue, and Sadie shot the next guy in line right between the eyes. Tears flowed freely down Cal's cheeks as he nodded. "Okay. Okay. He's about five minutes down the road. We gotta drive there." He gingerly stepped over the corpses and moved toward the back of the house. The others followed.

Cal had grabbed a set of keys when Brian told him to wait. Brian retrieved belts from two of the corpses. He then sprinkled the remnants of the liquor bottles on the floor, the furniture, the bodies, and the tattered curtains. After the room was liberally doused, Brian motioned for the group to move out.

Sadie exited first, gun at the ready and head on a swivel checking for the slightest suspicious movement and stood a safe distance from the remaining three men. She watched over them as they waited for Brian.

Brian had taken a candle from amongst the pile of drug paraphernalia that was on the kitchen counter. He had even gone as far as turning the gas on for the range before turning it back off. He had thought to burn the house down but at the last minute decided against it. Why attract attention? He locked the door and exited the house.

Chapter 15

on wagon he had taken from his mother. It took a minute to start and another few minutes to warm up. A cloud of blue exhaust hung in the still air engulfing the passenger side of the vehicle. Calvin and the one called Cooter sat in front while Sadie and Brian sat in the back flanking the third man who was part of Sadie's mugging. He was Darren Stancavage, the owner of the truck and the house.

They drove in silence, the tension palpable, down a gravel alley and on to the main road of the community. Brian noticed the absence of street signs. The houses all looked more or less the same. Cookie cutters with different hues of faded paint. Tar paper was fastened to portions of the exterior where the siding had blown off. Evidently upkeep was not a priority here.

The battered station wagon exited River Bank Village and traveled the same road Brian and Sadie had walked. They soon passed the property where they had left the Firebird. Jarrod was dutifully sitting in front of the car. He watched as the station wagon rumbled by.

Brian's thoughts wandered. Reviewing the past two days. He no longer was sure of the total number of lives he and his daughter had terminated. Like it mattered anymore. His emotional rollercoaster dipped into remorse, guilt, and worry again. He began feeling sorry for himself. He found himself staring at Sadie now. She made a gesture that broke him out of his self-pity.

He didn't grasp what she was trying to convey so she took it upon herself to speak up. "You said this trip would be five minutes. It's been ten."

"Yeah, well, we're almost there." Calvin didn't sound right, like he was hiding something.

Brian's feelings of pity were instantly replaced by anger and paternal preservation. Using one of the belts he had removed from the corpses, he wrapped it around Cooter's neck and the head rest of his seat and pulled it tight.

Startled, Cooter reacted by clawing at the belt. In doing so, he flicked the cell phone he had been secretly using in a low arc bouncing off Cal's shoulder and onto the console where Sadie quickly snatched it. She scrolled the screen. Cooter had typed a text to Bernie, but he had not sent it yet. It was a warning that Sadie quickly deleted.

Calvin grew brazen. The station wagon picked up speed. He gripped the wheel so hard his knuckles lost what little color they had.

"Slow down," Brian said.

The whine of the motor grew louder. Brian tightened the belt on Cooter's throat. He gagged and clawed frantically. He swiped at Calvin only to have his hand pushed away.

"Slow down!" Brian repeated more emphatically.

"Why? You're just gonna kill us all anyhow. If I'm goin' down, I'm takin' you with me."

As Brian cinched the strap even tighter around Cooter's throat, Stancavage saw an opportunity. He jabbed Brian hard in the ribs and swung a fist at Sadie. In the close confines of the backseat, he didn't have much force behind his punch, and she easily dodged it. She returned an upper cut to his jaw then jammed her pistol under his chin. He froze and their eyes met for an instant just as she squeezed the trigger.

The man's limp body fell onto Brian. He and Sadie angrily shoved the body over the back seat into the cargo area of the vehicle. It was enough of a distraction for Calvin to try to save Cooter. Cooter was making horrible gagging noises and rapidly losing his strength. With one hand gripping the wheel, he tried to loosen the belt around his friend's neck.

Brian grabbed Calvin's arm and twisted it down. He barked, "Stop the car!" at Calvin.

"See you in Hell, asshole!"

Looking over Calvin's shoulder, Sadie saw the speedometer was reading between seventy-five and eighty miles per hour. Thinking quickly, she reached between her father and the driver and shot Calvin in the right kneecap.

Calvin screamed and instinctively recoiled his leg. It was enough to no longer depress the accelerator.

"Stop the car!" Brian yelled again.

Through the tears and agony, Calvin saw a large tree looming ahead. The car was losing speed, but it would still be going fast enough to kill them all upon impact.

Brian saw the same thing and lunged over the seat. He elbowed Calvin aside and slammed the shift lever into Park. The back wheels locked up. As Calvin resisted Brian, he inadvertently cut the wheel hard left causing the back end of the station wagon to swing around. The car did three doughnuts before slamming into an embankment next to the large tree.

Brian was slammed into the door. Sadie was flung on top of him. A loud clanking emitted from the front of the car where the radiator had been pushed into the fan blade of the still-running motor. Sadie scrambled off of her father and frantically began searching for her pistol. She spotted it and snatched it from the lap of the now-deceased Cooter before Calvin had a chance to find it.

Calvin, however, wasn't finding anything. He had hit the steering wheel awkwardly and it was evident to Sadie that his neck was broken.

Brian coughed a few times. The wind had been knocked out of him but other than that he was fine. He clenched his jaw as he stared at the lifeless bodies in front of him. *Now what?*

Chapter 16

Erin and Sydney Moyer were sisters with Erin being a year older. The Moyer girls had been through a lot and all through high school they appeared to have handled it well. Their mother, a struggling actress and model, had gotten pregnant with Erin by a minor league baseball player in the Mets farm system. They did what they felt was honorable and united in a loveless marriage. A year after Erin was born, Carla Moyer gave birth to Sydney.

Two years later, Samuel Moyer walked out of their lives leaving Carla to raise two daughters on her own. Carla was more interested in her career. Before the girls were of school age, they were sent to live with Carla's uncle in upstate New York. The long car ride would be the last they would see their mother.

Uncle Jerry was a tough man. The girls had chores and were punished hard if they failed to do them. But, if the girls did perform their work, they were also rewarded with free time to do just about whatever they wanted. If Uncle Jerry had time, he would teach them to do things like shoot, cook, camp in the woods, hunt, fish, and anything else he could offer. By the time Erin and Sydney had reached high school, they could slaughter and butcher a steer, cut, split, and stack firewood faster than most boys and even a few men, and both could drop a running deer at over a hundred yards.

The girls were expected to keep up with chores, get good grades, and they had to participate in at least one sport of their choice. They each chose three sports. Both played soccer and basketball, Erin ran track and Sydney played softball all while making honor roll every marking period.

Erin was a senior, Syd a junior, when Uncle Jerry got hurt.

Uncle Jerry had not done well making ends meet with farming, but he had a small still that he used to produce moonshine. It helped bring money in, but it was a lot of work and he often wondered if there was a better way to make extra money. He had mentioned that to one of his clients one day when the girls were still young, and the client told him about meth.

It took some soul searching but before long Jerry had decided that if people were dumb enough to use that crap, he would supply it. He figured that he wasn't holding a gun to anyone's head to force them to use drugs. They didn't have to buy it but if they were going to buy it, he may as well be the guy who sold it. And sold it, he did.

Uncle Jerry had a very small but ultra-efficient meth lab that produced a rather lucrative income for him. He had the girls help him run it and while he never paid them directly, he had put money away for them for when they graduated high school.

At least that was the plan until a strung-out addict ransacked the lab. It had caught fire and exploded. Uncle Jerry had tried to stop the crazed man and was injured badly in the explosion. He lost a leg and a lung but worst of all, he lost his will. Two months after he got out of the hospital, Uncle Jerry said goodbye to the girls as they went to school then, an hour later, he put a bullet in his head.

Uncle Jerry had set up a will such that the girls got the farm. Once Erin had been able to get through school and graduate, things got a little easier for Sydney. While Erin had to quit track, Syd was able to keep going with her sports. They planned on selling the farm once Sydney graduated but bills were mounting.

One day while going through some of Uncle Jerry's things, the girls came across a composition book with a list of Uncle Jerry's customers and payments that had been made and were still owed. Some of the dealers had paid the girls after Jerry had passed but several had not. In fact, those who hadn't, owed enough that it would have made the difference between having to sell the farm and keep it for another year or two. The young women began to call in the debts.

A few of Uncle Jerry's clients settled upon request but it was a small percentage. Others had to be persuaded. One of the reluctant debtors had attacked the girls and wound up in the hospital. Word spread of the Moyer girls. More money came in and more reluctance was met with brutal physical punishment. Word spread further.

It was during a trip to New York City to collect from two deadbeat dealers that the Moyer sisters were first noticed by Mike. After some investigation, Mike learned that the women were efficient debt collectors. He made an appointment to meet them over dinner and they accepted.

The women carried themselves confidently and professionally. Plus, they were absolutely gorgeous. Mike immediately realized that their looks could be disarming, and he saw their potential. An offer was made and after some fine tuning, the women agreed to avail themselves to Mike should he need their services.

That was over five years ago.

Mike had employed them several times. They were efficient, ruthless when it was called for, and always successful. Mike never mentioned them to any of his associates. The Moyers didn't always kill, only when they needed to, so their surviving victims had talked enough to create a legend. Mike's associates were all aware of the Moyers and their reputation but had never concluded that they worked for Mike and that is just the way Mike liked it.

Recognizing that Hannah Turner might be used as a deterrent by Rollins men, Mike had sent the Moyers to Gettysburg. They looked young enough to blend with the college crowd, they followed instructions to the T intelligently improvising only when needed yet still remaining on task, and best of all, nobody would know they had been there. Indeed, they were ghosts, professionals of the highest caliber.

Mike had sent the Moyers to Gettysburg to babysit Hannah Turner. He didn't want Turner harmed by anyone unless her father failed to honor his debt in which case Mike would turn the Moyers loose on the college freshman. The fact that Rollins men had gone after the Turners at their home was very troubling. No doubt Rollins knew of Hannah at college and would be sending, or maybe already sent, someone to grab her. Somewhere Mike had a leak in his organization that jeopardized the elimination of Cooper Rollins. He knew he needed to work on that but first he had to handle damage control. If Hannah was used as a bargaining chip, Brian Turner would surely not fulfill his obligation.

Mike checked in with the Moyer girls but had gotten no reply as of yet. If Rollins had gotten to them, he would make an example out of them. It would be a message to anyone else thinking of going after Rollins. Mike honestly didn't believe the Moyers were dead, but his mind would have been at ease if one of them had responded to his text. He could only sit and wait. They were the best he had. His secret weapon. His plan B when all else failed. *I'm sure they're fine. Just busy doing their job.* He hoped.

*****

Erin and Sydney waited patiently for a full hour. They were not together though. They were at least two hundred yards apart, but they had synchronized their watches earlier that day. While most millennials used their phones for the time, the Moyers went old-school and used analog wrist watches because they didn't light up. Usually there was some source of light that was enough to see the hands on their time pieces.

Both women could have passed for college students, but Sydney was decidedly younger looking. Upon arrival to campus earlier in the day, she had purchased a Gettysburg College sweatshirt and a notebook at the bookstore. Those props, along with a pair of glasses and her hair wadded into a messy bun were all she needed to look like a stressed-out coed.

The Moyers were patient hunters and could wait all day for a deer to come to a meadow to graze. Waiting sixty minutes for the man in the Porsche to fall asleep was nothing. The hour had passed, and it was now time to act.

Sydney scurried along the shadows bordering the lot where Seamus Finney was parked. She then straightened her posture and cut a diagonal path through the lot but not directly toward the Porsche. She had a purpose to her walk, as if she were anxious to be somewhere.

Erin lingered in the shadows until she had visual contact with Sydney. Erin then zig-zagged toward the Porsche, careful to avoid being seen either directly or reflected in the vehicle's mirrors, until she had settled into a position for a guaranteed shot at the driver, if needed. She was still a good forty yards from the Porsche, but the man had intentionally parked in the open, as she would have, in order to see anyone that might approach him.

In the shadow of a parked car, Erin opened a bag she had slung over her shoulder and removed a syringe filled with an ultra-fast acting sedative, a black hood, and her silenced H&K VP Tactical 9mm pistol. What started as a moderately warm evening had turned into a cold, misty night. It was a miserable type of cold that went straight to a person's bones. Erin shivered as she waited for her sister to turn on the charm.

The Moyers wanted the man in the Porsche alive, but it wasn't a top priority. If Erin could safely use the hood and sedative on him without endangering Sydney or herself, she would. The key word in their plan was "safely." This man was truly a dangerous animal thus required utmost caution.

It wasn't long before Sydney sauntered into view. She walked straight toward the edge of the lot then paused, as if just noticing the Porsche. She conspicuously stared at it then altered her course. She approached the vehicle and peered in on the dozing man. Sydney gently tapped the window.

Seamus Finney opened his eyes and gave Sydney a hard glare.

"Are you okay?" Sydney asked loudly.

The man nodded.

Sydney waited for him to open the door. When he didn't, she spoke again. "Are you drunk?"

The man grimaced. "No."

"Why are you, like, just sitting here?"

Clearly this annoying girl wasn't going away. Finney turned

the key and lowered the window an inch. "I was trying to sleep. I am fine. Thank you. Good bye."

Sydney wasn't leaving. "Do you have some place to stay?"

"Yes. Here. Please leave."

"I could take you to the lobby of my dorm. It's warmer than a car."

Finney saw a potential opportunity. The dorms had key cards and only faculty and students could get in at this time of day. If this ditsy girl could get him in, he might alter his game plan. "Where's your dorm?"

Sydney pointed to a building that was not even near Hannah Turner's dormitory. Finney's mood soured. "Nah. I'm good. Please go now."

"It's kinda weird to be just sitting in a car at night in the middle of a parking lot. Maybe I could…"

Finney growled, "Leave me the hell alone? Yeah, maybe you could." He felt the weight of his Glock under his jacket. For an instant he entertained the notion of shooting the stupid girl and going into Turner's dorm like gangbusters and just taking her. He didn't need that kind of attention and rash decisions rarely ended well. He softened his tone and hoping the coed wouldn't call campus security, Finney whipped up a lie in an attempt to placate her. "Thank you for your concern but honestly, I am fine. I am having breakfast with my daughter. I got into an argument with my wife and had to blow off steam, so I came to campus early. I want to be left alone to sleep before I see her."

Good one, Sydney thought. She realized he probably wasn't going to move but decided to try one more time. "Who's your daughter? Maybe I know her."

Finney thought again about shooting her. Again, he decided against it, but the idea wasn't entirely unrealistic at this point. He fabricated a name. "Monique Johnson."

Sydney hesitated then shook her head. "Nope, doesn't ring a bell. Are you sure you're okay?"

"Positive."

Sydney knew she was beat. "Suit yourself." She shrugged and walked away leaving the man in his fancy car and her sister stuck beside another car on a miserable December night.

Finney watched in the side mirror as the girl walked away. Something didn't feel right. He hadn't survived in his chosen profession this long by ignoring his hunches. It wasn't a strong hunch. He watched for any movement, if she gave a sign or maybe spoke into some hidden microphone. A signal of any kind and he'd chase her down and put a bullet in her head, but she just walked.

He had to squint as the mirror was covered in misty droplets making it tough to see the ditsy coed. The girl ducked under some low tree limbs then reappeared as a silhouette on a poorly lit path. Finney continued watching until she was out of sight. He scanned the parking lot. Nothing. His hunch festered and fifteen minutes after the odd encounter, Seamus Finney found that he couldn't fall back to sleep.

Chapter 17

Brian and Sadie walked back to Jarrod's house. Calvin had taken them several miles away and it was getting late by the time they arrived and found Jarrod still guarding the old Pontiac.

The boy looked curiously at the disheveled state of his employers. They no longer had the baseball bats they had carried earlier. The pair also looked thoroughly exhausted. Jarrod stared at the pair waiting for them to speak. They looked defeated, and the boy felt maybe he should say something but he couldn't find the words, so the three people stood in silence.

Finally, Brian reached into his pocket and pulled out eighty dollars. He handed it to Jarrod who pocketed it quickly. Details. Brian should have checked the car first. No matter how tired he was, he could not miss any details. His gloom deepened. He turned to Jarrod, "Anyone stop by?"

"Nope."

"So, the car is just how we left it?"

"Yep."

Brian caught Sadie's eye. She raised an eyebrow, and he knew exactly what she was thinking. No witnesses. Brian shook his head. He wasn't going to kill this kid. Sadie's expression was non-committal, but Brian hoped she was at least a little bit relieved.

"Y'all wanna wash up?" Jarrod offered. Sensing their hesitation he added, "Ain't nobody home."

Neither Turner uttered a word.

Pointing at Brian's pant legs, Jarrod suggested, "You might want to run them through the washing machine."

Brian and Sadie looked down. Brian's pants had blood splattered all over them. He sighed loudly. Sadie had blood on her too. Both Turners nodded their acceptance to Jarrod's offer and the boy led them into the house.

They entered through a side door. The exterior of the house was faded but clean. The inside was even cleaner. After the house they had just been in, Brian and Sadie were both pleasantly surprised. The appointments and furnishings were mismatched but not abused. Hand-made draperies adorned the windows and the carpet was worn but clean. There was no clutter and the house even smelled pleasant.

Jarrod motioned toward the kitchen. Brian and Sadie began to wash their hands and face while Jarrod provided clean towels. The warm water felt great. Jarrod again offered to do their laundry and suggested they get showered saying he could provide temporary clothing for them and this time the Turners accepted.

Brian and Sadie searched the home for signs of other occupants but found none. Still wary, Brian chose to stand guard while Sadie showered and then she did the same for him. Sadie was given a brilliant lime green sweatshirt and matching pants to wear. Jarrod didn't have anything large enough for Brian, so he got black elastic sweatpants and a pink bathrobe.

Jarrod offered them food and still not wanting to trust the boy, the three of them made dinner together while the washing machine gurgled and churned in a room next to the kitchen. Jarrod fried some venison while Sadie was able to piece together a salad. Brian set the table. Nobody talked except for Jarrod's occasional offers of additional hospitality. The washing machine chimed, and Jarrod politely excused himself to move the clothing into the dryer.

Still wary, Brian took the time to find a secondary exit if needed and Sadie scanned the front of the house. No door but a large enough window. They made no effort to conceal their distrust when Jarrod re-entered the room. Oddly, the boy seemed to understand.

The three returned to the table to finish their meal. Finally, Jarrod's curiosity got the best of him. "You two drug dealers?"

The question seemed to catch both Sadie and Brian off guard. "What makes you think that?" Brian asked.

"I can't think of no other reason why you'd show up in some fancy car, leave town with Mr. Darren, Mr. Cal 'n' Mr. Cooter then show up without them and covered in blood. I'm guessin' they screwed y'all somehow and they done got what's comin' to 'em." The boy smiled as he spoke. "I guess I shouldn't be askin' y'all's business but, well, if that's the case… good."

Neither Brian nor Sadie spoke.

"Them fellers screwed up everything around here. I hope ya killed 'em good."

Brian and Sadie remained silent.

"Didja git Mr. Bernie too?"

The Turners exchanged glances. Brian shook his head slowly. This kid was too smart for his own good. He and Sadie had agreed no witnesses. Could he really kill Jarrod if he had to? The boy was walking a fine line and Brian decided to let it continue. "That was where we were heading when, uh, Calvin had a car accident."

Jarrod looked confused. "You shouldn't have needed to drive. Mr. Bernie lives next door to Mr. Darren."

Brian and Sadie could only stare in disbelief.

"You know this Bernie?" Brian affirmed.

"Oh, I know him alright. He stays here couple a times a week."

"Will he be back here tonight?"

Jarrod shook his head. "Nah. Prolly not for a good two days at least. He'll be too stoned to go anywhere 'till then." Jarrod paused. He looked ashamed. "Him and my mom. They'll be too stoned to come home." The boy paused again then said, "At least the house is clean."

Brian and Sadie wrinkled their brows. A facial expression that the father had unwittingly handed down to both of his daughters.

Jarrod noted their look. "Mr. Bernie likes the house to be spotless. Momma don't care, she's always too stoned but Mr.

Bernie, he wants it spotless." Jarrod rubbed his cheek and whispered, "Even then it usually ain't good 'nough."

Brian was stewing about being deceived. There was nothing he could do about it, but he wished he had somehow caught it before all that time had been wasted. He was deep in thought and didn't totally grasp what Sadie had commented to Jarrod. He got the gist of it from Jarrod's reply, though.

"Yeah. Mr. Bernie hits me."

Sadie's eyes hardened but her voice remained soft. "What does your mom do when Bernie hits you?"

"She gets upset. She doesn't like it but then she gets high and the problem goes away… for her."

Brian felt his pulse pounding throughout his body. He cut the rest of his venison only as something to do while he thought about their next move. It didn't take long. "Can you take us to Bernie? We don't know what he looks like so you'll need to point him out. From a distance, of course."

Jarrod grew solemn. "Yeah…" He was thinking, too. "The house you were in. The one where you found Mr. Cal and Mr. Darren. Did anyone… get out?"

"Get out?" Sadie repeated with a hint of nervousness.

"Yeah, my mom was in there."

Sadie was at a loss for words.

"No, Jarrod", Brian replied honestly and firmly. "There were no survivors."

There was an uncomfortable silence as Jarrod took a moment to absorb this information. He was small and underweight for his age, but his character made him appear bigger than his physical stature. His face flashed remorse but only for an instant before his features hardened. He offered a small but sincere smile. "Good."

Sadie was rocked by Jarrod's frankness. She left the table and walked to the kitchen window. It was dark now and she couldn't see out, but she stared anyway. Sadie had shot his mother and Jarrod *seemed glad about it.*

Brian and Jarrod ate the rest of their meal without conversation until Sadie returned to the table. She drained her glass of water and helped herself to another. Jarrod allowed her to get settled before making his proposal to the Turners.

"I'll take you to Mr. Bernie if you take me to my gram and pap's house. They live about fifteen miles from here in the direction you came from. If you're headin' back, it wouldn't be outta your way. Not much anyhow."

Sadie was slowly shaking her head unsure about bringing a kid along, but Brian disagreed. "We don't even know what Bernie looks like. We need the money back. I don't see that we have a choice. Jarrod's pretty self-sufficient but he still needs a family." Brian turned to Jarrod. "Your Gram and Pap, they treat you well?"

"Oh, yes, Mr. Lionel. They been wantin' to adopt me for a long time. They want me outa here. I'd get to go to a school with other kids, too. Not this boring home-school stuff. Dad's okay with it but Momma is the one that's holdin' things up. She wants money for me."

Brian caught a glimpse of Sadie. Her heart was breaking for Jarrod. She was now nodding at her father. "Okay," Brian said. "Let's make a plan."

Jarrod explained that Mr. Bernie would be in the lab around ten that night, but he wouldn't be cooking. Every Wednesday night, Bernie sold bulk product to a pair of guys from the big city. Brian and Sadie exchanged glances. They weren't sure what qualified as the big city. Kentucky didn't have too many big cities and none in their current vicinity. Jarrod continued to explain that the men were usually punctual so they should be at Bernie's lab just before ten. The trio decided to arrive about fifteen minutes earlier. They would take the Firebird and the old canvas tarp that was currently covering it. As before, there would be no witnesses. It was even more critical if Jarrod were seen as he was known locally.

Brian, exhausted, noted they had about two and half hours to wait. His neck had a kink in it from the crash and he was mentally wiped out. He offered to do the dishes after a one-hour nap if Sadie would help Jarrod pack. All three knew darned well that Jarrod didn't need help. Brian was being cautious.

Jarrod didn't seem offended by Brian's wariness. He showed Brian to the couch and got him a blanket. The couch was threadbare in spots and lumpy, but it was clean. It actually had a nice aroma to it, like dryer sheets. Brian was grateful for a place to lie down and too tired to care. Once Brian was settled, Jarrod and Sadie disappeared upstairs.

It didn't take much time for Jarrod to fill a single small duffle bag. It was more like a gym bag. He didn't have much in the way of belongings. Sadie noticed that he had taken a picture of when he was younger. He was with his mom and dad. They looked happy.

Jarrod saw Sadie looking at the picture. "That was about five, no, maybe six years ago. Momma wasn't using as much then and Dad was clean. They both had jobs, too. It didn't last long but that was a happy summer. That weekend we went to the county fair and rode the carny rides until I just about puked. That was the night before. The day we took that picture, we was fishin'. We packed sandwiches and some pop and fished all day." Jarrod shrugged. "That one summer was the only time that I can remember when we was a real family."

Sadie just listened. She felt she should offer her own story, but it didn't compare to Jarrod's. Sure, her mom had drunk for the past few years, but it was mostly at night, and she rarely missed an event due to drinking, at least until the past year. Sadie had been spanked once when she was about five and that was the only time and it hardly qualified as a beating.

Every summer that she could remember was a fun family summer like what Jarrod had described. Even when her mom's drinking had gotten out of hand in the past year or so, Sadie, Hannah, and Dad had fun. No, Sadie's life wasn't perfect, but it was nowhere even close to the hell Jarrod had been through.

An hour had passed but Sadie and Jarrod couldn't sleep so they did the dishes and cleaned up while allowing Brian to sleep a little longer.

At nine-thirty they woke Brian, reviewed the plan, and locked up the house. The nap had been just what Brian needed. His mind was clear and his thoughts lucid as he mentally played out every conceivable scenario that he could think of.

When they went out to the Firebird, Brian took one of the phones capable of voice notes and made a one-minute-long recording. Jarrod didn't understand but Sadie did. Details. The recording may not be needed but a phone took little room and could be invaluable. The threesome left for the lab to retrieve the Turners' stolen money and to give payback to a child abuser.

125

Chapter 18

There was no practical place to park the Firebird. The trio had considered leaving it at the Belcher residence; however, that would have meant a very long run back from Bernie's lab if they were being pursued. The car itself attracted attention, which was another issue. However a speedy getaway, or at least the option of one, took a higher priority. It was decided that they would drive the old Pontiac up to the final approximate two hundred yards, kill the motor, and push it to Stancavage's house.

Brian had just finished placing the final trash bag on the back half that Jarrod's greasy old tarp didn't cover when another car approached down the gravel road. Brian, Sadie, and Jarrod took cover as the headlights flashed over the backyard as the car turned into the neighboring driveway. The car was shut off and three men got out.

"That's him," whispered Jarrod. "That last guy. That's him."

He sounded overly excited, and Sadie patted his shoulder and made a calm down gesture with her hand. Jarrod looked like a five-year old being told to wait to open Christmas presents. He could barely contain his eagerness and Brian began to wonder if it would be a problem. He gave the boy an admonishing stare as only a parent can do. Jarrod wilted and contained his anxiety.

The three men scanned the area more out of habit than suspicion before unlocking the steel door and entering the building. Brian could tell from the sound that the door was thick and heavy. Possible solid metal or metal encapsulated gypsum board like a commercial fire door. It was thick regardless and breaking it down or shooting through it was not going to be an option. That wasn't the plan, but Brian always liked having choices.

Jarrod had told the Turners that there were cameras monitoring the perimeter of the building. It was decided that as soon as Bernie and his crew arrived, Brian and Sadie would have to sprint to the wall nearest the door and hide in the shadows. That way they could make their run before anyone could have time to check the monitors.

It was at least a seventy-yard sprint. The Turners had made their move as the door was closing. Fifteen seconds later, they were standing with their backs pressed against the cold steel building. Leaning on a short section of tree limb brought to wedge the door open if needed, Brian fought to quietly control his heavy breathing. Sadie, in much better shape, was hardly winded.

About two minutes had passed, enough for Brian to catch his breath, when Jarrod casually strolled into view. He walked straight up to the door and pounded on it loudly. Brian and Sadie could hear the whine of an electric motor as the camera closest to the door scanned Jarrod.

After a loud scraping noise, the door opened just enough for a man to poke his head out. "What do you want?"

"Momma sent me. She needs a little extra tonight."

The man looked disgusted by Jarrod. He withdrew into the building to repeat the boy's statement to somebody that the Turners presumed was Bernie. There was some back-and-forth between the guard and the person inside until the door swung open allowing Jarrod to enter.

Jarrod entered slowly. The impatient guard growled at him to hurry and pushed the door at the boy. Jarrod let the door hit his foot, slowing the closing action. He hoped Brian and Sadie were right behind him, but they hadn't moved yet. Just as the door was about to latch shut, a three-inch thick branch slid over the threshold. The ill-tempered guard was too focused on Jarrod to notice. Thinking quickly, Jarrod asked, "Where is he?"

Not even attempting to conceal his irritation, the guard grabbed Jarrod by the scruff of the neck and shoved him in Bernie's direction. The lab was dimly lit and even though Jarrod had been inside before, he pretended to not know his way. The guard shoved him again as he roughly guided Jarrod to Bernie.

With the doorman away from his position, Brian and Sadie slipped into the lab, removed the stick, and disappeared into the shadows. The door clicked shut. Sadie found a spot between several steel barrels that offered both cover and a respectable choice of shooting lanes just like she would if she were hunting deer in the woods. Her back was near the wall, and she had an ample view of her surroundings.

Brian moved away from Sadie but kept his back close to the same wall. He found a steel file cabinet in the corner that offered suitable cover and shooting lanes. He could see Jarrod and the guard approach Bernie and three other men. Brian frowned. *There must have been two inside already.*

The group was seated at a table. One of the men leaned over and used a clear plastic tube to snort a line of white powder. He handed the tube to the guy next to him who then did a line and passed the tube to the next guy. Everyone ignored the guard and Jarrod until they had each done a line. The guard stood dutifully with a meaty hand on Jarrod's shoulder waiting to be addressed.

Bernie eyed Jarrod then sprung to his feet. His movements were jerky. He wiped his nose twice then suddenly smacked Jarrod in the face. "Why are you here, shit stain?"

Jarrod reeled from the blow then quickly composed himself. Judging from how he handled the smack, it was clear to both Turners that Jarrod had been hit before. Emotionlessly he stated, "Momma needs a tweak."

Brian felt his pulse quicken initially then steady. His senses felt stronger, he felt like a predator. A quick glance at his daughter revealed to him that she was feeling the same way except maybe more angry. Their eyes locked for a flash. He gave a slight nod and Sadie slowly raised her silenced Sig Sauer as she readied herself to take a shot.

Bernie seemed jittery. He smacked Jarrod again. "A tweak? Damn it. That woman would smoke product as fast as I could make it if it were up to her." He looked at Jarrod suspiciously. "Why'd she send you? Is she so lazy she can't walk over from next door? She called you to come down?" He laughed manically. "Her little slave boy? Good for her!"

Bernie removed a sandwich bag half full of crystal meth from his pocket. He threw it at Jarrod. The throw was too hard, and Jarrod dropped the bag. Jarrod bent to pick it up when Sadie had had enough. Her Sig quietly spat a round that sprayed the side of the guard's head onto the men at the table.

Jarrod instinctively spun and dove for cover. It took Bernie a second to realize that his guard had been killed before he dropped to the floor and tried to grab Jarrod. He missed. Jarrod scurried away as Brian fired at another man. The man had moved just as Brian squeezed the trigger and Brian's shot was low and left hitting the man in the neck instead of the forehead.

The man clutched his neck with one hand and grabbed a modified Tech 9 machine pistol. With blood pulsing between his fingers, he shot erratically in Brian's direction. Brian took cover behind the filing cabinet as bullets slammed into the walls, the cabinet and floor around him. As the man bled profusely from the arterial wound to his neck, his shots were more concentrated on the floor blowing chunks of tile and subfloor onto Brian. By the time he had run out of bullets, the man was teetering on his feet. He dropped to his knees, then fell face down onto the floor and bled out.

A thick blue haze hung in the still air. It obscured Brian's view of the table where the men had been sitting. Brian figured if he couldn't see them, they couldn't see him and while the echoes of the gunfire still resonated, he took out the cell phone and played the recording then changed locations.

The recording Brian made was of him gasping for breath. He coughed and made gurgling sounds. There was wheezing and a few moans of agony inserted into the minute long recording. It was intended to be just long enough to pique a shooter's curiosity. And it worked.

Brian pressed his back into a tight corner created by one of the posts supporting the pole building. It wasn't much cover, but it offered a dark shadow that he could disappear into and a clear vantage point. He could see Bernie lying prone with his hands covering his head. Brian had a clear shot at him but needed Bernie alive to retrieve the stolen money.

The table that the men had been snorting drugs on had been overturned in the melee. Slowly, a man emerged from behind it, laser-focused on the coughing and wheezing sounds coming from Brian's former location. Weapon drawn, the man didn't even look to see if there were other shooters. With a nefarious sneer he honed in on the sound of the gasping. As he stepped over Bernie, Brian took a steady aim and fired a single shot that slammed into the man's head.

The man's body collapsed onto Bernie who squealed like a little girl. Bernie panicked and rolled out from under the corpse. He tucked his legs to his chest making himself into a tight ball and rocked. Brian watched Bernie and determined that he was too frightened to move very far. From Brian's position, Bernie would not make it to the door. He saw no other means of escape so all Bernie could do was hide somewhere in the building. The man's options were extremely limited.

Three bodies down. One to go.

Brian caught a glint of movement from across the lab. It was Sadie on the prowl. A wave of relief coursed through him. She was not only okay but she saw something he didn't. Keeping a mental note of where she was and where she was probably heading, Brian eased himself along the wall searching for the fourth man.

"Hold it right there." Emerging from the shadows came the fourth man with a gun pressed tightly against Jarrod's head. "Come out in the open so I can see you." Brian slowly left the safety of the shadows near the wall. "Before I kill you, tell me just who the hell are you and what do you want?"

Bernie had gone from a whimpering fetal position to standing fully erect, almost haughty in his posture.

Brian said nothing.

"Not such a bad-ass now, are you?" Bernie sneered. He surveyed the room. "Exactly what the hell is this all about?"

Sadie had to adjust her position. She wanted a clear shot on the man holding Jarrod but could not risk hitting Bernie, Jarrod, or her father. Each step was slow and deliberate as she carefully avoided debris on the floor. She maneuvered herself behind a large steel vat and slowly dropped to a knee. There was some tubing and glassware that she would have to shoot around or through, but it was the best line available to her.

"Cal paid you thirteen hundred dollars today. It wasn't his to spend. It belonged to me." Brian almost said *us*. Bernie and his man didn't seem to know about Sadie. "I'd like it back please."

Bernie gave Brian a blank stare for a few seconds then while making a sweeping gesture with his arm, incredulously asked, "This is all over thirteen hundred dollars?"

"Yes."

Shaking his head ruefully, Bernie replied, "You could have just asked. We could have discussed this."

"Oh really? Some guy just knocks on the door and asks for his money back and you would have been okay with that? You, Cal and I could have had a cup of coffee and discussed the mis-understanding?" Brian's reply was bitterly sarcastic.

Sadie fired a single shot. The man holding Jarrod dropped to the floor and Jarrod quickly retrieved the man's weapon. He seemed afraid to touch it, afraid to possess the power it held. Jar-rod stepped around the corpse and handed Brian the man's gun, clearly glad to be rid of it, as Sadie stepped from the shadows.

Momentarily horrified, Bernie stared in disbelief as the man's vacant eyes stared back at him, blood pooling under his head. He hadn't realized there were two shooters. He gazed at Sadie. She barely looked eighteen, if that. Bernie realized that he was alone now. Alone with a kid he had abused and now that kid had managed to get some muscle.

"May I have the money back now?" Brian asked.

Bernie's eyes darted from Sadie to Brian to Jarrod. He tried to think of a way out, but he was still buzzing from the cocaine. He could take them. The kid didn't have a gun and well, he was a little-shit kid. The coke made him feel electric. *I am smarter than everyone here. The guy's old. The girl's probably weak-minded.*

I go after him, take his gun, shoot her then him then, then, that little shit will pay dearly. Bernie could feel his entire body vibrating with strength and he made his move.

Brian studied Bernie as he apparently weighed his options. The man was jittery, seemed nervous yet potentially aggressive. Not like a cornered animal but different. He was clearly high on something, thus probably irrational. Brian didn't care. He just wanted the thirteen hundred back. And he wanted it back now. After a long silence Brian asked again, "The money?"

Bernie leaped toward Brian. It was ungraceful at best and Bernie over-estimated his athleticism. The leap didn't even cover half the distance between him and Brian. Brian watched the peculiar jump but when Bernie lowered his head and charged, not unlike a bull rushing a matador, Brian had had enough. He aimed and squeezed off shot that slammed into Bernie's lower leg shattering his tibia and dropping the man to the floor.

Clutching his wrecked leg, Bernie began to hyperventilate. Brian noticed some twine on a table and tossed the roll to Bernie. "Tie it off. Make a tourniquet if you don't want to bleed to death." Bernie, eyes filled with hatred, ignored him. Brian nonchalantly asked yet again, "The money. Where is it?"

Before Bernie could respond, Jarrod spoke up. "He keeps it over here." He shifted to a large steel locker, about two feet taller than he was, and opened the doors. There were lab coats, protective gear, rubber gloves, and gas masks hanging inside the locker. On the top shelf sat two revolvers and several boxes of ammunition next to a crisp black gym bag.

Jarrod gave Bernie a smug grin and slid the gym bag from the shelf. It was heavier than he had expected and plopped to the floor at his feet. The zipper was open revealing significantly more than thirteen hundred in cash.

"You little shit," Bernie hissed. "Leave that alone!"

"Shut up!" snapped Brian.

"Why should I? You're just gonna shoot me."

"I won't shoot you," Brian replied unconvincingly.

Jarrod took a step away from the bag. He had never seen so much money before. Like the pistol, he seemed afraid of its power. He was awed by the bundles of cash. So much so that he hadn't noticed Bernie crawling toward him.

Brian noticed. He grabbed Bernie by the back of his shirt and pulled him to a chair. Bernie resisted and Brian kicked him in the gunshot wound. Bernie only flinched then spat at Brian. He missed but the sentiment was clear. Brian slammed him into a nearby chair. He grabbed the spool of twine and began using it to restrain the coke-crazed man. The twine was thin, like what would be used for baling hay, so Brian wrapped several courses around Bernie.

Sadie toed the bag before kneeling beside it. She removed thirteen hundred dollars then after glancing at her father for approval, she rounded up and pocketed two thousand. "There must be twenty, maybe thirty thousand in here." Seeing Bernie sweating she added, "Maybe more?"

"We need to get going," Brian said. "We got what we came for." He eyed Jarrod. "You have anything to say to this guy before we leave?"

Jarrod stared at him, hatred oozing from his every pore. He approached Bernie.

"Oh? And just what do you think you're gonna do, ya little shit?"

The punch came quickly. Bernie wasn't ready for it, and it even surprised both Turners. Even Jarrod looked amazed at the way the drug dealer's head snapped backward when the boy's fist connected with the man's nose. Jarrod eyed Bernie as blood began to trickle from the drug dealer's nostrils. Overcome with pent up frustration, Jarrod unleashed a torrent of punches to Bernie's face and body.

Father and daughter made eye contact. It looked to Brian as if Sadie was thinking of stepping in, but he shook his head. Sadie got it. Jarrod needed this and Bernie deserved it. The Turners let Jarrod beat his oppressor until the boy was spent.

Jarrod dropped to his knees and wept. Brian helped the boy up and with his hand on Jarrod's shoulder, he guided the youngster away from Bernie.

Bernie was spitting blood, cursing Jarrod, and whimpering over his battered face. He spat a broken tooth then sneered at the boy. "This ain't over kid." Jarrod and Brian kept walking away from Bernie. "Hey! You gonna just leave me tied here? What now? Who is gonna…" Bernie's rant trailed off as Sadie approached him. Panicked he called after Brian. "Hey! HEY! You said you weren't gonna shoot me! HEY!"

Brian turned and from halfway across the cooking room he coldly stared at Bernie. "And I am a man of my word. *I'm* not going to shoot you."

The bloodied drug dealer turned to face Sadie. She had already leveled her pistol. Before Bernie could utter another word Sadie squeezed the trigger. Bernie slumped in the chair and Sadie calmly picked up the satchel of cash. Gingerly stepping over and around the bodies and debris strewn about the floor, she caught up to Brian and Jarrod. Sadie was calm. Cold even. Jarrod turned to take in a final look at the carnage, but Sadie gently urged him to keep going. As they neared the exit a sound made them all freeze in their tracks. Someone was knocking on the door.

Chapter 19

This nightmare just keeps getting worse. Brian backtracked to a TV monitor. The bright overhead lighting illuminated two men standing at the door. Both were dressed in neatly pressed, custom made suits. One was carrying a heavy duffle bag. None of the other cameras showed anyone else and the men did not appear to be law enforcement. One of the men knocked again and faced the camera with an impatient expression on his face.

Sadie had set the bag of cash near the door. She and her father were thinking the same thing, take cover while Jarrod lets the men in. She whispered encouragement to Jarrod then moved into the shadows. Brian was not far away, concealed behind a stainless-steel vat. He gave Sadie a nod who in turn gave Jarrod a nod.

Jarrod unlocked the door and held it open for the two men. The pair stepped in, and the boy latched the steel door behind them. As their eyes adjusted to the change in light, they regarded Jarrod with disappointment.

The one holding the bag shook his head in disgust. "Looks like Bernie really laid into you this time." He squinted then realized even though Jarrod was covered in blood spatters, he was not injured. "Or did he? What's this all about, son?"

Jarrod averted his eyes. He knew these men and they were always nice to him. They would slip him a fiver dollar bill once in a while or a fancy imported chocolate bar. He secretly hoped Mr. Lionel and Miss Sadie wouldn't shoot them, but he also knew business was business. Jarrod shamefully lowered his head and increased his distance from the men.

"It's about you slowly raising your hands," Brian said from the shadows.

The men didn't move. They didn't even acknowledge Brian. Clearly, they had been in tight situations before and remained quite calm. The man with the bag turned to Jarrod. "Did you set us up?"

Jarrod looked like he had just been kicked. "No sir! We was just leavin'. In fact, if you had been a minute later, we'd a been gone." He couldn't bear to look at the men. A tear rolled down his cheek.

"Well, this sure looks like a set-up to me, Jarrod."

"He's telling the truth," Brian said. Both men ignored him.

"It ain't no set-up!" Jarrod was panicking. He turned to Brian, "Tell 'em, Mr. Lionel. Tell 'em!" The boy turned back to the two men. "Look, we can just go and forget we even saw you. Right Mr. Lionel? We can just keep on goin'."

"I'm not so sure it will be all that simple, Jarrod," Brian replied. The two men had yet to look at Brian and he was pretty sure they weren't aware of Sadie lurking in the shadows. Brian eyed the men. "What's in the bag?"

They continued to ignore him, so Brian fired a shot that just missed the face of the man with the bag. The man never even flinched but the shot did get his attention. He turned to Brian and calmly spoke. "There is two hundred thousand dollars in the bag. We had a deal going with," the man nodded toward Bernie, "that guy."

"And what did he have for you?" Brian asked.

"He was to deliver several cases of meth."

The man was too calm. Brian didn't like it. He remembered seeing some large plastic crates stacked on the floor. He waved his pistol in the direction of the crates, quick to return his aim on the men. "Are those the crates?"

"They look familiar."

Brian thought for a second. "Okay, give Jarrod the bag and keep your hands up high."

The man tossed the duffle of cash toward Jarrod as Brian kept talking. "Jarrod, put the bag with those crates." Brian eyed the men. "Slowly, and I mean very slowly, remove your clothes down to your underwear."

"Really?"

Brian's tone was cold as steel. "Strip to your underpants or I shoot you. Your choice but don't take too long to decide. I have a deadline."

Jarrod dragged the bag to the crates. The bag was heavy, and he was drained physically and emotionally. Tears flowed freely as he wondered how he had ever gotten into such a mess. He knew. It wasn't him, it was his parents. He hated them and was glad his mom was dead and his dad was in jail. He hefted the bag on top of the crates.

The two men decided to comply with Brian. Slowly they removed their suit coats, shoulder holsters with weapons left inside. They removed their other weapons, spare clips, and the rest of their clothing.

There was a roll of packing tape near the crates and Brian motioned for Jarrod to toss it to the men.

Brian motioned the men toward a post. "One at a time, hug that post and tape your hands together."

The men did as they were told. While hardly pleased with their situation, they were astute enough to understand it was Brian's only safe way out. They watched in silence, still unaware of Sadie's presence, as Brian gathered Jarrod and the gym bag of cash. Brian ignored the small fortune that consisted of their duffel bag and the large cases of meth.

Jarrod stood next to the exit clutching the gym bag as Sadie emerged from the shadows. She said nothing. She just placed her hand on the door ready to move out as soon as her father was ready.

Brian found a small knife and placed it on the ground where the men could easily reach it. "Cut yourself loose when we leave." He trained his Sig on the men and began to back away. Once he reached the door, he shut off all of the outside lights, Sadie opened the heavy door, and the trio bolted out into the night.

They sprinted to the road, cautiously skirted the Mercedes that the two men had apparently arrived in, and ran to the Firebird. Jarrod was all but thrown into the back seat as Brian and Sadie rushed to get in. Brian fired up the motor and sped out of the hell hole known as River Bank Village. They were a good five miles away before Brian eased off the accelerator and began to breathe easier. "Okay, Jarrod. Where to?" Jarrod mumbled some simple directions, and the course was set to deliver the boy to his grandparents.

The trio rode in silence until Jarrod let out a loud sniff. Brian eyed the boy's reflection in the rearview mirror. Sadie turned around to face him. "What's wrong?" she asked.

"Why'd they piss their pants?'

Sadie was unsure of what the boy meant. Thinking he was referring to the two men they left behind she replied, "I didn't notice that they had. They seemed pretty calm to me. Like they had been in situations where guns were pointed at them before."

"Not them. The ones that…" Jarrod was being overly cautious in choosing his words. "Died. The ones that got shot and died. They pissed their pants. Were they *that* scared?"

Brian was forming an answer, but Sadie replied first. In a very clinical tone she said, "No. At least probably not. Have you ever gone hunting with your dad?"

Jarrod shook his head. "My dad don't do nothin' with me. He just gets stoned. I mean when I was little, we did stuff but I wasn't old enough to handle guns. He didn't go huntin' much neither."

"Oh." Sadie sounded deflated for a beat then continued with her explanation. "Well, when something dies, whether it's a deer or a rabbit or a person, all the muscles relax. The brain is dead so it can't tell the body to function in even the simplest ways like the muscles controlling the bladder. So, the bladder and bowels release when a body dies. It's just the way it is."

"So, they wasn't scacred?"

"No, they probably *weren't* sacred." Sadie emphasized her usage of proper grammar. Unseen by his daughter, Brian rolled his eyes at her thinly veiled correction. "There was too much going on to be scared. They probably had a lot of adrenaline and—what was that, cocaine?—pumping through their bodies to be scared."

"But Bernie pissed his pants before you… before he was shot."

Sadie paused to think of an appropriate response. Clearly seeing people die had bothered the boy and she was shifting from a sterile tone to a more compassionate posture. "Well, he probably was scared then, I suppose."

Jarrod was quiet for a beat. "Good." He didn't smile. He seemed to be satisfied that, in his mind, justice had been served.

The rest of the ride was silent save for Jarrod's occasional directives as to where to turn. It was an hour past midnight when the Firebird growled down a long gravel driveway. Brian hit the light override, and the car went dark except for the headlights. The driveway had a teardrop shape to it at the end and Brian piloted the car around such that it was facing away from the house. It was habit to park the car facing the most efficient exit.

Brian, Sadie, and Jarrod climbed out of the car. All three were exhausted. Jarrod retrieved his bag packed with clothes and little else. Brian grabbed the satchel taken from Bernie's lab. He removed one banded stack of bills and tossed it onto the driver's seat before closing the bag and joining the others.

Jarrod's grandparents had a small but tasteful home. Even in the darkness it was evident that the home was maintained with pride. The lawn was all the same length and the landscaping, even in winter, looked tidy. Nothing overly ornate or garish yet abundant enough to show the love the owners had for their home.

Inside two dogs barked a warning. A sequence of lights went on as the inhabitants moved from the bedroom to the front door. For a split second a thick shaft of light sliced across the porch before the overhead light went on. The dogs, two thick-bodied Rottweilers, emerged from the door followed by a balding man wearing a Washington Redskins T-shirt and striped boxers. He was holding a shotgun which he quickly pointed toward the trio approaching his home. The dogs, hackles raised and ready to attack, took positions flanking the man. "Y'all can just stop right there and explain who the hell you are and what the hell are you doing at my house in the middle of the night." His directives were driven home by the guttural snarls of the dogs.

"Pappy! It's me, Jarrod."

"Jarrod?" The man's demeanor changed instantly. So did the dogs'. They let out happy yips and charged off the porch to greet the boy. The man's stance became forceful again but not like it had been second earlier. "Who're you with, son?"

"Oh, it's Mr. Lionel and Miss Sadie. They… uh…" Jarrod stammered then stopped in midsentence. He wasn't sure what to tell his grandfather.

Brian took over. "Sir, our paths crossed with your grandson's today. What happened is best forgotten. It's my understanding that you wish to adopt Jarrod." Still holding the shotgun trained on Brian, the older man nodded once. "Well, that process may have gotten a little less muddled today." Brian tossed Bernie's bag of cash onto the porch. "This should help with the legal fees."

Jarrod had assumed Brian and Sadie were going to keep the money. He spun toward Brian, open-mouthed in surprise. "Mr. Lionel. I thought you needed that."

Brian shook his head. "We only needed what was taken from us. I did take a little extra just to be safe, but the rest is all yours."

Jarrod smiled and gave Brian a hug.

"Exactly who are you, mister?" Jarrod's grandfather was suspicious. For years his daughter, Jarrod's mom, had brought all sorts of shady characters to the man's home. Most of them he kicked out. He knew his daughter was no good and, difficult as it was, he didn't put up with her behavior. He made no effort to hide his distrust of Brian and Sadie.

"I am someone who is best forgotten." Brian didn't seem the least bit concerned about having a gun pointed at him. All but ignoring the grandfather, he held his hand out to Jarrod. "You are very brave and very smart. Do exactly what your grandfather tells you and study hard in school. Don't end up like Bernie, okay?"

Jarrod nodded and shook Brian's hand firmly. He turned his attention to Sadie unsure of how to say good bye to her until she grabbed him and squeezed him in a big-sister-like bear hug. The hug lingered then stopped. Sadie's smile faded. "You stay away from drugs okay?" Jarrod nodded, fighting the urge to cry. "If you don't, we'll be back," Sadie threatened.

Jarrod nodded again and hugged her once more. The boy turned and ran to his grandfather with the dogs trotting beside him. He stood on the porch and watched as the Turners walked away.

The Pontiac roared to life and Brian and Sadie left Jarrod to grow up in a loving home. After forty-eight hours of stress that involved saving Hannah from certain death, losing Lisa, and now three gunfights, both Turners felt good about delivering Jarrod to his grandparents. They needed to feel good about something.

Sadie turned her phone on and found the nearest motel. It took a half hour to reach and another half hour to check in, secure the Firebird, and get settled. They needed the rest. Both knew the next day would be hell.

Chapter 20

That stupid college kid was really nagging at Seamus Finney. He had to go for a walk. He wouldn't get a wink of sleep until he verified that the kid was a student or at least not a threat. Finney climbed out from his Porsche and walked straight to the last place he had seen the girl. The path continued toward some dormitories. Finney dropped a tissue, doing his best to make it appear to have fallen from his pocket accidentally should anyone be watching, and turned back to the car. Once he arrived at the Porsche, he climbed inside and stared at the image in his mirror.

The trees bordering the parking lot segmented his view of the path. Finney replayed the girl walking away in his mind and realized she had never passed through the final segment in his mirror. He could see the tissue clearly and he would have noticed if the girl had continued to walk on the path. He also could see if she had turned to the left. She hadn't. That only left one other direction and that was to the right.

Finney returned to the path and retrieved his tissue. He looked to the right and saw an untitled brick building that he previously hadn't given much attention to. All of the other buildings on campus had names. Either dorm names or honorary titles from large donors or past faculty worthy of such tribute. This building had nothing. It was two stories high and had a flat roof with another much smaller flat roof that protected an entry door jutted from the side about nine feet above the ground.

The misty air deposited droplets of moisture everywhere. Finney knelt on the walkway and studied the lawn between him and the building. The grass showed footprints heading toward the building. Finney followed. They led him under the small outcropping. He peered around the corner and saw several buildings, both administrative and class oriented. The buildings also had security cameras.

Finney pulled back and thought about where the kid might have gone. If she were a student, she may have gone this way to a class but not at this time of night. The only thing open was a library and that was in a different direction. The cafeteria was closed, and the dorms were in the opposite direction. Essentially, there was no good reason he could think of why a student would travel this way at night, particularly on a Wednesday. It wasn't party night.

Erin observed Finney as he went to the path, dropped a tissue, returned to his car, then back to the path where he knelt and studied the grass. He was thinking and that was bad. She and Sydney preferred not to communicate when on a job. They relied instead on timing, but they also always had throat mikes and ear buds in case their timing went south on them. Erin clicked once, then whispered, "Boyfriend on the prowl." She received two clicks back indicating that Sydney understood.

After making certain that the man was still on the path, Erin sprinted to the Porsche. She unscrewed the caps on both passenger side tires. She pulled a book of matches from her pack and jammed a pair in each valve. It was enough to allow air to escape without a loud hiss that might garner unwanted attention. Once the air was steadily leaving both tires, Erin began to follow the man.

Finney was becoming agitated. His thoughts wandered briefly. He needed to get at least an hour of sleep and this kid was up to something. He thought about just grabbing Hannah Turner and leaving but that still wasn't the most rational method of taking her.

Back to the college girl. *She came this way.* Finney was confident that no other student had come through since, and the misty crap falling from the sky would have covered anyone's tracks but the most recent passerby. Finney studied the grass again from under the low roof. The only prints going away from the outcropping were his. He tested the door, but it was locked. His gloved hand left a dry mark on the handle.

Finney stepped back and looked at the edge of the entry roof. Two hand prints. The kid went on the roof. He cursed to himself. If she were on the roof, she probably saw his every move. That could have been a fatal mistake.

The assassin from Philadelphia stepped back and launched. Grabbing the edge of the roof silently with strong gloved hands, he began to pull himself up. Something grabbed his left leg and punched it. Finney immediately dropped and found himself face to face with another woman. In her hand was a syringe with a broken needle.

The woman stomped hard on Finney's foot simultaneously landing a hard uppercut to his jaw. She used the heel of her palm instead of a fist. It was a move that had been taught. The foot to distract, the shot to the jaw to concuss an attacker, or victim depending on perspective. Finney may have been impressed if he wasn't the object of her aggression.

Reeling from the hard blow to the jaw, Finney stumbled backward and pulled his Glock. It was kicked from his hand before he got off a shot. He regained his balance and began a counter-maneuver. Finney stepped toward the woman as if to throw a punch then dropped and swept her legs from under her. She dropped hard and rolled away from him.

Finney grabbed for his backup; a small .38 he kept in a holster above his ankle and found the other part of the broken needle. The woman had tried to use a syringe on him and stabbed his holster. He fumbled for a moment, scratching his hand on the needle, then drew his weapon.

From her rooftop vantage point, Sydney had watched the man right to the point where Erin tried to sedate him. When she saw Erin go into a fighting stance, she dropped from the parapet to the outcropping. The man on the ground had drawn a second pistol and was pointing it at Erin when Sydney dropped. She landed perfectly with one foot on the man's arm and the other on his thigh.

Finney was a powerful man. The student dropped on him from the entry roof. He held his grip on the pistol but under her weight the gun barrel went into the ground. A muffled shot sprayed bits of dirt and turf into the face of the first woman. Finney knocked the younger woman aside with a head butt to the stomach and sprang to his feet.

Erin threw a punch at Finney, but he parried and countered with a punch to her cheekbone. She toppled into a shrub and fell to the ground. Sydney smashed an elbow into Finney's nose. He grabbed her by the hair, but it was a wig. Sydney threw another punch, but Finney caught her arm and bent it behind her. He slammed her body into the steel column supporting the roof and was about to go for her throat when Erin raked her fingers over his face in search of his eyes.

That was enough for Finney. He let Sydney go and flipped Erin over his shoulder directly onto her partner. The two women clamored to get to their feet and resume the battle, but Finney had retreated. He scooped his Glock from the wet grass and bolted for the path and the parking lot.

Rounding the corner of the building, Finney slipped twice in the wet grass but caught purchase on the walkway. His daily training regimen was brutal, but it prepared him for times like these. He was at full sprint and hardly winded when he arrived at the parking lot. While still running, he hit the key fob to unlock the Porsche and then he hit the remote start.

The car was idling when Finney approached from the back. He immediately noticed it was sitting lower on the passenger side. *Touche. It's what I would have done. These girls are good.* The tires were completely flat.

Finney never slowed. He banked hard right and headed for the dorms with the two women now in hot pursuit. He had a good head start on them and was just about to the edge of the lot when a bullet sparked on the macadam next to him. Fueled by a rush of adrenaline, he ran even faster, covering the end of the lot and adjacent strip of grass in a fluid, all-out sprint. Reaching the shadows of a tree line, Finney changed direction away from the dorms.

From the opposite end of the lot, Erin and Sydney saw their quarry enter the shadowy treeline but could only assume where he headed from there. They were well aware of the possibility of the man setting up for a shot at them. They had no choice but take cover. If he was running, he would be gone. If he set up for a shot, he would give away his location. If he were smart, he would circle around and take his shot from their flanks.

Suddenly the Moyers felt like they were in a fishbowl. They had no choice but to retreat and wait him out. They sprinted to the nearest car and crouched behind it. Now they were behind a rock in a fishbowl. It still wasn't safe, but it bought them a few seconds.

Erin nodded toward a light illuminating the west side of the lot. Sydney understood and leveled her silenced Heckler Koch. Erin had hers pointed toward the other light on the eastern side. Sydney fired once, then again blowing the light out on the second shot. Erin's gun spat a nine millimeter round into the light on her side and instantly the duo was in total darkness. They wasted no time getting out of the lot and back to a secure place where they could watch Hannah Turner's dorm room. It was going to be a long night.

Chapter 21

Thursday

After shooting out the lights in the parking lot, Erin and Sydney had run in the opposite direction from where they last saw Seamus Finney. They maintained a varying distance between each other to make them a more difficult target yet still able to maintain visual contact in case Finney came after them. The jaunt back to their unmarked van was uneventful and they took turns repairing and modifying their disguises while the other sister kept an eye out.

The scrum with Finney had damaged their makeup. They both wore prosthetic noses, wigs, even their chins and cheekbones were enhanced. They didn't have time to invest in a full makeover, but a new wig and glasses did wonders. They wore reversible jackets which were changed and after a quick check and reload of their weapons, the Moyers returned to campus in the same manner as they had left, maintaining a distance and heads on a swivel.

Erin and Sydney set up in triangular vantage points. Erin posted in the cover of a small copse of pines. She could see Hannah Turner's dorm window, now dark, and the front entrance of the large rectangular residence hall. Sydney had found cover between two large exterior heating units next to another dorm. She could see Turner's window and the back exit. The only way the man could approach Turner would be from inside the dormm and while that was certainly possible, it was the least probable scenario. Now it became a waiting game.

The waiting was part of the job. Sometimes the women would be required to hole up in position for days. While those situations were rare, they had done so in order to strike an unsuspecting target. There were still a few hours before daybreak. The Moyers assumed if the man were to make his move, it would be during the time the students were heading out for class or breakfast. It's what they would do.

The hours soon passed. The bone-chilling dampness of the night before had moved east. Bright morning sunlight gradually spread over Gettysburg College and with it the happy chirping of birds. The air was still cold, but the sun offered some soothing warmth. Squirrels scurried at high-speed foraging for food. The squirrels that lived on campus were as accustomed to stale pizza crusts as they were to acorns as dietary staples.

It was seven fifteen when, just like the squirrels, the students began to emerge from their burrows. At first it was a trickle of early risers, but it didn't take long for the trickle to become a steady stream of students. Some heading to an early sports practice, some heading to breakfast at the dining hall, and some off to class.

Hannah Turner emerged from her building dressed in sweats, hair in a braid, and a backpack slung over one shoulder. She was flanked by two friends with two more trailing behind in the same level of attire. All five were chattering loudly about an upcoming class and how annoying their roommates were. Their breath fogged a cloud around their faces as they talked.

More students emerged from other dorms creating a temporarily dense confluence where the paths converged. Greetings were joyfully exchanged between morning people and grunted or ignored by those who functioned better at night. The crowd flowed together for about fifty yards before dispersing toward their destinations.

A campus maintenance worker approached on a John Deere Gator painted in the school's bright blue and orange colors. The man pulled up to a trash receptacle near where the student flow began to fan out. Erin watched as the man lifted the lid of the trash barrel. He seemed preoccupied. She whispered into her throat mic, "Check out the trash man."

Sydney clicked her mic twice indicating that she got the message. The man's back was toward her. He was wearing loose fitting custodial overalls and a woolen cap pulled low over his ears. Sydney couldn't discern if it was the man from the night before or not.

Turner's group emerged from the throng of students and the man stopped fumbling with the trash container. He studied his surroundings quickly then moved toward Hannah Turner.

Erin whispered, "It's him." She didn't wait for a reply. Erin broke from her concealed location and moved to a group of students. Using them for cover she positioned herself such that the man would have had to look over his shoulder to see her. She continued shrinking the distance to the man by moving from group to group.

When Erin got within twenty yards, she slid her hand into her coat pocket. There was a case of two syringes containing a strong sedative cocktail, one syringe had a broken needle as a result of the earlier encounter with the man, and a Vipertek VTS-989 stun gun.

Having dealt with the man earlier, she wasn't convinced she could use a TASER from a distance. Disabling him would have to be up close and very personal. The stun gun would go through clothing, but Erin wanted to be sure, and she was going to aim for skin. She would have only one shot with the pocket-sized stun gun. If she missed her mark, the man would overpower her quickly and it would be up to Syd to shoot him.

The man swept into Turner's group. He grabbed Hannah by her arm and whispered something in her ear. With the stun gun in her left hand and the undamaged syringe in her right, Erin snuck behind the man. A few inches taller than Hannah, the nape of the man's neck was exposed when he bent to whisper to her. It was the perfect target. Erin planted the stun gun on the bare skin and sent a temporarily incapacitating burst of voltage into the man.

He dropped hard to the pavement. Erin sat on top of the convulsing man and plunged the syringe into his neck emptying the contents in a desperate thrust. She used the stun gun once more as Sydney arrived on the scene.

Syd cuffed the man and shackled his legs while Erin sent a third blast of electricity into him. Sydney then pulled a black cloth hood from her pocket and put it over the man's head. While Erin strapped a gag over the hood and across the man's mouth, Sydney quickly gathered two smart phones that students were using to take videos. Without any explanation she pulled them apart, took the camera card out and smashed it. Then she smashed the phones themselves. The students were stunned and offered no protest.

"Anyone else want to try to take a video?" Sydney scanned the crowd of close to twenty students. None touched their phones. "Good. I am Dr. Marta Klondike from Grundig Psychiatric Hospital in Harrisburg. We ask that you not take any video as this patient comes from a high-profile family who values their anonymity."

She paused to assist her sister in lifting the man to his feet. The effects of the electric jolts had diminished and although the man was woozy, he was very much aware of what had just happened to him. He was just beginning to resist when the sedative took over. If it weren't for the Moyers holding him up, the man would have collapsed unconscious onto the ground.

Sydney turned to Hannah Turner. "You're a pretty lucky young lady. This man had some plans for you."

Hannah looked stunned. "I don't even know him."

"No doubt," Sydney agreed. "But he knows you. I'm guessing you have a Facebook account?"

"No," Hannah shook her head. "Nothing but email."

Not missing a beat as she concocted the story, Sydney asked, "Do your parents have an account where they might post pictures of you? Proud of their little girl?"

"Mom does."

"Uh huh. That is his M.O. He learns all about people on social media then tracks them down and, well, it hasn't ended well for the people he has stalked."

Hannah and the crowd seemed skeptical until Erin put on a pair of gloves and began removing weapons from under Seamus Finney's jacket. The curious students stepped back with a collective gasp as she disarmed him of two pistols, a knife, and duct tape. Sydney continued addressing the crowd. "I know it's hard, but we really need to keep this to ourselves. This man's family is aware of his psychosis and has deep pockets to make sure that if anyone posts a video on line, the posting will be traced and the person responsible will be sued. You have been warned."

Erin noted a small blood stain on the back of the coveralls. She nodded to Sydney. Somewhere there was a dead maintenance worker. That wasn't something they could concern themselves with now. They had to go. As the Moyers pushed through the crowd, Sydney thanked them for their cooperation.

Once clear of the students, the women picked up the pace. Together the Moyers were a formidable team, quite capable of dragging Finney but it was very slow going. Two wrestlers offered to help, and the Moyer sisters accepted. After assuring the wrestlers that Finney was completely unconscious, the athletes hoisted the limp man and carried him to a white van with Grundig Hospital emblazoned on the side panels. Erin unlocked the back doors and the young men gently placed Finney inside.

Sydney thanked the wrestlers as she hastily ushered them from the van. She didn't want to allow the young men any more opportunity to scrutinize the van than what they had already done. Erin had secured the back doors and was now in the driver's seat starting the vehicle. Sydney explained to both young men that the plain interior was needed with patients like this man. A simple carpet was fine as escaped patients were often tranquilized. The men seemed to believe everything she said and even commented that escapes must happen often if they had a special recovery van. Sydney rolled her eyes and casually laughed, "If you only knew!" Not wanting to allow the conversation to continue, Sydney quickly climbed into the van with her sister and the pair sped off.

They were no more than a mile or two from campus when Erin found a driveway enshrouded with trees. She backed the van into the driveway only far enough to not be readily seen from the road. Both sisters hopped out and peeled off the fictitious hospital banner revealing brightly hued lettering that read Millers Florists. Erin rolled the hospital banners together while Sydney peeled a film of fictitious numbers that had covered the license plate revealing another film with another false license plate. Once the banners were safely stored in a cardboard tube, the pair were on the road again. They passed a police car, strobes flashing and siren blaring, as it rushed in the direction from where they came. Someone must have reported the escaped patient or found the body of the maintenance worker.

Sydney made a phone call as the pair headed north on Route 34. She was given an address in Bendersville. It was about twenty minutes away. A simple drive north on Route 34 then bear left onto South Main Street.

Twenty minutes was a luxurious amount of time. Sydney moved from the passenger seat to the back of the van. Seamus Finney was still unconscious. She lingered over his rugged good looks. While probably fifteen years her senior, he was an attractive man. He had an athletic frame and obviously took good care of himself. He actually looked approachable and kind while he was unconscious. Sydney had looked into his eyes though. He was an alpha predator. Ruthless and cold. Just like her.

A black duffle bag was stuffed behind the driver's seat. From it she retrieved a roll of plastic sheeting. She peeled off a section and shoved it under the unconscious man. He was muscular and heavy. With the limited room in the van, it took all of her strength to roll him enough to get a good amount of plastic under him. Once that was accomplished, Sydney removed a syringe from a small kit, filled it with a potassium chloride solution, and slid the needle into his carotid artery. After she emptied the contents, she repeated the procedure twice more giving Finney a large enough dose to kill ten men his size.

Sydney watched as Finney's body seemed to tense just a little then his vital signs stopped and his eye lids slowly relaxed exposing deep blue eyes that no longer seemed so evil.

Sometimes she wished she could date. She went out once in a while, but those times were few and far between. Wary of anyone who approached her, she often rejected any man's attempts to get to know her. She never put herself in places such as bars or singles mixers so the only time she could meet a man would be a chance encounter. A successful assassin does not allow himself, or herself, to believe in chance or coincidence, thus such encounters were greeted with intense suspicion. Hardly a way to find a boyfriend. Sydney didn't have time for such thoughts right now. She had work to do.

The younger Moyer sister removed sharp scissors and a heavy trash bag from the duffle. In a matter of minutes, she had Finney's clothes cut off and stuffed into the trash bag. His body was wrapped in a cocoon of black plastic sheeting and sealed with duct tape. Sydney then stripped her own clothing off and changed back into her Gettysburg College outfit. Her clothes were stuffed into the bag with Finney's. She applied a prosthetic nose and chin, a wig, and colored contacts.

Erin pulled the van to the shoulder of the road and quickly switched positions with Sydney. Sydney drove as Erin stripped off her clothes and changed into something more casual. She too altered her appearance adding several clip-on earrings and temporary tattoos to go with the wig, contacts, glasses, and a clip-on nose ring.

The pair found the address given to them. Across the street was a small diner that had a few family cars and two police cruisers parked in the lot amongst a majority of construction vehicles. If the locals like it, it must be a good place. They parked the van and gave it a good wipe-down before locking it. They walked over to the diner and found a booth with a window that offered a view of the van.

A gum-chewing waitress sauntered over to the women. "Coffee?" Both nodded. "What else can I gitcha?"

Famished and feeling the drain from the long night, the Moyers decided to take the time to eat some breakfast. They both ordered the Number Six – Hungry Man's Special. The waitress eyed the women from head to toe. "Oh, to be young again."

Erin and Sydney had almost finished their multi-course meal when a blue Range Rover pulled into the same lot their florist van was in. A Latino man, small in stature but with a confident gait, exited the vehicle and walked toward the diner. He entered and just before the hostess offered to seat him, he enthusiastically waived to the Moyers. In a heavy Spanish accent, he explained that he was meeting friends here. The hostess stepped aside, and the smiling man headed toward the sisters.

"Sophia! Caroline!" He hugged each of them then sat down. "How are you doing? Wow! It's been a long time. You look great!"

"Carlos!" Erin greeted the man with a kiss on the cheek.

The Moyers were fond of Carlos and had done business with him several times in the past. He and the sisters only knew each other by their aliases but that was not a concern. All three were consummate professionals and they respected each other accordingly.

Carlos ordered a cup of coffee but no meal and the three chatted away until the Moyer sisters were done eating. They left a hefty tip and exited the diner. The trio crossed the street and stood near the Range Rover. Erin reached into her pocket and removed the key Carlos had slipped in during one of the hugs. She nodded to him. He slid his hand into his pocket and found the key to the van. He nodded back and smiled. *"Los cerdos comen todo pero los dientes." Pigs eat everything but the teeth.*

The Moyers waved goodbye and got into the Range Rover. Time to go back to Gettysburg and continue to babysit Hannah Turner. They had the better part of two more days of watching her. Depending on what their handler would tell them, after Friday night they would either leave her to continue her education and enjoy a successful life or they would be meeting Carlos for breakfast again.

*****

"Man! That was freaky!" Darryl, one of Hannah's friends on the wrestling team, shook his head. He had helped carry the psychiatric patient to the hospital van. "It totally creeped me out and I wasn't the one he was stalking!"

"Thanks," Hannah grumbled. She was a tough kid, but everyone had their limits and hers was clearly reached. She needed to go to her class but was still visibly shaken. A crowd of her friends surrounded her with words of amazement and support. Hannah blocked them out. She pulled her cell phone from her pack and hit Dad on the speed dial. It went straight to his voicemail so she left an excited message. She tried Mom but also went to voicemail. Hannah tried Sadie's phone and that, too, went to voice mail. She texted her father and debated on calling one of her grandparents. After a slew of comforting words from friends, Hannah began feeling better and decided not to involve her grandparents.

It was scary but it was over. Disaster prevented. She saw no reason to worry over it. She was still a bit shaken but felt that a distraction would help. She decided to go to class and would call Dad again later.

Chapter 22

Both Turners slept until mid-morning. They needed it. Brian was the first to rise. He had showered and put on fresh clothing. He changed into his hunting boots and soaked his regular shoes in the bathtub. He would throw them in a dumpster later as they had crusted blood spatters from multiple sources on them. He had just finished dressing when Sadie began to stir. Like her father, she had slept deeply and it took a moment to clear the fog from her mind.

"You okay?"

Sadie yawned and smiled. "Yeah, I feel great." She stretched with a grunt and rolled out of bed. "I slept like a rock. Or a log, or a baby, or whatever. A shower and some breakfast and I will be ready to run a marathon."

Brian gave her half a smile. "No regrets?"

The teen looked blankly at her father. "About what?" There was a hint of that special tone that teenagers use when they think a parent is an absolute idiot. Sadie, and Hannah for that matter, never used that tone to the extent that other kids did with their parents but on rare occasions it came out ever so slightly.

"Yesterday."

"It had to be done. Plus, we helped a kid out. Jarrod's life will be much better because of us."

Brian smiled. "Yeah, I suppose you're right."

Sadie picked up one of her dirty socks and whipped it at her father. He easily dodged it. "Thou art disgusting."

"The apple doesn't fall far from the tree," she giggled and disappeared into the bathroom with an armful of clean clothes.

Brian watched his daughter with a proud parental smile until the bathroom door closed. He made a small pot of coffee from the complimentary supply that the motel provided and ruminated on the fact that he was proud of his little girl for not being crushed by guilt for killing so many people. He wasn't sure how many at this point. He tried to discard the perverted pride that he couldn't help but feel.

Brian checked on the Firebird through the slits in the blinds. It looked okay from his vantage point. The coffee pot ceased to gurgle, and Brian poured a cup then settled into a chair. He clicked on the TV while Sadie showered. The local news had long been over, and his choices were limited to morning talk shows and one national news show. He chose the news.

Just before a commercial break, the show went to local news headlines and an anchorwoman appeared cheerfully updating the viewers about the weather, traffic, and a police investigation into what appeared to be a shoot-out between rival drug dealers at the River Bank Village outside of Owingsville. She didn't go into any significant detail other than to plug the midday news for more information.

Brian turned off the TV and found a classic rock station on the small bedside radio. As Mott The Hoople played their most famous hit, Brian Turner focused on the next step. They needed more drones, maybe some fresh clothing, food, and to travel across a good portion of the state of Kentucky.

The elder Turner stared at his phone. The battery had been removed and Sadie had used a pink hair tie to keep the battery and phone together. He either talked or texted Hannah every day and didn't want to raise any suspicions on her end. He knew she also spoke with or texted Lisa every day too and well, that wasn't happening any more. He took a sip of coffee and put the battery into the phone.

After a series of electronic noises, the phone indicated several messages. Brian scanned them. Hannah had left a voice mail and had texted. Elaine, Lisa's perpetually inebriated mother, also had texted multiple times. There were a few texts from clients, but they were used to Brian taking a few days to communicate. It was a contractor thing.

The texts from Elaine were troubling. Lisa blamed Brian for virtually every disappointment or inconvenience known to mankind and therefore so did her mother. Elaine hated Brian and only texted when she was good and drunk and wanted to pile on a rant that Lisa had generated. Brian stared at the text then opened it.

WHAT THE HELL DID YOU DO TO MY BABY? SHE DOESN'T ANSWER HER PHONE. WHERE ARE YOU? YOU MUST HAVE REALLY MESSED UP THIS TIME.

That was the gist of all seven of the texts from Elaine except for the most recent one that mentioned she was looking for someone to drive her to his house. Elaine had lost her driving privileges due to repeated D.U.I. offenses and the last time she drove she wrecked her car. It would take her a few days but eventually she would find someone to drive her unless she decided to use a taxi. She was too cheap for that. At least Brian hoped so. He couldn't imagine how he would handle his mother-in-law finding the mess that awaited him when he got back home. *If* he got home.

He wished he had thought to take Lisa's phone with him. Details. Brian cursed himself for not covering every detail. He was under duress when he vacated his home, of course, but if Elaine showed up, his carelessness would come back to bite him.

Brian rubbed his temples, took a deep breath, and concluded that there was absolutely nothing he could do about his mother-in-law at the moment. He would talk it over with Sadie once she was cleaned up and ready to go.

The next texts were from Hannah.

I GOT A 98 ON ORGANINC CHEM TEST! TINA GOT SO TRASHED SHE PUKED IN HER BED AND SLEPT IN IT! THAT'S ALL FOR NOW.

Most of the other texts from Hannah were updates on her classes and campus life. Except for the final one. DAD CHECK YOUR

VM. WILD SHIT WENT DOWN THIS MORNING. IM OK. GOING TO CLASS. WILL CALL LATER. WHERES MOM?

Brian listened to his voicemail from Hannah. She excitedly relayed the events of the morning regarding some escaped psych patient had been stalking her and two doctors subdued him before he could attack her. Brian closed his eyes and steepled his hands as he listened. He was trying to come up with a plausible reason why Lisa didn't answer her phone and why he and Sadie were difficult to reach.

"Now what?" Sadie was leaning against the door jamb, dressed in clean clothes. A white towel was wrapped around her head absorbing the moisture from her long curls. She held her sneakers up and wrinkled her freckled nose. They had blood stains on them. "Who are you talking to?"

"Nobody. Hannah texted and left a voice mail. She said somebody had come after her today but was stopped by his psychiatrists, or something like that." Brian's skepticism was evident in his tone.

Sadie's demeanor changed. "Was she hurt?" she growled.

"Doesn't sound that way. She said she'd call. She also wants to know where Mom is, and she'll probably ask why I was hard to reach too. And…" Brian let out a long sigh as he often did when reminded of his mother-in-law, "your grandmother left me a few loving texts as well. She wants to know why Mom isn't answering her texts. She said something about coming up to the house."

"How can she? She lost her license and wrecked her car."

"I guess she'll call a taxi. I don't know. She didn't elaborate."

Both Turners were silent.

"I'll call Hannah," Sadie suggested. "I'll tell her you and Mom had a big blow out and that's why you haven't been in touch."

"Okay, and how are you going to tell her? By a phone call? Do you ever call her?"

Sadie looked momentarily perplexed but then got what Brian was saying. "No, I don't call that often."

"Right. You guys Instagram each other. So do that but make

sure the background is something that she would see at home. Pine trees or sky. Nothing that says Kentucky."

Sadie nodded. "Details."

"Exactly." Brian rubbed his chin pensively. "Now for that lovely grandmother of yours. I will send a text saying the same thing. Big blow out, I'm at work, Mom is probably too drunk to talk."

He studied Sadie as he spoke. She remembered all the good times with Lisa even though there hadn't been many since she had started drinking so heavily. It hurt Sadie to think of her mother as a lush. Of course, after Tuesday that was now in the past too. If Sadie was hurting over her mother's passing, she wasn't showing it. One more thing for Brian to worry about… later. No time to psycho-analyze his little girl now.

Brian turned to his phone. ELAINE. I DON'T KNOW WHERE LISA IS BUT I WOULD GUESS SHE IS PASSED OUT ON THE COUCH. I AM AT WORK. I WOULD CALL BUT I DOUBT LISA WOULD ANSWER. LOVE YOU.

He probably shouldn't have ended with sarcasm, but it just felt right. Brian tapped send and hoped his mother-in-law would leave him alone.

Sadie sent an Instagram to Hannah. She sent several like she would normally. In one she told of the big fight between her parents, in another she griped about a teacher that she knew Hannah had had and didn't care for, and in the third, she just made a weird face and insulted Hannah. All of the pictures were taken by the window at such an angle that they had the sky in the background.

The motel room became abnormally quiet as the Turners contemplated the lies they had just fabricated. If Elaine traveled to their home and found Lisa and the four dead men, well, Brian didn't even want to think about that. It was out of his control. His mother-in-law was lazy. She probably would not try to go to the house, at least not for a few more days, he hoped.

Brian and Sadie gathered their possessions, swept the room for anything they may have missed, and checked out. After breakfast they disposed of any clothing that had blood on it and hit the road again both very anxious to get the job done and put this week of pure hell behind them.

Chapter 23

The Turners crossed most of the length of Kentucky stopping at Walmarts, hobby stores, and a grocery store as they completed the collection they had begun the day before. They bought new clothing as well and new running shoes for each of them. The back seat was full of boxes and bags. Sadie had begun consolidating the packages but was soon diverted by the task of modifying the drones. She was engrossed in the schematics of one of the drones. They had been on Route 24 West for only a few miles when lights flashed in the rear view mirror.

"Shit," Brian muttered. He glanced at the speedometer. He was doing the posted limit. At least close to it, he might have been two or three miles per hour above but ordinarily that wouldn't get him pulled over. He realized he had not exchanged the Pennsylvania license plate with his borrowed Kentucky plate. He doubted that was the problem, but it was a detail he had not fully addressed, and it annoyed him.

"What do we do?" Sadie was concerned. They had made it this far without any police interference and only had approximately thirty miles left before they reached New Concord.

Brian thought for a second. "Well, we didn't do anything wrong, right? I mean, I don't know why he would want to pull us over. We're only driving and shopping. And I can out run the patrol car, but I can't out run the radio." He backed off the throttle as he reasoned with himself and Sadie.

"I guess." Sadie wasn't convinced that stopping was the right thing to do but she also had to admit that running seemed to be the worse option. "I don't like this." She patted her pistol under her winter jacket. "What do I do with this?"

"I don't know. It's not a legal set up, I don't think. We'd better leave them in the car. Just slide it under the seat but be sure you can grab it quickly if needed." Brian downshifted, removed the pistol he carried and slid it under the seat.

Neither Turner liked the prospect of shooting a cop. Killers and drug dealers were one thing, but a cop was another story. He probably had a family. Sadie felt sick just thinking about having to shoot him. That was a last resort, though.

Brian was nervous. There was no reason that this guy should be pulling him over. He habitually checked the car for faulty lights or cracked lenses, anything that would attract the attention of police. A faint sensation of paranoia crept over him. Something wasn't right.

They hadn't passed a car in a while and the highway was devoid of homes and businesses. It was one of those stretches where it felt like they had been driving in a tunnel of forest. The remoteness both comforted and concerned Brian. He pulled to a stop on the shoulder of the road.

The cop parked behind the Firebird and shut his strobes off. Brian watched in the side mirror as the cop spoke into a small radio before getting out of the cruiser. The cop spit a stream of brown chew juice. He adjusted his belt then he spat again as he sauntered up to the car. Brian had already rolled the window down.

There were no pleasantries exchanged. "License and registration."

Brian passed the documents to the officer.

"Where you heading, Mr. Breckenridge?"

"Visiting relatives for the holidays."

The cop peered into the car. He eyed Sadie and smiled. It wasn't a warm or friendly smile. It was creepy. She withdrew into her jacket and stared at the Firebird's twin hood scoops. The cop's eyes lingered on her face, smooth and pretty. Her hair was long and naturally curly. She was one good looking young lady. *Very* young lady.

The cop returned his attention to Brian. "Relatives, huh? Where do they live?"

"Tennessee."

"Exactly *where* in Tennessee?"

Brian couldn't think of any towns in Tennessee other than Nashville and he wasn't entirely sure which part of the state it was located in. He changed the subject. "How come you pulled me over, sir?"

The cop ignored the question. "I need the two of you to step out of the car."

Something didn't feel right. Brian repeated his question.

"I suspect you might have been drinking. Please step out of the car." The cop's unfriendly demeanor turned even colder. "Now!"

The cop had positioned himself such that he could see both Brian and Sadie. Neither would have been able to draw a weapon from under their seats without being shot first. Brian and Sadie slowly got out of the car.

"Face the car, Breckenridge. Hands on top." Brian turned and placed his hands on the roof of the Firebird. "Now, Sadie, hands up where I can see 'em. Walk around the car." She hesitated, her eyes met Brian's hard stare. "Let's go," barked the cop.

Brian could tell, thankfully, that Sadie had picked up on the cop's error. He referred to Brian as Breckenridge. The car was titled in Lionel Breckenridge's name and that was the license Brian had handed the man. But the Lionel Breckenridge ID that Brian had set up was not married nor a father. There was no way the cop could have known about Sadie unless he had been informed prior to pulling them over and that information would not have come through the law enforcement channels.

The cop was holding handcuffs but watching Sadie. Brian waited until his daughter had walked around the back of the car. Brian feigned submissive compliance and did not resist at all when the cop grabbed his left arm to cuff him. As soon as Brian felt the cold steel of the handcuff close over his wrist, he pivoted hard and raised his elbows. Brian had taken several years of mixed martial arts. Close quarters fighting prevented throwing punches, but elbows worked very well.

The first twist brought Brian's right elbow crashing hard against the cop's cheekbone. It didn't do any damage other than to stun the man. The second twist jammed his left elbow into the officer's ribs. Again, no damage but the idea was to clear some space and knock his assailant off balance.

Brian was now able to spin and face the cop. Still too close to throw a punch, Brian grabbed the man by the ears. He slammed his forehead into the cop's nose, crushing cartilage and breaking bone. With the hit to the nose, the cop's eyes would tear and impair his vision.

Still in close quarters, Brian raised his knee hard into the cop's groin. Reflexively the cop doubled over in pain and stepped backward. This also gave Brian space. He spun and kicked hard into the man's knee causing it to bend in a direction nature had never intended. The resulting pop was loud and disgusting. The cop, fumbling for his sidearm while screaming in agony, fell in Sadie's direction.

Sadie pounced. She grabbed for anything she could find. The cop had fallen on his side where the holstered service pistol was. Sadie could not grab the weapon, but she got the next best thing, his TASER. The cop flailed wildly, still unable to see through tear-clouded eyes, and managed to grab Sadie by an ankle until Brian kicked him in the ribs, cracking at least one of them.

The cop released Sadie's ankle and she stepped back. He rolled onto his sore ribs and reached again for his pistol when Sadie fired the TASER. Sixty thousand volts coursed through the cop's body. He froze in a twisted, full-body cramp. Sadie released the trigger. The stunned cop gasped for breath. Before he could recover Brian grabbed the officer's pistol and a key ring with about fifteen keys on it.

Brian stuffed the gun into his waist band then found the key to unlock the handcuffs. He told the cop to roll over. When the man resisted, Sadie sent another pulse of electric through his body. Using his foot, Brian rolled the cop onto his stomach and knelt down driving his knee between the cop's scapulae. He pulled the man's arms back and quickly cuffed him.

Breathing hard, the cop rolled onto his back. "You stupid fucking assholes! You have no idea who you're up against," he hissed. The cop then smiled a dark, nefarious grin. "There's a crew on their way now. You have nowhere to run." He glared at Brian. "You're gonna be strapped to a chair and made to watch as crowds of men take turns on your daughter for days on end." He cackled and smiled a tobacco-stained grin. "And I'm gonna be first in line." Sadie hit him two more times with the TASER. The cop's bladder released with the second blast.

Brian scanned the horizon with both his eyes and ears. Nothing… yet.

Going through the cluster of keys, he found the one that opened the trunk of the police cruiser. It was packed with flares, a riot gun, caution tape, and myriad other police paraphernalia. Brian scooped it all out and tossed it into the backseat of the cruiser. In the corner of the trunk lay a Kevlar vest. Body armor. Brian tossed that into the Firebird. The cop could do nothing more than watch. His vision had cleared but he was breathing heavily and drooling from the repeated jolts of electricity. Blood and snot had crusted on his mustache, his eyes dark pools of venom.

When Brian had the trunk completely cleared, he returned to the police officer. Sadie kept the TASER at the ready. Brian wondered how many blasts the batteries had left. He worked quickly stripping the shoes, socks, and pants from the cop. The cop cried out when Brian straightened his wrecked leg. With the man's hands cuffed behind his back, Brian had to use his small pocket knife to cut the jacket and shirt off the cop. He yanked the barbed TASER ends out. The cop was so drained from the TASER that he barely made a noise when the barbs were yanked from his skin and offered little resistance as he was stripped down to his soiled underpants.

Brian dragged the man to the trunk but needed help from Sadie to lift him into the trunk. The cop began to fight. Brian grabbed the barbs and jammed them into the cop's abdomen. Sadie hit him with another jolt of electricity, and the cop wilted in defeat. It was still an arduous task to get the limp officer into the trunk. Even without him resisting, the portly, middle-aged man was difficult to maneuver, but the Turners prevailed.

Father and daughter scanned the area to remove any signs of struggle. It looked clean enough. Sadie double checked the area while Brian got settled in the police car. The TASER wires were long enough to reach the front seat from the trunk. Sadie set the TASER on the floor next to the driver seat. She passed her father the pistol from under the seat of the Firebird. Brian tucked the gun inside his coat and started the cruiser.

Brian nodded to Sadie. He scanned the horizon again. Still nothing but he could practically *feel* Rollins' men approaching. "Go at least two roads up. Then let's get the hell off Route 24. We'll have to take back roads from now on. First, I want to talk to this guy so find a road with some woods to hide in," he stressed with a paternal finger wag, "but not the first one we come to. It's too predictable. Feel free to go fast." Sadie nodded and fired up the mighty Pontiac engine.

Cruising at seventy-five miles per hour, they were making good time until Sadie did exactly what Brian had said not to. She got off at the first exit onto Purchase Parkway. Heading south, she drove hard and fast into Draffenville. Not too happy with his daughter's choice, Brian cussed under his breath but had no choice but to follow her.

Draffenville turned out to be a small town and they quickly found a country road leading out of it. Sadie actually seemed to know where she was going, and Brian's ire lessened. After a few more twists, Sadie slowed the Pontiac and turned into a long gravel driveway. It led far into a wooded area before emerging onto a flattened cornfield. Perfect.

Brian first disabled the radio and onboard computer in the police cruiser. He then opened the hood and using some of the tools from the small kit he had removed from the trunk, he disconnected the battery cables. If there was any type of locating device on the police cruiser, Brian was hoping it was now disabled. Sadie approached the cruiser and Brian handed her the TASER.

Standing to one side, he cautiously opened the trunk and shined a flashlight beam on the man. "Get out."

The cop looked like a cornered animal. Eyes wild with a mix of rage and trepidation. "I'm fine right here. I think I'll stay." The officer was going to resist anything the Turners wanted him to do.

"Suit yourself," Brian said with a shrug. He produced a screwdriver from the tool kit and several empty coffee cups of varying sizes. He told Sadie to keep an eye on the cop. Brian knelt beside the rear of the cruiser and thrust the screwdriver at the gas tank. After several failed attempts, Brian found a rock and pounded the screwdriver through the heavy gauge plastic. Gas poured freely filling cup after cup until Brian plugged the hole with a stick. Gas continued to leak but only in drips.

Smelling the pungent odor of petroleum, the policeman began to panic. "What are you doing?"

"I'm going to torch your car," Brian replied casually. "I don't want any fingerprints or DNA left behind." Brian leaned in to the back of the cruiser and removed a handful of bullets from the cop's duty belt, two road flares, and the officer's night stick. He then dumped gas over the rest of the gear they had removed from the trunk. Another cup of gas was distributed over the steering wheel, dashboard, and computer.

"With me in it?" the frightened cop asked.

"Your choice, not mine. I invited you to leave."

The cop began to flop in the trunk. With his hands cuffed behind him, cracked ribs, and a wrecked knee, the man didn't make much progress.

"So now you want to get out?" Brian taunted.

The cop didn't respond. He kept trying to roll out of the trunk but failed. Brian set the final cup of gas on the ground and helped the man roll out. The cop flopped on the ground and cried out in pain. Brian grabbed him by the arm and Sadie took the other arm and pulled. With his good leg, the cop pushed himself along the ground and they managed to get the police officer to a safe distance from the cruiser.

Cold and exhausted the cop lay in the hard dirt of the cornfield. While December in Kentucky wasn't known for being cold, it wasn't exactly warm either and the crooked cop had only his underpants on. He was already shivering. His spirit seemed broken so Brian thought he would try his luck. "So, Officer, I'm curious why you pulled us over."

The cop mulled an array of responses before deciding on the truth. "There's a BOLO out for you."

Sadie looked at her father questioningly.

"I believe that's an acronym for Be On the Look Out," Brian said to her. He turned to the cop. "Why?"

With renewed belligerence, the cop snarled, "We don't care for Yankee assholes in our neck of the woods."

"Fair enough. How'd you know her name?" He nodded toward Sadie.

"I got it from a local truck stop advertising whores."

Brian produced the nightstick and swung it hard onto the cop's good knee. The first swing caused the man's kneecap to shift to the side of his knee, but Brian didn't stop. He crashed the club into the man's knee multiple times. The officer howled in agony, but Brian didn't stop until the joint was horribly disfigured.

Brian repeated the question. "How'd you know her name?"

The cop was breathing heavily. He grunted, "You're not hard to find, Breckenridge. Police have records of everyone, you know."

Brian fixed the cop with an icy stare. "Lionel Breckenridge has no family. How did you know her name?"

The cop looked away. Brian wanted to know exactly how the Lionel Breckenridge ID had been traced to him, but time was now working against him. If this guy knew he used an alias, then others did too. This was a complication he didn't need.

Brian jammed the end of the nightstick into the man's chest and asked again. "Why are the police looking for us?"

The cop looked like he wanted to cry. "You're wanted for questioning in a crime in Pennsylvania."

Brian growled. "What crime?"

"Murder."

"Bullshit!" Brian thought for a moment. "Murder of who?"

"Tommy Kincaid."

"Tommy Kincaid," Brian repeated. "Who's that?"

"How the hell do I know?" the cop snarled. "You think I know everyone from Kentucky?"

"I thought the crime was in Pennsylvania. Who said anything about Kentucky?" When the cop pursed his lips indicating he wasn't going to answer, Brian stated, "I think you know this Tommy Kincaid. Who is he?"

The cop said nothing.

Brian stared eye to eye with the cop before he resumed swinging the nightstick. This time it was an elbow. The cop rolled trying to avoid the blows, but Brian kept swinging. If he couldn't hit the elbow, he hit a shoulder. Anything with a bone. The cop kept rolling, winding the TASER leads around him until Sadie pressed the trigger. Instantly, the cop cramped, and Brian had a clear shot at the man's elbow. He swung five, ten times, then a few more for good measure. The man's elbow was mush. Sadie released the trigger.

The cop was going into shock. His skin looked pale. He was shivering and tears flowed freely from his eyes. Brian grabbed him by the hair and asked again, "Who is Tommy Kincaid?"

The whispered reply came in gasped bursts. "Rollins… sent him… and his boys… to kill you."

Sadie's eyes widened. "He killed Mom!" The cop's body arched as she sent more voltage into him. Brian didn't intervene as s his daughter tortured the man, he only watched. After allowing her to get it out of her system, he reached into his jacket and pulled out the silenced pistol. He put a single bullet in the cop's head.

The pair dragged the policeman's corpse back to the cruiser but this time they just shoved the body under the car. A steadily growing pool of gasoline had developed under the leaking plug.

Brian removed the stick and filled two more cups with gas. He doused the hood of the cruiser with one and the other he used to make a trail leading away from the cruiser. He took a road flare and lit it. Making sure Sadie was at a safe distance, he tossed the flare onto the trail of gas. The cruiser burst into flames.

The Turners walked to the Firebird in angry silence, neither feeling a hint of remorse. Their shadows cast jet black against the malevolent red glow from the ambient light of the flaming patrol car. Above, through the naked tree branches, the stars sparkled brightly in the clear December evening. Neither noticed. They focused their blame on Dr. Cooper Rollins. Mike was at fault too but it was Rollins' men who killed Lisa. It was Rollins' dirty cop who pulled them over and it was Rollins' people who were hunting them. It was Rollins who would pay the ultimate price for the hell bestowed upon the Turner family.

All business, Sadie put the battery back into her phone and waited for it to boot. Both Turners habitually removed the batteries of their phones to save the charge and prevent tracing their location. Once it was on, she went straight to Google Maps. "Do we have paper and a pencil?"

"Yeah," Brian said softly. *Smart kid. She's got a hell of a future if I didn't screw it up.* He kept a note pad and several pencils in the Firebird's glove box. "All back roads. It will take longer but I don't see that we have a choice. Don't plug in the destination. Just expand the map."

Brian leaned over her shoulder and helped plot the course. Sadie wrote the road names on the pad then turned off her phone and removed the battery.

"You drive," Brian told his daughter, his voice devoid of emotion. "I have a call to make."

Chapter 24

The phone in Mike's pocket vibrated. He didn't answer. After a minute he excused himself from a late dinner with some of his associates and left the private room. He grabbed his coat and stepped outside. On this night he had told his driver to stay home. He wanted to drive alone. Mike got into the Lincoln Navigator and drove to the middle of a vast parking lot at a shopping mall. His wasn't the only car in the lot but it was the only car within a hundred yards of anything. He could see if anyone approached.

Mike hit redial, and the phone only rang once before Brian Turner's irate voice barked, "How'd they know about Lionel Breckenridge?"

"Who the hell is that?" Mike snapped defensively.

"Don't bullshit me, asshole!"

"Whoa! Calm down. Why don't you tell me about this *Breckenridge* guy? Tell me what you know and maybe I can help fill in the spaces."

Silence. Turner wasn't talking. Mike heard him let out a long breath and he heard what sounded like a motor in the background. He gave Turner a minute before nudging him to talk. "Hello?"

Another deep breath then Brian Turner replied, "It's an alias I set up back in the day. It is completely separate from me. The only thing we have in common is a driver license photo. The Kentucky cops have a be-on-the-look-out for Breckenridge. How did that happen?"

Mike was shocked. "You have an alias? Wow." Most of the people Mike had called in favors from, were average people just like Brian Turner had become, or so he thought. Turner had managed to keep his nose clean for over thirty years. He was a carpenter and a family man. That was all pretty normal. The alias was not. Mike was intrigued but he and Turner had bigger issues to deal with. "I know nothing about this other name of yours. Maybe you tell me how they found out?"

Again silence. Mike knew Turner didn't trust him. He also knew Turner had no choice. He could help Turner or leave Turner on his own. Mike wanted to help get the job done and with the deadline in less than forty-eight hours, Turner was his best chance at this point. When Turner didn't respond Mike kept the conversation flowing. "So, let's backtrack. The Kentucky guys were at your house and things didn't go how they had planned. You and your kid left. How?"

"How? What do you mean *how*?" snarled Turner.

"I mean walk me through what happened next. Step by step."

"I didn't want to be followed so I took their car instead of mine. I mean you and these Kentucky guys knew where I lived and knew our cars. I figured taking their car was more of an unknown."

"And that's what you're driving now?"

After a short pause, Brian replied, "No." Turner went on to explain the steps he took to get from his house to Gettysburg College including the use of the Firebird. Mike knew what happened after they had reached the college.

"You parked the car from Kentucky close to your rental home. They probably had some kind of tracking locator on it, most of the newer cars do these days." Mike thought a moment. "If it were me, I'd have sent a local guy to find you. It would take too long to gather another crew from Kentucky. So, again, if it were me, I'd send your info to the local guy. He'd probably take your picture and walk around to see if anyone knew you. Since you parked right at your rental, well, it probably wasn't a very long walk before someone recognized your photo. They do a search on the alias you've maintained and voila… cover blown."

Again, silence.

Mike continued. "So, you're in a fancy car. It sticks out like a sore thumb, but I agree that you need it. It's still gonna stick out even with Kentucky plates. You on back roads now?"

"Yeah." Turner was silent again only for a moment. A horrible thought crossed his mind. "They know about Hannah, don't they?"

Mike hesitated for a beat before answering. "Yeah. I'm sure they do." He could hear Turner wilt on the other end of the phone call. The last thing he needed was for Turner to bail and try to save his other daughter. Fortunately, Mike had been through this kind of mess before and had made plans earlier in the day. "Don't worry about her. I got it covered."

Turner said nothing. He wasn't about to divulge that he knew about the mental patient and how the person had been removed from campus. He was hardly relieved to have one monster protecting his daughter from another monster but at least Mike's monster was doing what Mike said he would.

Mike picked up on Brian's concern. "She's gonna be fine as long as you hold your end of the bargain. I won't allow anything to happen to her."

Brian couldn't help but notice how Mike's Brooklyn accent weakened and his grammar had gotten better. It was still him, but he was letting his guard down for Brian. Oddly, it made Brian come closer to trusting the man. "How do you propose to protect her? Did you kidnap her and have her locked up somewhere?"

"No," Mike fired back quickly although the thought had crossed his mind. "No, I have eyes on her at all times. She is fine."

Brian could not remember ever feeling so helpless. He had to admit that he was too far away to do anything to protect Hannah. He felt like he would cry but after surviving the past couple days, he had no more tears left in him. Like it or not, he and Sadie had hardened. Brian moved to another aspect of the job. "Okay. Considering the Kentucky police are now looking for us, the target's redneck buddies are looking for us, and now we have to take back roads, I might need another day for this job. I still plan…."

"No!" Mike interrupted. His voice grew softer. "No. I can't allow that. It has to be done by Friday night."

Brian was surprised by the reaction. He pondered for a beat then realized Mike might be in a tight spot. He needed Rollins dead by Friday for some reason. "Why? What's happening on Friday? Or is it Saturday? There's something going on that you don't want this guy involved with. Right?"

This conversation was not going the way Mike would have liked. It was now he who was being silent.

"Well, I'll see what I can do. It may take an extra day but if I can get the job done by Friday, I will. No promises." Brian almost smiled when he said that.

"Friday," Mike growled. "It has to be Friday. And yeah, there's a deal going down on Saturday that has to be… diverted."

"Where and when? Maybe finishing the job then would be better."

"No, too much going on. It has to be before. I don't have an exact time. Not yet. I won't know the exact time until midnight and the job has to be done by then." Mike eased off. He actually liking Brian Turner. He would still kill him in a heartbeat, but he'd feel remorse over it. Turner had spunk. Mike hoped the job would be completed. "I can't have it any other way."

Brian nodded. He wished he could look Mike in the eye but that was unlikely. "Understood. I'll do what it takes. Any chance you can get the police off my case?"

"No. You have to treat each one as being controlled by the target. You're on your own. I wish I could help make it easier, but my hands are tied. All I can do is protect your other kid."

"Fair enough."

There was a long awkward silence that Mike eventually broke. "So, how'd you find out the cops were after you?"

Brian told him about being pulled over, the cop's slip in using his daughter's name, and then taking the cop to a remote location for questioning. Mike asked, "So, where's the cop now?"

"Still back in the lot where we left him."

"How do you know he didn't walk out?"

"It didn't end well for him. He isn't walking out."

Mike had to smile. This guy was too much. He'd called in favors before, some worked out and few had not but nobody had ever been like the Turners. "I noticed on the news that there was quite a drug war down your way. Coincidently, it was in the vicinity to where you had me pull that address. Know anything about that?"

Brian was silent.

"You're leaving a trail of bodies."

"Are you suggesting that what I've done wasn't justified?"

Mike's smile faded. Turner had been through hell. He lost his wife, almost lost Hannah, he was obviously involved with the River Bank shootings that were all over the network news, and now he was running from authorities en route to committing a murder. He and Sadie had killed in self-defense. It was probably justified. Even if it wasn't, Mike didn't care as long as the job was done on time. "No. Just making an observation."

"Look, I gotta go. I'm on *deadline*."

Mike couldn't help but smile at Turner's little barb. The guy definitely had spunk. "Okay. Check in later if you can. Keep me updated." Mike didn't wait for a reply. He ended the call and stared at a lamppost in the parking lot. The Favors have always been crapshoots. Somehow, Turner was different. Mike had confidence in this guy. It'll work out… he hoped.

Mike rolled the phone in his hand as he contemplated his situation. There was not much he could do except monitor things. He typed a quick text to another number. HOW'S IT GOING?

Five, ten, fifteen minutes passed and there was no response. *Shit*. Either the babysitters he'd sent to Gettysburg College were busy… or they were dead.

Chapter 25

An hour after their encounter with the Kentucky State cop, Brian and Sadie stopped to decompress. Both had to use a bathroom and they needed gas. The station they found was just about to close but the kindly man stayed open just for them. Brian washed his face in a rust-stained men's room sink before meeting Sadie inside. They paid for a full tank, plus a five-gallon jug of fuel, and some snacks and water. The man commented on the Firebird and Brian talked to him about it in his best imitation of a southern drawl. After some friendly chit-chat, the Turners were back on the road.

Ten minutes later, Brian turned into a farmer's path along a partially harvested cornfield. He shut the car off and opened a bag of salted cashews while Sadie worked on the drones. Brian studied the photos that Mike had provided him, but he needed a closer look. Against his better judgement, he inserted the battery in his cell phone and googled Rollins' address.

Zooming in, Brian could see a small plateau within sight of Rollins' stately home. He gave Sadie a nudge. "If this were Pennsylvania, I'd bet you a milkshake that there would be a tree stand right here." He pointed to a spot just inside the trees bordering the grassy plateau. "I think there are a lot of deer hunters in Kentucky too, but I won't bet you a milkshake on the tree stand."

Ignoring the tree stand comments, Sadie looked at the image. "I could set the drones up in the field and find a tree to climb so I can see where to fly them."

"That's what I was thinking," agreed Brian.

Brian zoomed in on the house, the yard, the land. There was what appeared to be a perimeter fence. The driveway was gated, and a small guardhouse was to the left of the gate. There were three boats at the dock, but the image also had leaves on the trees. It was not current.

Sadie glanced at the image again. "I might be able to see the road from there, too." Good thought. "You know, in case someone comes while I'm still up there."

Brian went back to his home screen. There was another text from his mother-in-law. WHERE IS LISA? SHE IS STILL NOT ANSWERING HER PHONE.

That was the last thing Brian needed. Lisa and her mother talked a minimum of four times a day. He ignored the text but secretly wondered when the hag would actually exert the effort to get to their house. There was nothing he could do about it now. *Worry about the immediate problem and handle the rest as they come.*

Hannah had texted too. He yearned to talk to her. He replied to her text telling her that he was neck deep in clients and would have to chat with her tomorrow or the next day. Brian shut the phone off and removed the battery.

Sadie continued working. She had removed the cameras on the drones and modified the servos. In place of the cameras, she attached a red Solo cup lined with aluminum foil. She had Brian hold the drone, careful not to interfere with the blades, then she turned it on and tested the rigging. The cup dumped most of the way, but it wouldn't completely empty. Sadie would have to pitch the drone as she dumped.

She then told Brian to let go of the drone. It hovered easily with the empty cup. The next test was to see how much liquid payload it could hold. It came to about three quarters of a cup. Sadie asked, "Do you think gas weighs the same as water?"

Brian shrugged.

Sadie shrugged too. "If there's a difference, it can't be much." Sadie had an open bottle of Snapple and poured it incrementally into the Solo cup, testing the drone with each pour. She was happy to see that they could fly with a substantial quantity of liquid. It even dumped well.

She kept working and rigged three more Solo cups each equipped with a three-foot-long rocket fuse. One last test flight with the fuse and several ounces of Snapple. The fuse would be used for the final flight of each drone. Once Sadie had completed modifying each drone to suit their needs, the Turners began the final leg toward their destination.

Remembering a late-night trip home from a long day at the Jersey shore with a pre-Lisa girlfriend, Brian suggested driving in thirty-minute shifts. Sadie would go first, and he would try to sleep. They would switch off for the next two hours, which would bring them very near Rollins' home. Had they been able to take main roads, the trip would have been significantly quicker.

Sadie eased onto the deserted country road. The white noise of the motor quickly lulled Brian to sleep. At the thirty-minute mark, Sadie woke him up and showed him what roads to look for before they switched. This went very well for three uneventful shifts.

Brian was nearing the end of his second shift. He figured they were getting close. It had been about two hours since their last stop when they checked the layout of the land and the maps. The road he was on led to Rollins' driveway. How far in they had to go was still a mystery.

Had Brian used a GPS he would know when he would arrive to the minute. They didn't have that luxury as they didn't want to use their cell phones in case they were being monitored. He could only estimate and keep his eye open for road signs. What he saw made him feel sick. It wasn't a road sign that caused Brian's stomach to turn.

The road traversed a stretch of rolling hills. The Firebird would climb a hill then dip into a valley then back up a hill like a low budget roller coaster. As they crested a hill, Brian saw taillights far in the distance. Just as he began his descent into the ensuing valley, he glimpsed blue and red flashers and the taillights of the car glow brightly.

Brian gasped and hit the brakes hard causing his slumbering daughter to slam into the shoulder strap. "What's the matter?"

she asked in a panicked voice. She had already drawn her pistol.

Among the many modifications Brian had made to the Firebird, were two switches for the lights. One was a switch that killed all of the lights except the headlights. The other killed the headlights as well. While the second switch was redundant—he could have used the actual factory switch to turn the headlights on and off—it was near the rest of his added controls thus easier to use if he were in a hurry. He flipped open the console and flipped the two switches putting the Firebird into total darkness. Even the dashboard lights were off. "I think we have a check point up ahead."

"A what?"

"This is the only road going to Rollins' house, right?" Brian spoke as he backed the car up the hill.

"Yeah." Charged with a jolt of adrenaline, Sadie was fully awake now. "Yeah," she repeated more pensively as she saw what her father had seen. "They're expecting us."

Brian checked the rear view as he crested the hill. They were surrounded by the night. Far ahead, the lights were still on. Brian and Sadie could make out the swinging of flashlights as the people carrying them walked around the car. "Yup," Brian whispered. "They're looking for something and I would agree that it's probably us."

Looking at the aerial picture, Sadie guessed they had at least a two-mile hike carrying drones, gas can, and multiple guns including a deer rifle. And that was two miles straight through woods. The drones would be damaged before they made it half way even if they could carry everything. "Now what?' she asked Brian.

"I don't know." He actually did know. He had an idea, but he really didn't like it. He pushed it aside and thought out loud. "The 'Bird is built for a lot of things but ramming a checkpoint isn't one of them."

"I think there's only one thing we *can* do," Sadie said with what Brian perceived to be a hint of cold detachment. Or maybe, was it enthusiasm he detected in his daughter.

Brian ignored Sadie. "We can't drive around them."

"Dad. We need to get in and get out quickly. We are doing this to save not only ourselves but Hannah as well. I think you know what we have to do."

Brian continued to ignore Sadie. They sat in silence until the car that had been traveling ahead of them turned around. Headlights shown from a distance. "Oh, shit."

Brian remembered a turn off about half a mile back. He spun the car around and was heading down the hill in the direction the came from. He hit the headlight switch and stomped on the gas pedal. They soon found the turnoff.

Whipping in quickly, Brian turned the car around in case they needed to make a fast exit and shut off the motor. Sadie was already rooting through the bags of items they had purchased earlier. She found one of the two camouflaged boat covers they purchased. Waterfowl hunters used the covers to make the watercraft a floating blind. It was designed to fit a twenty-two-foot boat but it worked just as well on an old Firebird.

Working quickly the father-daughter team covered the classic Pontiac and eased back inside. Brian suggested they rolled the windows down a crack so they could listen. Another five minutes passed when they heard the car pass by.

A few minutes later, Sadie broke the silence. "Dad. You know what we have to do. I don't see any other way."

Brian let out a long, defeated sigh. She was right.

Chapter 26

Friday

It was shortly after midnight. Brian and Sadie sat in the darkness while he came to terms with what he was about to agree to. Sadie had been altered in the past few days and Brian had no idea how to undo it. It was something he didn't have time to concern himself with but, as her father, he was worried. He couldn't help it.

Sadie was right, though. Brian knew what had to be done to give his girls and himself the best chance of survival. Another deep breath then Brian pulled his gun. He double checked that the clip was at full capacity. Sadie did the same. They both packed two more clips and a second gun before easing out of the Firebird.

Brian showed Sadie where there were extra keys hidden in case she had to leave in a hurry. She just went along with it to appease her father but had no intention of ever leaving him behind. A quick hug and they were on their way.

The Turners walked right down the deserted road toward the horizon where they had seen the strobe lights. It had to be at least a two-mile jaunt over rolling terrain. With each rise they searched the darkness but saw nothing. They had crested yet another hill when they heard voices in the night air. Not a hundred yards before them were the silhouettes of two vehicles blocking the road.

To the left of the road was dense forest that led all the way to Rollins' home. To the right was a field of winter wheat that was past its harvest time. Sadie and Brian went right, climbing a steep embankment and entered the waist-high wheat field. They moved in a large arc and soon found themselves within earshot of the road block.

There were three distinct voices talking about the upcoming college football bowl games. Cigarettes flared bright orange as the men took drags. The conversation shifted to the job at hand. One man said, "I'd be shocked if they showed their faces here."

"Well, it seems pretty certain. We just don't know when," a second voice offered. The man flicked his cigarette to the ground and crushed it with his foot. "I mean, really, they're amateurs. It can't be that hard. They're gonna screw up. Hell, they already screwed up by using a classic muscle-car. I mean it's kinda easy to spot."

The third man snorted. "Remember, Custer doesn't want the girl touched. He's got some bidders for her. He said he'd split the money with us we deliver her unmarked."

"Custer's a pig."

"Yeah, but he's a pig that'll pay us a good fee once he sells the daughter. Just think of the pig who wants to buy her."

The men all laughed.

Brian felt rage boil inside him and fought the urge to blindly attack. He caught Sadie's expression of horror and quickly composed himself. Any moral debate Brian or Sadie may have had about eliminating these men just became much easier to decide. Motioning her to ease backward, the two belly-crawled to a safe distance where they felt they could whisper a plan of attack.

"I'm not going to be sold!" Sadie hissed.

"Calm down," Brian replied. "Put that out of your mind. Anger will only cloud your thinking. Now, let's go back up there and end this. You take the guy on the far right, I take far left and we both go for the middle. Do *not* shoot to injure. Understand?"

It was the first time that Sadie had detected the hatred in her father's tone. In the past forty-eight hours she had undulated from a victim's mentality to predatory assassin and back again more times than she could count but his mood had been pretty consistent. He was concerned but not panicked and fairly even tempered. At least he had been more even tempered than she had been. Hearing about plans to be sold to the highest bidding pervert made her angrier than she had ever experienced. Her father, however, just turned ice cold, methodical, and calculating. He became a predator. She had to do the same. She willed the rage from her mind and focused on eliminating the hurdle that faced them.

Brian was waiting for her response. The emotional knot in her throat suddenly dissipated to nothing. Her heart rate slowed to normal. She felt the cool night air on her cheeks and every pebble under her as she lay in the field. Her senses were on full alert. She was back to being a predator. A single nod to her father was enough to set them in motion.

The pair snaked back to where they both had clear views of the three men. Brian leaned his foot against Sadie's. One of the men lit another cigarette. The flash of the lighter illuminated his uniform. Another cop. Another dirty cop. And he was the one farthest right. Sadie leveled the Sig and slowed her breathing. Brian had done the same. He could see Sadie in his peripheral vision. She was ready. He nudged her foot once… twice… fire.

Sadie's first shot slammed into the dirty cop. Fittingly, the bullet passed through his tainted badge before perforating his heart. Using the suppressed gun, the sound of the round hitting the man was actually louder than the shot itself. The cop toppled backward into his cruiser then crumpled to the road.

Brian had a clean shot on the man to the left. His bullet struck the man's right temple and blew the left side of his head out in a dark spray. As with Sadie's first shot, the impact made more noise than the shot. The man dropped instantly.

Time seemed to slow to a crawl. The third man who was in the center didn't immediately comprehend what had happened. At least it seemed to Brian and Sadie that it took a full two seconds for him to process that his two partners had just been killed.

The Turner's wasted no time in taking their next shots. Sadie went with the sure thing and put a sternum-crushing shot into the center of the man's chest. Brian confidently went for the head and placed a shot that entered the man's skull at the bridge of his nose. The man's torso snapped backward, and he dropped to the ground.

Brian and Sadie rolled to their feet and scrambled down the embankment. The cop that Sadie had shot took his last desperate gasps as she knelt beside him and whispered, "I'm not for sale." His panic-filled eyes met hers. He knew she had won. His expression of fear and defeat soon vanquished into the vacant stare of a dead man. Sadie smiled as the last inkling of life left the dirty cop.

Brian knelt between the other two bodies to make sure they were dead. He was all too familiar with stories of hunters thinking a deer was dead only to have it revive in the back of their trucks. With large portions of their heads missing, it was obvious that the men would not be a threat but Brian still felt that he needed to check. Neither had a pulse.

Deep in thought as a revised plan was forming, Brian stood up to survey the scene. *These assholes were expecting a Firebird but now we just inherited a police cruiser and an Excursion.* His thoughts were shattered when Sadie shrieked, "Dad! Look out!"

Brian bent at the waist and lurched forward but not before a searing pain raked along his back. He fell onto his stomach and rolled to his right. Emerging from the Excursion was a knife-wielding man. His pants were down, bunched at his ankles and prevented him from being able to jump so he had to lunge at Brian.

Sadie arced her pistol as the assailant awkwardly pounced from the truck and pumped two rounds into the man as he flew toward her father. She could have gotten a third off, but it would have been too close to Brian. The man belly-flopped on Brian and began thrashing wildly.

The man plunged the knife toward Brian's chest, but Brian blocked it by grabbing the man's wrist. The man's body slid off Brian and pinned his other arm to the ground. Brian raised his knee hard jamming his thigh into the man's unclothed groin. He repeated raising his knee while still holding the man's arm to prevent another stabbing attempt. The man arched his back in an attempt to thwart the attack on his groin and that was enough room for Brian to slam his forehead into the man's nose.

Brian pulled his head back for another shot at the man when Sadie's foot swung in front of his face. She kicked the man hard in the throat. The man gagged horribly and began losing strength. Sadie kicked him hard in the ribs and the man recoiled enough for Brian to get leverage to roll out from under him.

Sadie jumped on the man's arm that held the knife. Brian recovered his pistol and fired a point-blank shot into the man's head. The man's body went limp.

Running on full adrenaline, Brian sprang to his feet. He held his finger to his lips for Sadie to be silent. Then he motioned that they check the police cruiser first. It was empty and they quickly moved to the Excursion. The front seat was empty. The next row of seats was folded down. In the back was a naked woman, maybe twenty years old.

The woman sat up unsteadily. "What's all the commotion out there?" Her words were slurred and slow. She eyed Brian and smiled. "Did you butt in line?" The woman's eyes were red and glassy. She held her head unsteadily and had problems focusing on Brian. She was obviously high on something.

This was the last thing the Turners needed. Brian let his guard down and rubbed his head. The motion created a brand-new wave of pain emanating from his back. He caught his breath and winced. *Shit.* As if things weren't difficult enough. Now he had a damaged back and a prostitute to deal with. Not to mention the four bodies lying in the road. And keeping his daughters alive. The burden overwhelmed him.

Sadie's gun spat from the front seat of the Excursion. The prostitute's head snapped backward, and she collapsed leaving a hole in the rear window surround by blood spatter. Brian spun around to see Sadie frowning at him from the front seat.

He snarled, "What the hell was that?"

"We can't have her come with us. She was a junkie whore. She'd only slow us down or give away our position."

Brian grabbed his daughter by the shoulder. The pain in his back fueled his anger. "You don't just kill someone! What's that matter with you? She could have…" He was looking for the right words.

"Could have what, Dad? Could have gotten us killed? Yeah, you're right. She couldn't even sit up straight. Maybe if this had occurred *after* we killed Rollins, we could have taken her somewhere, but she would have been too much to handle now."

"And *you* made the decision to end her life. That's wrong. We should have discussed our options, Sadie, but you had to be judge, jury, and executioner. You can't just act, Sadie! What if she was being forced to do that stuff?"

"We *did* discuss our options. No witnesses, *remember*? Besides, it didn't look to me like she was here against her will." Sadie waited until Brian was about to counter before adding, "I guess *she* wasn't sold to the highest bidder."

Again, Brian knew deep down that Sadie was right. The young woman would have been an insurmountable liability and she was probably willingly prostituting herself to fund a drug habit that Rollins was all too happy to accommodate. But *killing* her was wrong. It was an impetuous solution to a very complex problem. *Wasn't it*?

And what was happening to Sadie? She just shot the woman and acted casually about it. *We've killed....* Brian lost track of how many people he had shot, how many his little girl had shot, and of course, the total had now escaped him. There was probably a large percentage of soldier, war heroes even, who had not killed as many as he and his daughter had. Like the number would have mattered.

He felt Sadie's stare. Confusion ran amok along with myriad other emotions in his mind. Deliberately meeting her eyes, Brian growled, "Don't lose sight of the fact that I am still your father." The comment didn't make sense in regard to their current situation, but it was all Brian could muster. His back hurt and his shirt was soaked in blood. "Let's clean this mess up and get back to the Firebird. We can toss the bodies down the hill there."

Sadie went straight to work without saying a word.

Chapter 27

After rolling the five bodies over a steep embankment, Sadie took the police cruiser and Brian piloted the Excursion back to the Firebird. His back fired bursts of pain with every turn of the steering wheel reminding him of just how stupid he had been to not check the truck. Details.

Both Turners were still angry with each other when they arrived at the old Pontiac. Neither spoke until communication was absolutely necessitated. Brian cracked first. "There's a field…"

"I know, Dad," Sadie interrupted sharply. "We've discussed this."

Brian wanted to turn her over his knee for a well-deserved spanking. He had spanked her once when she was little. It was all he had needed as from then on, the threat of a spanking was good enough. She was far too old for that now, but her insubordination pissed him off. He realized the spanking might have been more of a release for him than a punitive consequence for his daughter. *A spanking for shooting somebody without permission.* Brian snorted at the ludicrous thought. Thankfully, Sadie was too busy loading the drones into the cruiser and didn't notice.

"Before we go, I need you to sew me up. There's a med kit in the Bird."

"What?" Sadie stopped while holding the last drone.

"My back needs stitches. I can feel it. If I could reach it, I wouldn't ask." Brian retrieved the med kit as he spoke. Inside was a bottle of rubbing alcohol. He was surprised at how well it was sealed as it had to be thirty years old. He handed it to Sadie and lifted his shirt.

Sadie said nothing and there was a long pause before she unscrewed the cap. The gash was horrible, maybe four inches long and gaping a quarter inch at the center. Brian bent over and waited. Sadie dripped the alcohol onto the cut and Brian did his best not to scream at the top of his lungs. He grunted and squeezed his hands so hard that his forearms began to cramp.

To her credit, Sadie kept going. It would have been worse had she stopped and started again. She threaded the curved needle and plunged it into her father's back. She looped the needle through about twenty times. Brian never flinched. The needle was nothing compared to the excruciating pain of the rubbing alcohol.

There were several bandages in the med kit, but the adhesive had long since gone dry. "Nothing sticks, Dad. I can *sew* a bandage on if you want."

Brian snorted. He smiled at Sadie as he tucked his shirt in and moved his arms. He could feel the stitches pull but the pain was still nothing compared to the cleansing process. It would have to do. "I think I'm good, Doc. Thanks." He grinned at his daughter who looked a little pale. "You okay?"

She nodded. "Yeah. You?"

"Good as new… sort of."

There was a short silence between them. Brian put the med kit back into the Firebird. After double-checking that they had loaded everything they could possibly need, the Turners draped the camouflage cover over the old Pontiac and finalized their plans. They put on the camouflage hunting gear they had purchased. Camo gloves, hats with easily removable camo face netting, and camo pants. They had already been wearing their camo sweatshirts although Brian's now had a bloody hole in the back. Brian had Sadie put on the Kevlar vest taken from the cop who had pulled them over outside of Draffenville. She argued at first, but he insisted and finally she complied.

Brian made sure Sadie could find the hidden keys if needed and told her that if he were unable to go, she must leave him.

Another unresolved argument ensued and both Turners stomped into their respective vehicles, each furious at the person whom they loved more than anything else the world could offer.

Brian led in the Excursion. Sadie followed in the police cruiser. She had all of the lights off. They hoped that from a distance it appeared that there was only one vehicle driving. In a matter of minutes they had arrived at the driveway that would take them to Dr. Cooper Rollins' home. Brian stopped the truck about twenty yards in.

Sadie pulled the police cruiser into the driveway and parked it sideways between two large elm trees. Cars would not be able to drive in or out without moving the police cruiser. She gathered the drones, which were in a camouflaged bag intended for hauling goose decoys. She slung the bag and two five-gallon containers of gas over her shoulders. The gas cans had makeshift straps made of rope and were filled with only three gallons each, but they were still heavy and awkward to carry. She had two pistols, extra clips, and a box of ammo.

She had a lot of weight awkwardly balanced on her athletic frame. She felt like a miner's mule from the old west. They were always depicted as overloaded with bags, sleeping rolls, pans and everything else the miner would need. For a moment, Sadie stared where her dad was sitting in the Excursion although she couldn't actually see him, then she turned and pushed through the woods toward the clearing.

Brian watched his daughter until she disappeared. In his mind's eye images of her growing up flashed in rapid sequence. In the delivery room when he stared at her as she fussed on the incubation tray. He held his finger out toward her and she wrapped her little hand around it. In that moment of introduction, the entire planet shifted. He pictured her and Hannah at the beach, both in pig tails and covered in sand. And of course, all the times they went to work with him. From the days when he paid them in ice cream for cleaning up to the days where they were actually beneficial to have on site and earned money.

Realizing there was a decent chance he may never see her again he whispered, "I love you, Peanut." He wanted one last hug and to apologize for being angry with her, but that opportunity had passed. A lump was forming in his throat, but he forced it away. He had a job to do. Brian put the truck in gear and slowly continued down the driveway.

The headlights shined on a brick guardhouse and a heavy iron gate mounted on a thick curved brick wall. A black iron fence that matched the gate disappeared into the woods in both directions. Two men were huddled by the guardhouse. They smiled at the sight of the approaching Excursion.

Brian slowed as he approached the pair. His silenced Sig lay on his lap under the camouflaged face veil. Brian found a pair of sunglasses in a case clipped to the visor and put them on. There were cigars in metal tubes laying in the console tray. He removed one and lit it. Brian wasn't a smoker, but he wanted to look like the man he assumed would have been driving the Excursion.

Slowly Brian eased the big truck to the gate. He lowered the window as the two men eagerly approached. One, carrying a six-pack of Miller Lite and a bucket of fried chicken, said with a heavy southern drawl, "I hope y'all didn't wear that whore out. I thought you'd be here a half hour ago. I've been lookin' forward to this all day!"

Brian blew a thick cloud of blue cigar smoke out the window. As he did, he raised the Sig and spat a bullet into the forehead of the first man. The second man floundered for his weapon, but it was under a heavy winter coat. Brian didn't hesitate and fired a forty-five caliber bullet that slammed a hole directly between the man's eyes. The man dropped and Brian pointed the Sig at the guard house and waited.

There was no movement from the guardhouse, so Brian slowly exited the big Ford. He approached the guard house, head on a swivel searching for any other men. Cautiously he opened the door. A full ashtray, a radio tuned to some station playing a twangy bluegrass song, and a pile of empty beer cans was all he found.

Brian returned to the truck and lowered the side door window before turning off the ignition and put the key in his pocket. He removed his Remington 700BDL .243 deer rifle and set it gently on the ground. He had five rounds in the gun and another ten rounds loose in his pocket.

Not taking any chances, he checked for a pulse on each of the men before hefting the corpses into the back seat. He shoved them through the open window which was significantly more work than opening the door, but it didn't activate the dome light. Brian scooped up the six-pack and bucket of greasy chicken that the first man dropped and threw it all into the truck, too.

He slung the rifle over his shoulder and crept into the woods. Brian found a heavy limbed oak tree that was located perfectly in front of Rollins' home. It was a moonless night. Brian climbed the tree mostly by feeling his way limb to limb. He found a suitable branch at what he estimated was about fifteen feet above the ground. The limb supported his weight and was located under another branch that he could rest his rifle on.

Although Brian had plenty of ammunition it was the first shot that was the most critical. It had to count. Any shots after that would be hurried and he may have bullets coming in his direction as well. He made himself as comfortable as he could and pointed the rifle in the direction of the house. Two lanterns flanked the massive front door. They were actual gas lights that provided a soft flickering glow that gently illuminated the front door. Brian checked his shooting lanes. Through the Nikon 3x9 scope he could not only easily see the door but the peep hole and the heavy brass knocker.

As Brian studied the door through his scope, another thought occurred to him. Dr. Cooper Rollins had the same propane lanterns between each of the garage doors and two more along the sidewalk. Brian could assume that there would be the same type of lanterns on the back of the house too. It was an ostentatious accessory in his opinion, but it would make Sadie's job a little easier as long as she recognized the lanterns for what they were.

The gas lights meant there would be a tank to store the propane. If Brian had built the house, he would have put the tank in front. The lake was in the back and with the driveway to the right that ruled out those locations. The propane delivery company would want the tank located within reach of the driveway.

From the surveillance photos, there was no service entrance so that logically ruled out the left side of the house. The tank had to be in front.

Brian scanned the yard through the rifle scope. It was too dark. He couldn't see anything that resembled a lid to a propane tank. It had to be there. He filed that thought away and resumed waiting. It was all up to Sadie now.

Chapter 28

Sadie was sweating like a mad woman. Hefting the drones, gas, and weapons uphill through the forest while wearing body armor and her camo hunting gear was no easy task. She unzipped her jacket to try to regulate her temperature, but it only helped a little. She rolled her sleeves up but that revealed two arms that had long lost their summer tan. She felt like they glowed in the darkness. Probably paranoia but she wasn't taking a chance. She would keep her sleeves down and sweat. She stopped for twenty seconds to let the cool air wash over her then she marched on.

It seemed to her that she had hiked at least two miles by the time she found her way to the meadow that she and her father had seen on the surveillance photos. Although there was no moon, the difference in the grass from the woods was easy to see. It took a moment for Sadie to get her bearings then she marched to the east.

Sadie had taken no more than twenty steps when a deer snorted loudly and crashed from the edge of the woods. From the sound of it, there were a few deer in the herd, and they all moved at the sound of the snort. Sadie felt like she would have a heart attack. A moment later and the night was silent again except for Sadie being able to hear her own heartbeat. She was shaking.

The teenager took a knee and breathed in the cold winter air. She held the neck line of her vest open and a wave of humid air swelled up over her face. She could smell her own sweat. Whatever. She wasn't in a beauty contest. Her pulse slowed to a near normal rate. Sadie stood and pressed on.

The meadow turned to the south. Sadie carefully lowered her load. She counted her paces in order to find the drones and gas, as she walked the perimeter of the meadow. Peering through the naked tree branches Sadie soon saw the soft glow of the gas lamps. She studied them for a moment, not sure why the lights acted so differently. Then, she remembered her friend's house. They were a well-to-do family and had outdoor lights that were actually small fires, torches lit by propane. Her job just got a little easier.

Retracing her steps, Sadie gathered the drones and gas and moved them back to her vantage point. She would have to fly the drones behind her first then loop over the trees, but she could watch everything from just inside the woods. Thankfully, the drones had two small red lights that would allow her to see them for a little while at least. As long as she got them pointed in the right direction, she should be able to see them in the ambient light from the house.

Sadie loaded the first Solo cup with gas. It was lined with aluminum foil so the fuel wouldn't dissolve the plastic. The drone sounded like a jet in the still December night as she piloted it over the meadow and arcing above the trees. She lost track of the red lights but could hear it. Soon, she caught sight of it again as the flames of the house lights glinted off the shiny white plastic rotors.

Sadie aimed for the back of the house first but quickly realized she could not see where the drone was going. She had it hover while she quickly moved deeper into the woods to the east. It was hard to find but eventually she saw the reflection of the lamps on the white plastic again.

She guided the drone about twenty feet above the house and flicked the switch that would have operated the camera. The camera was removed, and the switch activated a servo that wound a string attached to the Solo cup. The first few ounces of gasoline were dumped onto the roof of the home, and some ran down the cedar siding on the wall.

Sadie repeated the procedure with the same drone. She would bring it to a landing in the meadow, fill the cup with several ounces of gasoline, run back to the woods, and fly the drone to dump more gas. Once the back of the house was coated with about two gallons of gas, a few ounces at a time, she moved to the south side where the garage was.

The battery indicator was reading a low level, so Sadie switched drones. She didn't need to run as deep into the woods to watch the second drone as it coated the custom wooden garage doors. Careful to avoid the propane lanterns, Sadie splashed gas on each door and the roof.

The northern side of the house was impossible to see. Sadie splashed what she estimated to be about a gallon on the roof and about a half-gallon on the lawn. The process had taken a terribly long time. In fact, to the east through the spider-web of leafless tree branches, the sky was getting ever so slightly brighter. But she was done and now it was show time.

Sadie filled a cup half way with gas. She piloted the drone to the back of the house. She sprinted into the woods to her vantage point and watched as she sent the drone through a window above the back door. She spilled the contents of the Solo cup right before impact in an attempt to drizzle enough gas to hit the lanterns yet also have some dump inside the house.

The sound of glass breaking tore through the pre-dawn quiet of the woods. After a seemingly eternal second of silence came a loud whoosh as the entire back of the house ignited. The fire covered the cedar siding and flashed inside the broken window.

Sadie marveled at the flames for a second then rushed to get the next drone. She had poured gas in the cup before sending the first one so the second was ready. She flew the drone into one of the lanterns flanking the garage doors and another loud *whoosh* blasted the early morning air.

The third drone strike was different. Brian and Sadie had purchased a rocket fuse, neither knowing there would be propane lamps. Sadie lit the fuse and sent drone number three over the house to the north. Once clear of the house, she killed the motor. It plummeted like a rock bouncing off the roof and out of sight.

The north side roof did not immediately ignite but there was a whoosh from the gasoline in the lawn and soon Sadie could see a bright glow from the north side.

Embers were beginning to take flight and soon the entire roof and three sides of the house were engulfed in flames. Sadie watched as one of the garage doors opened and fire immediately spilled into the garage bay. The door reversed direction and closed halfway before the flames burned through the wires controlling the opener. It froze in place giving the fire plenty of air to draw from. The garage filled with flames and smoke.

Sadie piloted the fourth drone with the final payload, two ounces of gas and four .45 caliber bullets. Among the many items the Turners had purchased on their trip down was a small candle. Brian had drizzled wax over the four bullets to seal them. It was those four bullets that were now in the cup of gas. The wax was intended to delay any liquid from penetrating and ruining the gunpowder.

With the house fully illuminated by fire and emergency lighting, Sadie could easily see the south side chimney. She piloted the drone directly over the flu that had smoke coming out of it and dropped the gas and bullets into the furnace.

Men and dogs poured out of the only safe exit remaining, the front door. Sadie didn't stick around to watch. She had to get moving to help her father. Leaving the empty gas cans and drone control, Sadie chambered a round in her Sig and ran through the woods toward her dad. The crack of a rifle report sounded loudly above the now roaring flames.

Chapter 29

Brian had grown stiff from sitting in the tree. Initially, it was comfortable, but one can only sit in a tree for so long. Plus, his back was throbbing. He could feel every stitch as it tugged on his skin. *Stupid.* He should have checked to see if anyone was in the Excursion and now he was paying the price.

The sound of the drones had brought his focus back to the plan but even that took forever to implement. The Turners had no idea how long it would take to spill six gallons of gas on a house a few ounces at a time. It turned out to have taken even longer than the worst-case scenario Brian had considered. Dawn was not far away.

The odor of gasoline grew more pungent as Sadie made pass after pass after interminable pass with the drones. Brian was again beginning to fidget when the first burst of flame lit up the back of the house. After that, he felt nothing. Every sense focused on the front door. His breathing slowed, his hearing sharpened, his eyesight hone perfectly in anticipation of the slightest movement.

The entire house was engulfed in fire when the front door finally opened. Three dogs poured out first. Brian could hear the iron gates sliding open. They must have had a control inside as well as in the guard house. He should have thought to buy a chain to seal the gates. Too late now.

The dogs barked loudly and began sniffing the ground. They moved back and forth methodically heading toward the open gate. It was only a matter of time before the dogs found his trail.

A crowd of men burst from the front doors. Inside Brian could see flames covering the floor and smoke billowed from the open doors. The men hurried out and formed a protective circle around three other men. Brian counted eight body guards each holding a pistol at the ready. Adding the ones being protected there were eleven men. That was more than he had hoped for. Again, too late now.

The fire illuminated the entire front yard. Half the distance from the driveway Brian saw the source of fuel for the fancy exterior light. Just about the surface of the expertly manicured lawn was the cap of an underground propane tank. *Noted.*

Brian found his target. He steadied his breathing. Keeping the crosshairs on the head of Dr. Cooper Rollins, Brian slowly squeezed the trigger.

A massive spray of red mist blew into the air. Rollins dropped as did the man immediately next to him and one of the body guards. Rollins had to be dead. Brian was too good of a shot to miss that one plus he saw the spray. Through the scope Brian saw the third man inside the protective circle fall to his knees next to Rollins. He was wailing loudly. Rollins and the second man were not moving. The bodyguard was struggling to get up.

Brian moved his scope toward the propane tank lid. He tried to visualize just how deep the tank would be, but he really didn't know much about their design. The dogs were barking and moving toward him now. Brian pumped two rounds into the tank lid hoping to maybe get lucky and break a valve. He returned his attention back to the crowd of men, put the cross hairs on a bodyguard and dropped him. His fifth and final shot went into Rollins' chest just for insurance.

By now the remaining bodyguards had seen the muzzle blasts from Brian's rifle. They scattered for what sparse cover they could find and began to return fire. Tree branches splintered all around Brian and one bullet even tore through his sleeve, but it didn't hit skin. And now the damned dogs had arrived. With noses to the ground, they were working together to narrow their search for the intruder.

Reluctant to drop to the ground amidst three large and ill-tempered Dobermans, Brian chose to reload his rifle. It was far from his best option, but the dogs presented a problem he would rather deal with after dispatching some more bodyguards.

The remaining men no longer needing to protect a corpse, fanned out and returned fire from multiple directions. Brian got two more rounds off killing two more bodyguards, but the survivors saw the muzzle flash and shot at it.

Bullets blasted into the tree all around Brian. The dogs were now a secondary concern. Brian tried to get one more shot off when a bullet tore into the side of his abdomen. It felt like a punch to the gut backed by a Mack truck. The shot slammed into him so hard he lost his balance and toppled backward from the tree. Brian clipped a branch on the way down and actually landed on his feet but the pain in his side doubled him over.

The dogs had watched him fall and one of them pounced. Brian raised his hand defensively and the big Doberman clamped on it. Instead of pulling back, Brian shoved hard. His hand slid deep into the dog's mouth prompting the animal's gag reflex. The big Doberman spit Brian's hand out with a cough. The dog regained its composure and was quickly joined by the other two. The three of them instinctively began working as a pack. They circled around Brian who was kneeling at this point.

Brian shifted his position and leaned his back against the big oak. The fire was growing in intensity and an undulating orange hue glowed on the ground and trees. Flames reflected in the dogs' eyes making them look satanic. Brian slowly reached for his pistol. It was tucked under his outer camo shirt and between the hole in his side and the gash in his back it took all of his might to move without screaming.

One of the dogs pounced but its chest exploded before the animal reached Brian. He never heard the shot that Sadie fired from her silenced Sig. A second dog clamped onto Brian's leg. He wore jeans and camo outer pants which prevented the dog's teeth from penetrating his skin, but it still hurt like hell. Brian finally found his gun and placed the muzzle against the dog's head in a direction that wouldn't hit his own leg. The gun spat a round that ended the dog's life. Sadie took out the third dog with a single shot.

"What the hell are you doing here?" Brian snapped trying not to sound grateful. "You're supposed to be going back to the car!"

"And so are you but you look like you need some…" Sadie never finished her admonishment toward her father. The air from the teenager's lungs seemed to be pressed out of her as a bullet slammed into her back. Her body flew forward draping over Brian.

In the glow of the flames Brian could see two men fast approaching. The first held his gun ready for a second shot. Brian aimed at his chest and fired. The man bent backward as the bullet struck dead center into his chest. The second man quickly ducked behind a tree. When he tried to return fire, Brian peppered the tree with three rapid fire shots.

Sadie was gasping for air that just wouldn't fill her lungs. At least not at first. Brian was horrified as he watched his daughter struggle for breath. She looked like a fish out of water. He hugged her body and kicked the ground pushing himself and Sadie around the trunk of the tree. He had to crawl over two of the dead Dobermans while holding his daughter and keeping his Sig ready to shoot.

The man behind the tree fired a shot at Brian but hit one of the deceased dogs. With a strong kick, Brian moved to the safer side of the big oak. He let Sadie go and she slid off him to the ground still gasping for air.

Thinking Brian was tangled in the dogs and Sadie, the man decided to attack. He left the cover of the tree and ran straight at the Turners. Brian easily dispatched him with a shot to the throat. He landed with a crash of broken branches and dried leaves. Brian heard another sound above the fire and shouting bodyguards. Sadie was breathing again. Her breaths were in exaggerated, heavy, wheezing gasps but she was breathing.

Sadie was on all fours gulping air. Her face contorted in pain with each breath, but she could breathe. Soon the athletic teenager was standing. "Let's go." Her voice harsh and croaky yet full of determination.

"No. I'll hold them off. You go. I will only slow you down. Get out of here," Brian said. He was bleeding heavily from his side now and there was something else coming from the wound, too. The smell was horrible. He had hunted long enough to know what a gut-shot deer smelled like. It was an odor like no other. While Brian didn't smell that particular exact odor, he smelled something enough like it that he knew that he was badly damaged.

"Dad, this isn't a time to argue. I'm not leaving you. Either we both go, or we both stay. What's it gonna be?"

"God damn it, Sadie! You have your whole life ahead of you. Get out of here!" Brian snarled. The voices of the remaining bodyguards were getting closer. Brian actually fleetingly considered putting a bullet in his own head. It would end the excruciating pain and leave Sadie nothing to stay and fight for. It was a stupid panicked idea. "I am your father, and I am telling you to go!"

Sadie said nothing. She winced from the pain of just breathing and took a knee beside her dad. She held her pistol out, ready to fire. Clearly, she wasn't moving. Brian was so angry at her that he couldn't find the words right away. He felt his face turn red and for an instant the rage inside him overpowered the pain. He was about to yell at her again when the front lawn exploded.

Chapter 30

Travis Farley was relaxing with a smoke. He had nothing else to do. He had taken his turn with the prostitute, and she was now entertaining one of the other men at the road block on the southern side of Rollins' property. The girl they brought along was the only action they had seen all night. Not a single car had come by. Jerry Sutcliff, the cop, was sleeping in his cruiser. It was a quiet, clear night and frost had blanketed the ground. Farley could hear Sutcliff snore.

There was a faint smell of wood smoke wafting in the air. Farley assumed it was from a distant woodstove but then he wasn't so sure of that either. The smoke had a pleasant cedar-like character to it, but it also carried a faint asphalt-like smell that made him think it might not be from a wood stove. Farley took another drag from his Camel and the cigarette smoke overpowered any other aromas.

It was peaceful. The stars were out, and an owl hooted from some distant tree. Farley enjoyed being outside on nights like this. It was boring work, sitting and waiting to check passersby, and that's why they had a girl from one of Rollins' several brothels come along, but it was work nonetheless and he liked the pay. The complimentary passes to the brothels were a nice perk of the job as well. Farley took another drag from his smoke and then all hell broke loose.

A loud rifle blast shattered the stillness of the night. It was followed by several gunshots then more rifle reports. The sound was coming from Rollins' house. By the time Farley had roused the slumbering cop and alerted his partner, the volley of gunshots had intensified. From the direction of the gunshots, Farley could see an orange glow growing over the trees.

Farley led the way in his Suburban as his partner and the hooker were getting dressed. The police cruiser was right behind with its lights flickering blue and red on the barren winter branches of the trees lining the road.

Within two minutes Farley was at the driveway but found it blocked by an abandoned police cruiser. He got out and tried to open the door only to find it locked. "Jerry! You got keys for this?"

"What, you think all cop cars are universal? *No!*" came the smartass reply.

Farley jumped back into his truck, put it in four-wheel drive, and rammed the cruiser aside. He tore down the long driveway with Jerry behind until they came to the big Ford Excursion parked in front of the sliding iron gates. The truck was reflecting an orange glow from the now visible fire. Farley correctly assumed it was another road block and did not invest the time in looking for keys. He began to nudge the truck forward when the propane tank exploded.

Dirt and sod fell from the sky peppering Farley's truck and Sutcliff's police cruiser. Through the windshield Farley could see trees toppled from the blast and flaming debris igniting the dry leaves on the ground. Before he knew it, the flames were spreading, illuminating the woods in a malevolent orange glow that threatened to trap them.

He shifted his truck into reverse and hit Sutcliff's cruiser hard enough to crack the grill. Taking the hint, Sutcliff backed his police car all the way out to the driveway entrance while simultaneously describing the scene to his dispatcher over the radio. The two vehicles flanked the driveway entrance and were immediately abandoned.

Guns drawn, Travis Farley, Officer Jerry Sutcliff, and Farley's young partner, Sam Manning, ran down the driveway. The curious prostitute followed at a safe distance. Heat from the growing forest fire was intensifying. The group had ventured as far as the Excursion when a man wailing like a child ran to them. Fire had engulfed the nearby trees and formed a flaming tunnel around the driveway from where the man came.

The man was Martin Benner. He was in his mid-fifties, with a slender build, and flamboyantly effeminate. Benner was wearing a pastel blue, full length satin nightgown. He was shoeless and covered in blood, dirt, and soot. Martin Benner and Dr. Cooper Rollins were life partners and had been together for well over twenty years.

None of Rollins' men understood the connection. It was one thing to be gay, that they accepted, but Dr. Cooper Rollins was a retired general practitioner and very conservative Republican-type of person.. He dressed in tasteful but affordable clothing. He was refined yet still affable and easily approached. He was also a shrewd businessman, owning a few legitimate businesses such as a carwash and two bars, along with several criminal enterprises like fourteen brothels, an employment agency staffed by human trafficking, and a burgeoning counterfeiting operation.

Benner was flamboyant to the point where he made people uncomfortable with his lavish attire and wild gesturing when he spoke. He loved to go shopping with his conservative partner's money. He was often kept apart from Rollins' more nefarious endeavors, yet Benner had made his presence known often enough for all of the people in Rollins' employ to recognize and politely tolerate him. The couple were the embodiment of the cliché "opposites attract."

Wailing hysterically, Benner tried to hug Farley but was rudely pushed aside. Undaunted, Benner moved to the prostitute. She held him and tried to comfort him, but Farley was already barking rapid-fire questions. "What happened? Is anyone else in there? Where's Dr. Rollins?"

"Everyone's dead!" wailed the man. "Everyone is dead! My Cooper is dead!" Benner flailed his arms dramatically and cried hysterically. "Men came from all directions. It was an army of murderers. They were shooting everywhere. My Cooper, my beautiful, precious Cooper is dead!" Benner shrieked loudly into the woman's shoulder.

The fire forced the group back toward the road. Flames soon engulfed the Excursion and embers from the burning trees rode the heat until settling downwind and creating new fires. The situation was getting worse at an exponential rate. After moving Farley's Suburban and Sutcliff's cruiser even farther away from the driveway entrance, all they could do was wait for the firefighters.

Rural life had plenty of rewards but it also had some drawbacks. One of them being that any emergency can have a delayed response. It took twenty minutes for the firefighters to arrive and by then several acres were ablaze.

Farley watched helplessly as more fire companies arrived. Periodically he would grill Benner for answers, but the result was always the same. The man was in shock and oscillating from being nearly catatonic to having out-of-control hysteria. Betsy, the prostitute, tried her best to soothe Benner but he was inconsolable.

Equally frustrated and disgusted by Benner, Farley moved away from the group. He needed a moment by himself. He lit a cigarette and his moment abruptly ended when Sutcliff approached. Sutcliff had told everyone he knew that he had given up smoking but the truth was he had just given up buying cigarettes. Farley handed him the pack of Camels and Sutcliff removed one and handed it back to Farley.

Sutcliff cleared his throat twice before Farley tuned in. The police officer needed a light. Farley fished out his father's old Zippo lighter and lit the man's smoke. Farley's father had died in a moonshine running accident and the battered old lighter was one of the few things of his father's that Travis had. It never left his possession.

After a few drags, Sutcliff said, "You may as well get it over with."

Farley nodded but did nothing.

"It's only going to get worse. He has to know." Sutcliff took another drag and slowly exhaled a blue cloud that slowly dissipated into the cool morning air. "He can't shoot you. I mean, well... he just wouldn't."

Dalton Custer had made it explicitly clear that he was to be disturbed only under the most extreme conditions. He wanted a day off before what promised to be a huge weekend. The assassination of Dr. Cooper Rollins was certainly qualified as extreme, but Farley was still hesitant.

Farley actually found some comfort in Sutcliff's words. He doubted Custer would shoot him, so he pulled out his cell phone and made the call.

Chapter 31

One or possibly both of the shots Brian had taken at the propane tank must have connected. Gas had leaked out of the tank and, being heavier than air, pooled in a low spot on the ground. The tank was due to be filled that week; thus it was only at about one quarter capacity of the liquid gas. Had it been full, the tank would have acted more like a torch than a bomb.

Turf and dirt rained over Brian and Sadie. Some trees toppled but the big oak that Brian had used held strong. An uprooted tree had one of Cooper Rollins' bodyguards pinned under it. The man was flailing franticly as smoldering bits of debris landed all around him and began to ignite the dried leaves and organic detritus that lay on the forest floor. He was probably screaming but Brian could hear nothing but intense ringing from the blast. He couldn't bear to see the man burned to death, so Brian leveled his pistol at the man's head and squeezed the trigger.

Sadie was patting out a small area on her sleeve that had caught fire. She wasn't burned but the shirt was ruined. She motioned to her father to get up and this time he obliged. Using the rifle as a cane, Brian followed Sadie into the woods.

The Turners sprinted, as much as they could, for what seemed an eternity but was actually a little over a hundred yards. Sadie had to stop, her heavy breathing was making a crunching sensation below her left scapula where the bullet had hit.

The intensity of Brian's pain was growing exponentially. It felt like a combination of a sucker punch to the gut and a kick to the balls. He dropped to a knee and vomited. In the dim light he tried to see if there was blood in what he spit up, but it was still too dark. Determined to outrun the fire, he wiped his chin and began loping through the woods.

The Turners maintained a surprisingly decent pace considering the physical condition they were in, particularly Brian. He had to vomit about every hundred yards. His shirt was soaked with blood and perspiration and his entire right leg was crimson. He was feeling weaker with each step. And thirsty. He desperately needed a drink which made him think he was losing a lot of blood.

By the time they reached the road, Brian could barely stand. Their hearing had returned enough to communicate with each other. It took a moment to get their bearings. Sadie turned to her father, "The Firebird is up the road a bit. Maybe two hundred yards."

Brian wasn't going to make it. Sirens were blaring and a volunteer firefighter's pickup truck with its blue lights flashing sped by. Sadie ducked into the roadside ditch to avoid being seen. Brian was still far enough in the woods to avoid detection. He leaned against a tree and involuntarily slid down the trunk leaving a trail of red spots on the bark.

"Dad!" Sadie said. "Dad, I... I'll get the car. Just hang on." She tried to conceal the desperation she was feeling. It didn't work.

Sadie started to run toward the road but had to duck back into the cover of the woods when a fire truck came blaring past. Once out of sight, Sadie bolted for the Firebird. She had to quickly seek cover two more times before finally reaching the car. She found the keys, stuffed the camo cover inside and sped off to get her father.

Sadie pulled the car around and drove off the road as far as she dared. She hastily covered the car again and dove into the woods just as another volunteer fire fighter sped by. The camo cover worked well in the low morning light.

Brian was almost unconscious when Sadie returned to him. She dragged him to the car and quickly shoved him into the passenger seat. Another siren was blaring toward them, and she climbed over her father pulling the cover over the car as she held the door shut. Shards of pain blasted through her back into her chest, but she ignored the agony. The fire truck sped by, and Sadie backed out the door. She buckled Brian in and pulled a wad of gauze from the medical kit to try to stem the bleeding from his wound. Then she retrieved his rifle. It was the only thing that could tie the Turners to the mayhem associated with Rollins' death.

Sadie scurried under the camo tarp, shoved the rifle into the back seat, and climbed behind the wheel. Her heart pounding, she took a moment to gather her thoughts. She only remembered seeing one road about three miles away where she would be able to turn. It didn't matter which way she went, they just needed to get the hell away from Rollins' estate. She would need her cell phone. They might be able to trace it but *they*, whoever they may be, would probably be concentrating more on the fire.

"Hey," came a soft, ragged voice. Her dad's breathing seemed labored. Exerting what seemed to be his last reserves of energy, he slowly lifted the console lid. He showed her three switches that he hadn't mentioned earlier. "In the back are canisters of twisted steel barbs. Only use one at a time. You flip a switch, and the barbs will spread across the road. Anyone behind you will get four flat tires."

"James Bond stuff?" Sadie smiled weakly.

Brian only nodded once then closed his eyes. "I'm proud of you, Peanut."

Sadie's eyes welled up. "Dad?" She grabbed his hand. "Dad?" Brian didn't respond. "I'm not done with you yet. And we have an argument to finish. DAD!"

Brian squeezed her hand lightly then drifted off to what Sadie hoped was sleep. He needed medical attention, and he needed it fast. She fired up the motor, rolled down the window, and from the driver's seat she pulled the camo cover in through the window. She wadded the cover into the back seat and pulled out onto the road. Three miles to the next intersection.

Sadie stomped on the gas and speed-shifted through the gears. She crested a hill at sixty miles per hour just as two police cars sped past her. She *felt* the first cop making eye contact and in the flash of the moment, Sadie realized the cop recognized who she was. She caught a glimpse of brake lights in her rearview mirror and swore loudly.

The road was rolling but straight and unlike Pennsylvania, the surface was smooth, devoid of potholes. The old Pontiac had eclipsed ninety miles an hour with plenty of power to go faster. In under two minutes she had reached the intersection. Braking hard and skidding just a bit, she made a sharp right. Her phone with Google Maps displayed flew off its perch on the console and under her foot. She gently kicked it aside while simultaneously hitting the gas and trying to work the clutch.

Sadie risked a glance to get her phone and when she successfully found it, there were two cops in the distance behind her. She glanced at the phone again. *Shit!* The road ahead had curves. She would have to slow down. *Dad said this thing was built for road racing. Let's see what it can handle.* Sadie made sure her Sig was next to her, but she had lost count of how many bullets she had fired. There was no time to check now.

The road banked hard left then right. A hilly quarter mile of straight asphalt followed by more turns. Sadie was taking turns at double their marked speed, but the car held fast to the pavement. Glancing at Google when she could there was nothing but twisting, rolling roads in the area. The country roads were a blessing in that she was not exposed the way she would be on the highway but they were a curse in that she couldn't evade the police. Then she spotted something on the map that gave her an idea. A creek meandered across a small road. The intersection for that road was a mile away.

Sadie double checked the map to make sure it wasn't some rural dead end. It wasn't. It was a tiny road that had a bridge. Sadie hammered the gas pedal and Firebird lurched faster. Two hard turns and the intersection was upon her faster than she expected. She hit the brakes but still blew past.

Her phone flew from her lap, Brian's arms fell off his lap, but the shoulder harness kept him from impacting the dashboard, and the rifle and camo cover fell from the backseat. Sadie shifted into reverse, found the intersection, slammed the shifter back into first and hammered the gas again. Just as she piloted the car into a wooded section, she caught another glimpse of her pursuers. A third car had joined the chase.

Sadie had to slow the Pontiac on this road. It was paved but also had a copious amount of loose gravel on it. It didn't matter how well built the modified Firebird was if the tires couldn't grip the road. She drove as fast as she dared, and the cops were soon in her rearview mirror. *This had better work.*

The bridge came into view, and it was even better than she had hoped. It was a single lane bridge with thick stone walls. Sadie flipped the console and hit a switch. There was a bang from the back of the car. She didn't have time to see if the barbs had spread as she drove over the bridge twenty miles per hour faster than sanity would suggest.

The bridge was humped, and the Firebird left the ground. The car landed hard, and Sadie slammed her face into the steering wheel but maintained control. Her eyes teared up and blood dripped from her nose, but she kept driving. She risked a glance in her mirror just before entering a hard curve. The lead police car, presumably with four flat tires, didn't make it over the bridge. If it worked like she had hoped, the car would have created a block in the bridge, and with any luck the other cars would have crashed into it. She would never know.

Sadie sped through the dusty back road as fast as she dared. The car occasionally slid in gravel then caught purchase, rocking her and her father as it jolted back and forth. Before long she came to another intersection. It was a larger road that would allow her more speed. Sadie turned right and hit the gas.

She drove for thirty minutes without seeing a single police car. During that drive Sadie began looking for a place to stop so she could check on her father. The sun had crested the eastern horizon making her squint, but it was still early and there were no vehicles on the road yet. She was in a rural area so there weren't many people, but it was a school day and a work day so Sadie expected people to be going about their routines shortly. The Firebird would be noticed.

Sadie checked on her father. His breathing was steady, and he looked like he was sleeping. He needed medical attention, and that was more of a concern than being seen in a classic car. Sadie decided to Google the nearest hospital. He would die if she didn't.

After rounding a bend, Sadie found herself driving between two large fields. In the distance was a farmhouse amidst several outbuildings. The driveway was long, and she would pull in there to search for help. As she drove closer, she saw a sun-bleached sign that read *Animal Clinic*. Below that in smaller text were two names, *O. T. Detweiler V.M.D., B. K. Detweiler V.M.D.*

Sadie had helped her father on several jobs for a veterinarian back home. She remembered the vet was concerned about security because the majority of animal drugs were the same as human drugs just labeled differently. Sometimes addicts would view veterinary clinics as easy marks and rob them of their pharmaceuticals. She also knew that her dad's client had done work as an EMT. It was worth a shot. Sadie pulled in.

The gravel driveway divided two large fields, one plowed under for winter and the other had unharvested hay growing in it. The driveway fanned out to a large lot surrounded by several barn-like buildings. One had a large overhang on the front and sides. Two tractors were parked under it but there was an empty space to the side. Sadie backed in such that the Firebird could not be seen from the farmhouse.

After reloading her Sig to capacity, she removed the battery from her phone, and whispered to her dad. "I'll be back soon. I'm going to try to get help. Don't go anywhere." She smiled at her joke. There was no reaction from Brian. Disheartened by the lack of response, Sadie slid out of the car and retrieved the camo netting from the back seat. She hurriedly draped it over the front of the car, stuffed the pistol in her waistband, and slowly walked to the farmhouse.

She knocked on a faded screen door and heard a stirring inside. Soon a woman that Sadie judged to be in her mid-sixties, answered the door. Seeing Sadie's bruised face, dark bags under eyes, and stains of smoke, forest detritus, and blood, she exclaimed, "Oh my word, child! What on earth happened to you? Come in, come in. Let me help you." She had a comforting voice and a heavy southern drawl.

"It's not me that needs help. It's my… friend. He's hurt real bad."

"Worse than you?"

"Please help me?"

"Of course." The woman stepped out the door then stuck her head back in and yelled, "Otto! Get outta bed. We got an emergency outside!" Not waiting for an answer, the woman ushered Sadie to show her her friend.

Sadie led the woman to the Firebird. She was about to remove the netting when a helicopter appeared in the distance. Sadie studied it as it flew nearer. She let go of the netting allowing it to drape over the car and she pressed against the wall under the big overhang. The copter continued on its path and Sadie relaxed. Her behavior did not go unnoticed by the woman.

"Well, I was about to ask why you didn't go to the county hospital. I guess that answered my question."

Sadie didn't say a word. She lifted the netting and opened the door.

The woman gasped. "He's been shot!" She knelt beside Brian and looked at his wound. The smell coming from it was pretty rank. "And the bullet hit an intestine. Honey, you really should get him to a hospital."

"I think you might be a better option." Sadie wasn't trying to sound menacing, but her tone let the vet know she meant business.

The two stared at each other for a few seconds until the awkward silence was broken when the woman's husband, Otto, came around the corner. "Holy shit, what happened to him? Is that a bullet wound?"

The woman nodded. "Honey, let's get a cart and move him inside. They can't go to a hospital."

"Why the hell not?" Otto protested. "He needs…"

Sadie didn't utter a word. She gently brushed her camouflaged jacket open to reveal her Sig stuck in her waistband. Otto got the hint. He brought a large cart used for hauling sick goats and sheep and parked it next to the Firebird. When the three of them lifted Brian onto the cart it became evident to the veterinarians that Sadie was injured too.

The trio got Brian inside the clinic and into a surgery room. Dr. Barbara Detweiler warned that while they were very clean and sterile for animals, they were not up to the cleanliness standards of human treatment. Sadie said to do their best, then she sat down.

"You aren't looking so good yourself. Let me take a look while Otto preps *your friend*."

"I'll be fine." Sadie shook her head and felt dizzy. "Just get him fixed up."

The stainless-steel table in the veterinary surgical room was big enough to hold large dogs but not humans. The woman doctor began removing Brian's shirt while Otto called upstairs to their granddaughter for help. Sadie heard the exterior door creak open, and the screen door bang shut. Footfalls thudded from the second floor of the clinic and resonated down the steps as their granddaughter ran to catch up with Otto. Again, the screen door banged closed.

Sadie watched as the man returned with sawhorses followed by the young woman carrying some heavy planks. They disappeared once more only to return with a full sheet of three quarter inch plywood and a sheet of plastic. The plywood was set on the planks and the plastic sheet covered the makeshift table.

The woman said, "Maggie, wipe the plastic."

The younger woman did as she was told. She opened a sterile gauze pad and poured a surgical cleanser from a brown glass bottle. By the time she had wiped the entire plastic sheet the animal doctors were lifting Brian from the cart to the table.

In the process of moving a shirtless Brian, the woman saw the gash in his back and the haphazard stitching. Smiling at Sadie, she asked, "Is that your work?"

Sadie never answered. She was slumped in a chair fighting a losing battle to remain conscious.

Chapter 32

Custer had to be dreaming that his phone was ringing. The ringing stopped and Custer lapsed into a deeper sleep. The ringing started again. It was not a dream. Reaching across the sleeping woman who lay next to him, Custer snatched the phone from his nightstand. "This had better be beyond important."

"Um… Mr. Custer, sir? This is Travis. I…"

"Spit it out, Farley!"

"Dr. Rollins is dead."

Custer's ire was replaced by shock. Now fully alert, he propped himself up on his elbow and told Travis Farley to repeat the statement.

"Dr. Rollins is dead. I haven't seen the body, but Martin said he was shot. He said The Geek was killed too." Farley paused more out of fear than to let the news sink in. "Martin said everyone else is dead, too."

Custer listened intently. "How did this happen?"

"I'm not sure yet. Martin is a mess, and I can't talk to him with all of his drama." Farley steeled himself in preparation for what he had to say next. "Plus, the house is on fire. *Everything* is on fire."

"Fire?" Custer growled.

"Yeah. Martin didn't say how that happened but the house, the woods, everything is on fire. They're trying to put it out now, but they have to stop the forest fire before they can get to the house.

There was an explosion when I got here. At first, I thought it was a bomb but I'm guessing it was the propane tank that exploded."

Custer rubbed his eyes. His anger took a new angle. "And just how the fuck did this occur with two road blocks checking every goddam car that came down that road? Were you asleep?"

"No," Farley panicked. "No, sir. We were up all night. Nobody came our way. I got there at midnight. The other guy went home. It was me, Jerry, and Sam. Nobody came down that road."

"And the other road block?" snarled a now thoroughly enraged Custer.

"I don't know. I might guess they are dead. Ben's ride was used to block the driveway at the gate and the cop car was blocking the drive up farther. I had to push it out of the way with my Chevy. I couldn't look around much because of the fire. Then the explosion and Martin and all hell broke loose." Farley was scared. He was trying to give details, but they weren't coming in the sequence they occurred. "We heard gun shots from where we were at. That's why we packed up and came over to the house."

Custer said nothing.

"You'd best get over here, Mr. Custer." Farley waited a beat. "Sir?"

Custer had already ended the call.

Custer angrily shoved the sleeping woman out of his way with such force she landed flat on her back on the floor. Before she could voice a complaint, he yelled, "Get out!"

Confused, she replied, "I thought you wanted me for the whole day?"

"Get out!" Custer roared. "If I had time to clean the mess, I'd shoot you in the head and throw you in the lake."

The woman was about to fire an insult, but Custer grabbed a baseball bat. She cursed and quickly grabbed her clothing. As she was picking her clothes up, Custer kicked her, sending her sprawling. She scrambled to her feet as Custer started after her with the bat in hand. Clutching her clothing, the woman scurried through the tiny apartment, flung the door open and ran naked into the frigid morning air. The frost-covered grass felt like spikes on her bare feet as she sought refuge from the crazed man.

Custer had grabbed her stiletto heeled shoes and cell phone that she had left behind. He stepped outside and threw them at her. The shoes fluttered harmlessly to the ground, but the phone hit her in the back. Crying, she grabbed her things and scrambled to an open outbuilding that housed boats waiting for repair.

Dalton Custer got dressed and stormed out of the apartment that he inhabited more than his house. He started his BMW 735i and stomped on the gas pedal. Spitting gravel, he tore out of the parking lot and onto the road. On normal days, with normal traffic, at normal speeds, it took just under thirty minutes to get from the boat shop to Rollins' estate. Running stop signs and passing two school buses with their lights flashing while children boarded, Custer made it in just over twenty.

The irascible former Philly cop emerged from his car and everyone, but Travis Farley seemed to shrink away. Instead, Farley stepped forward and initiated conversation. "We still haven't been able to get to the house. The fire's too hot but they are containing it."

"Containing it. What the hell is that?"

"The fire was spreading real fast, Mr. Custer. The fire fighters had to stop the spread first then start knocking it down. They're saying it might be another hour yet and even then it's gonna be hot." Farley paused. "We found the guys from the other road block. All dead. Their bodies were thrown over the edge of the road. They even killed the whore. A fireman found the dogs."

Rage seething from every pore, Custer said nothing. He just stared at Farley. On some level he had a glimmer of respect for Farley. Nobody else had the balls to approach him. Custer calmed his tone. "Martin is the only survivor?"

Farley nodded.

"Why?"

Farley didn't have an answer.

Custer brushed past Farley and marched up to Benner. "What happened?"

Benner sobbed. "They killed Cooper."

"No shit. I'm aware of that. They killed *everyone,* right?"

Martin Benner nodded. He looked like a toddler being punished by a parent.

"So why are you here?"

Benner looked confused. "What do you mean?"

"These guys, whoever the hell they are, killed everything in sight, right? Rollins, The Geek, all the men, the guys at the road block, the whore…" Custer stepped uncomfortably close to Benner. "They even killed the dogs, Martin. The *dogs* are dead, Martin!" Custer leaned even closer to Benner and snarled, "So why is it that *you* are still alive?"

Benner's breathing became heavy. Again, he pouted like a toddler. His chin trembled. His hands shook as he wiped his nose. "I don't like what you are implying, Dalton."

Custer squeezed his eyes shut. He hated Martin Benner. He had hated the man from day one. And he really hated talking to him. Benner's flamboyant queerness disgusted Custer and to top it off, Benner not only used Custer's first name, but he pronounced it in the most peculiar manner. He made it sound like two separate words instead of two syllables. It came out like Dahl Ton with over-emphasis on the T.

Custer snarled, "From the beginning. Tell me everything."

Benner reiterated the events of the evening. Slightly less panicked, his account of the attack was in a more logical order. Again, he referred to many attackers which Custer delved into a little deeper. "How do you know there were so many attackers? Did you see them?"

Benner pondered the question carefully before conceding, "No." Custer raised an eyebrow and Benner defended his position. "But bullets were flying all over the place. I heard them. There just had to be a lot of men out there."

"Is it possible you heard sounds from the fire?" Custer had interviewed many eyewitnesses over the years. No matter how intelligent or sober a person was, under extreme duress their mind often filled in the blanks. Sometimes a car that a witness initially said to be red was actually another color, but the witness had focused on the taillights. In this case, the crackling of the fire could have sounded like multiple shooters. Custer had learned to ask the right questions to pry the actual events from witnesses.

Again, Benner thought hard. He was mostly preoccupied by the death of his life partner. He seemed defeated when he shrugged, "Maybe."

"And is it possible that many of the gunshots you may have heard were coming from our guys trying to pin down the assassin?"

"Assassin? Are you saying one person did all this?" Benner fanned his arm dramatically gesturing to the massive amount of destruction. "Seriously, Dalton. One person? I don't think so."

"Why not? Once started, a fire takes on a life of its own. One person strategically starts a fire then waits for his target to funnel out to where he is most vulnerable. Like shooting fish in a barrel. It's pretty smart if you ask me."

"I didn't ask you, Dalton!" Benner was growing hysterical again. "We were finally going to be married! And now my Cooper is dead! Where were you to protect him?"

Custer narrowed his eyes. "Don't go there with me."

Benner began crying and sought comfort from Betsy. Custer removed himself from Benner's presence. The man disgusted him. All gays disgusted him. He had been in Rollins' employ for over two years before learning of his homosexuality. If Custer had known sooner, he never would have taken the job. By the time he learned of it, Custer had already developed a respect for Dr. Cooper Rollins and, as difficult as it was, Custer looked past the man's sexual preference. The flamboyant Martin Benner however, was a much different story.

Ironically it was Benner who suggested that Rollins hire a security detail after Rollins was stabbed by a pimp who viewed him as a rival.

Cooper Rollins had been a popular family doctor in a very conservative area of rural Kentucky. He had made an easily mistaken misdiagnosis of a child once and the family that Dr. Rollins had watched grow up over the years decided to go for some easy money and sue him. The mistake was hardly life threatening but with the help of an unscrupulous attorney, the family made a malpractice case against Dr. Rollins that was the topic of gossip throughout the region Rollins served.

During the trial, Rollins' homosexuality was brought to light. Rollins' practice was located in a very conservative region of the Bible Belt. Consequently, he began to lose patients. The family was awarded a paltry settlement but the damage to Rollins had been devastating. It seemed as if the entire community had turned against him. The only one who'd remained loyal to Rollins was his boyfriend, Martin Benner.

Rollins could no longer maintain his lifestyle and fell into a deep depression. He moved in with Benner but remained depressed until the day that a young woman showed up at their door. She was a hooker who had been badly beaten by a john and sought medical attention from Rollins.

The woman wanted to compensate Dr. Rollins but just being able to help somebody was enough for him. She insisted and Benner suggested renting a room to her. It would be some income and she could continue her business in a safer place. The woman agreed and shortly thereafter asked if a friend could move in as well. That started an enterprise.

Rollins and Benner grew a prostitution business by treating their employees with dignity and fairness. Rollins was the front man and Benner, using his degree in accounting, handled the behind-the-scenes work. Eventually they needed a manager, and Sheila Carter was hired as a madam to oversee the now several brothels. As the business grew, so did the tempers of local authorities and rival pimps. Using payouts and coupons to the brothels, Rollins made arrangements with the right people to keep law enforcement looking the other way, but the rivals were another matter.

As the prostitution business continued to flourish under Madame Carter's insistence of going beyond simply satisfying customers, it garnered the attention of another type of person. Requests to accommodate fetishes became a challenge for Carter. Unbeknownst to Rollins and Benner, she began bringing in *employees* who were not necessarily willing participants. She allocated one brothel specifically for this, and thus another facet of Rollins' and Benner's business had blossomed – human trafficking.

Accommodating the growing list of fetishes was done at outrageous prices and soon one of the customers offered to buy the *employee* of his desire. Madame Carter was all about the money and began selling people at auction. By the time Benner and Rollins had learned of Carter's actions it was already immensely profitable. Profits were triple what the other brothels were producing, and Benner suggested that maybe it was a way to screw the community that had screwed Dr. Cooper Rollins. Rollins still harbored enough resentment to agree.

It was about that time when Rollins had survived a stabbing attack from a rival pimp who rightfully blamed Rollins for the loss of his clients. Benner suggested they get a security specialist and through a rumor, Rollins became aware of a retired Philadelphia police officer who had returned to the area. He was a regular at one of the brothels. Carter knew him and facilitated a meeting between Dr. Cooper Rollins and Dalton Custer.

Rollins was a fantastic judge of character and immediately offered Custer a job. He knew exactly what he was getting when he hired Custer. He also knew it was best to keep a man like Custer far away from a man like Benner. It had been another two years before Benner and Custer met. After that Rollins did his best to keep the two apart. Benner just assumed everyone he ever met liked him. Rollins knew that was not true. He knew Benner's flamboyance made some people uncomfortable. One of those people was Custer.

Over the years Custer had thwarted several attacks on Rollins and his business interests. He also conducted strategic counter attacks or preemptive strikes to keep competition at a comfortable distance. And on the rare occasion that somebody did harm the enterprise, Custer made sure the persons responsible were found and made an example of.

Custer did his best to not dwell on Benner out of respect for his boss. In turn, Rollins made busy-work for Benner or sent him shopping when Custer was scheduled to be at the estate. Eventually Rollins and Benner purchased two bars for legitimate businesses to hide some of their profits and to get Benner away from the illicit dealings that as of three years ago also included counterfeiting. It was an uneasy tightrope on which Rollins had managed to balance for the nearly twenty years that Custer had worked for him.

The balancing act seemed to go unnoticed by Benner, but Custer was much more astute. He realized very quickly what Rollins was doing, and he had appreciated it. But Rollins was now out of the picture. Custer needed Benner for the transaction that was scheduled later that night but after that, Custer had absolutely no foreseeable use for Benner in the future.

Plus, Benner knew too much about the business. There was a trust issue. Benner's knowledge was fine when Rollins was around. Rollins' death changed that as well. Benner was weak. Custer glanced back at the weeping man. With a little help from Custer, Benner might soon be reunited with Rollins.

Custer walked toward the house. The driveway had melted and the air was rancid with asphalt and wood smoke. Custer didn't get far enough to even see the house before his shoes began to stick to the hot driveway. With nothing else to do, he decided to go to a diner and get some breakfast.

Returning to the group, he motioned to Farley. "I'm gonna grab a bite. You drive."

Chapter 33

The Detweilers went to work on the Turners. Brian's wounds were obvious and required the most amount of attention. Otto and Maggie began working on him.

Sadie was overwhelmed with fatigue. She was fighting just to stay upright in the chair. Her head was pounding, and she wanted to lie down, but Barbara didn't allow that just yet. The vet kept Sadie in the chair and helped the teen remove her sweatshirt. "Is that a bulletproof vest?"

Sadie only nodded. It felt like she had a golf ball in her throat, and she sensed her chin tremble slightly. Everything was piling up. The stress of the confrontations she had had over the week, the loss of her mother bothered her even though Mom had been lost to alcohol years before, her concern about her sister, her father being wounded, her own wound, and the race away from the Rollins estate all combined to build a crushing pressure on her. Along with the physical toll, Sadie was about to shut down. She didn't even offer much help when Barbara removed the body armor.

The vest had done its job by stopping the projectile from penetrating, but the force of the bullet had broken some ribs in Sadie's back. From the massive blue area, Dr. Barbara Detweiler realized that several blood vessels had been damaged. Maggie broke away from Otto and Brian to assist her grandmother in getting Sadie to the x-ray machine. It, too, was designed for animals, and thus was smaller than what one would find in a hospital but still equally effective.

After snapping two x-rays, Maggie went back to helping Otto. Barbara grabbed a clean blanket and had Sadie lay down on the floor. It was the only place for the teen to go and still be under medical supervision. Dr. Barbara Detweiler then retrieved a seldom used human anatomy book just to verify her general understanding of the human circulatory system.

Using a fine-point Sharpie, Dr. Barbara Detweiler made some marks on Sadie's back outlining the bruising. Then, using her beloved Echo, she set a timer for five and ten minutes. If the bruising grew significantly past the marks, then the vet would have to sedate Sadie and open her up. She hoped that wasn't the case.

Otto had been an army field doctor before settling into a veterinary practice. He had dealt with gunshot wounds and non-sterile conditions during two tours in Viet Nam. Compared to the battlefield, his veterinary operating room was as sterile as a regular hospital. He had Maggie assist him by holding a tray of surgical tools and monitoring Brian's pulse.

"Gram?" Maggie asked during a lull while Otto was involved in deep cleansing of Brian's wound.

Barbara grunted.

"The news showed a fire at Cooper Rollins' place. Neighbors reported hearing gunshots, too."

Both Otto and Barbara paused. They exchanged glances then Otto solemnly went back to work. Barbara eyed Sadie for a moment. She picked up the girl's shirt and sniffed. The semi-conscious girl smelled of wood smoke combined with a subtle whiff of gasoline. It was all beginning to make sense. Barbara smiled and whispered to Sadie, "Didja get him?"

Sadie didn't react.

Otto sniffed. His eyes watery, silently he leaned toward Maggie. She dabbed his eyes, and he went back to work on Brian. Barbara joined him. With a choppiness to his words, Dr. Otto Detweiler said, "These two will not die. Not here. Not under my watch."

Tears flowed from Barbara's eyes. Maggie dried them with another tissue. Barbara took a deep breath and steeled herself for the job of saving Brian and Sadie. "Okay, I'm good." She turned to her granddaughter. "Now listen. Go move their car into the barn. Back it in and cover it with a tarp and then stack every empty box you can find on it. Make sure there are no helicopters or planes flying when you move it. When you come back, lock the doors. Okay?"

Maggie nodded and left the operating room.

Once the Firebird had been hidden, Maggie returned to the veterinary surgery room. Sadie was sound asleep on the floor. Otto and Barbara had cleaned and sutured Brian's intestine and were flushing the wound in preparation of closing that too. They had discovered that the bullet had passed through Brian, hitting the side of his large intestine enough to open it.

Closing the wound in the organ was not nearly as precarious as closing the wound in his muscle and skin. If any fecal matter was missed, it would lead to an infection that could be fatal. If the infection didn't end the man's life, the trip to the hospital would as he would most assuredly be found out by Rollins' men. The Detweilers were extremely thorough.

After they had done all they could for Brian, the Detweilers moved on to Sadie. The x-rays revealed a slight fracture of one rib and another that was broken to the point of detachment. They decided to sedate her and repair the rib.

Army field surgery was unlike anything that would occur in clinical conditions. One had to improvise and do so very quickly. Otto was a very good field surgeon. He and Barbara used a small plate from inventory that was intended for repairing bones in animals. It was the same thing a surgeon would use in a human only with slightly less customized engineering. Sadie was sedated and the procedure took under two hours.

Barbara had cleaned herself up from the surgeries while Maggie and Otto handled the final details of Sadie's procedure. The operating room was not quite ready to be cleaned so Barbara returned to the kitchen where two half-eaten breakfasts were still on the table. She busied herself by starting to put the breakfast food away. She was scraping dishes into the bucket to feed the hogs when she heard a car crunching down her gravel driveway.

She peered between the frills of the white window dressings to see an unmarked police car parking. She recognized the two men inside and immediately ran back to the surgery room devising a plan as she ran. She instructed Maggie to load two syringes with sedatives and hide behind the door if it were to swing open. She wedged Sadie's pistol into Otto's waistband at the small of his back.

Barbara returned to the kitchen. She dumped the warm contents of coffee creamer into a half-full glass of orange juice creating a curdled mixture. She then found the top of the onion she had cut for fried potatoes. She grabbed a napkin and set the cream and juice mixture on a table next to door. Just as the men had reached the porch, Barbara squeezed the onion below her nostrils and inhaled deeply. It burned and instantly made her eyes watery.

One of the men pounded loudly on the door.

Barbara waited. Maggie had left the sign on the door such that it read CLOSED.

The man knocked again, even louder.

Sniffing and watery-eyed, Dr. Barbara Detweiler appeared at the door. In an artificially hoarse voice she croaked, "We're closed today."

"Open up, Barbara. We have some questions for you."

Barbara made them wait a beat then unlocked the door. Her nose was red and runny, her eyes glassy and red. She coughed. "What?'

The men pulled away from the sick woman. "Uh, wow. You look terrible. Maybe we could talk to Otto."

"He's in bed. He's got it worse than me. Maggie, too. What do you want, Skip?"

The man sighed. "Any abnormal activity here today? Strangers coming by or did you hear or see a hot rod car come through?"

Barbara gave him a look as if to say 'You're kidding, right?' "Skip. Except for when I…" Barbara feigned a cough. She turned her head away from the men and continued coughing out of their view. Quickly she took a mouthful of the orange juice and cream mixture. Using the napkin to wipe her nose and mouth she reappeared face to face with the men then pitched forward and spit the mixture onto the porch floor splashing their shoes.

The men jumped back and swore.

Barbara wiped her mouth. "As I was saying, except for when I am puking, I have been asleep."

Clearly disgusted and wanting to keep their distance, the men backed off the porch and onto the side lawn. "Well, we're looking for some suspects. You didn't see anything?"

Frowning, Barbara coughed in his direction. "No."

Skip seemed skeptical. He knew the history between Detweilers and Rollins. "You won't mind if we look around then."

Barbara sniffed and coughed, not bothering to turn her head or cover her mouth. "Come on in."

Skip's partner, a younger man that Barbara recognized but didn't know his name, shook his head. "I ain't going in there. That shit's for real. I'm going back to the car." He didn't wait for Skip's reply.

Barbara gestured for Skip to come in.

He hesitated then shook his head. "That's alright. Just keep your eyes open."

"I don't think so. I'm going back to bed." Barbara closed the door and locked it. She watched the men return to the car, scan the area, then get in and leave. She couldn't help but grin as she watched them drive away.

Chapter 34

Dalton Custer and Travis Farley had been sitting in Custer's office back at the boatyard. They had had a lengthy conversation starting over breakfast rehashing what they knew versus what they suspected about the hit on Rollins. Custer told Farley about Seamus Finney. He felt it was safe to assume Finney had failed to kidnap Hannah Turner. Farley asked if they were going to go after the hitman responsible for Rollins' death, and Custer backed away.

The murder of Dr. Cooper Rollins might be a fortuitous occurrence for Custer. He saw no reason to pursue the hitman at this point as he was no longer a threat and they had much more pressing concerns now. Custer knew Brian Turner had done the job as one of those damned favors that New York employed. Turner was a family man and although he certainly had proven to be resourceful, he was not schooled in the ways of the criminal world. Once the dust settled, Turner would go back to the perceived safety of his mundane life and let his guard down. If needed, Custer would eliminate the Turners later, but they were no longer a threat. He didn't divulge Turner's name to Farley and Farley knew better than to press.

The conversation shifted from the hit on Rollins to how they would handle the shipment due in that night. They talked all through breakfast and continued their discussion on the ride back to Rollin's estate where Custer had retrieved his car. Farley followed Custer to the boatyard and once inside the office, the mostly one-sided conversation had resumed.

"I'm concerned about tonight," Custer reiterated for the umpteenth time. Farley only nodded. "Really concerned. These new suppliers are too easily spooked. Benner needs to man up and quick." Custer sighed.

Even after spending the past several hours with Custer, Farley was still uneasy about volunteering any insight or ideas. Still, it had to be said. "What if he doesn't? What if they do get spooked?"

"I don't even want to think about that."

"Don't we… you… have to? I mean a Plan B would be a good idea, right?"

Custer eyed Farley. Travis was a good guy. He liked the man and as the day had progressed, Custer began to think Farley was pretty smart. He also was helping keep Custer on an even keel. Custer could occasionally act impulsively and with the pressure he was currently under, there was a better than average chance of him doing something rash. He got that. Farley seemed aware of it too and was doing a great job of respectfully keeping Custer on task.

"No, we do not have a Plan B." The reply had an edge to it that Custer partially regretted. Farley was only trying to help. "It would be a hit to our reputation if it fell through. We have buyers for over sixty percent. Buyers that will want their deposits back. That's bad enough," Custer rubbed his chin thoughtfully. "What would really piss me off is missing out on the auction. I've seen pictures of some of them. The pretty ones will bring big bucks."

Farley ruminated on what Custer said. "Do we have the funds to return all of the deposits?"

Custer's eyes flared with anger. "We will *not* return the deposits!"

With utmost caution Farley pressed on. "If we don't, we lose a lot of otherwise happy customers. These are all people who know business. I mean we can certainly assume that if they are going to spend forty to sixty thousand dollars on a single girl, right? They should know that things happen. If we keep their money, we lose them in the long haul. And then, maybe, they talk to someone who might make problems. If we bite the bullet and give the money back, then we keep them as customers for the long haul. It's just good business, right?"

The fire in Custer's eyes died down quickly. Farley was right. After a long and awkward silence Custer relented. "Martin knows the numbers. He is also the contact guy… or whatever." He rubbed his eyes. "I guess Plan B is to keep the business going. Like you said, we eat the deposits, go back to how we were before we got wind of the new supplier. We still have our old contacts, so I guess nothing changes." Custer frowned. "I hate to blow this. Those Chinese girls got our clients all excited. They bring a premium compared to the Latinas we've been supplying."

Energized with confidence, Farley held up a finger. "Okay, so it's a punch in the gut but one we can handle. We give the money back then try to get our own deposit from the new guy, right?" He didn't wait for an answer. "But…" He wagged his finger again. "But what are the new guys gonna do with four truckloads? That's over two hundred people? They can't very well take them back or even safely find another buyer at this point, right? They may never do business with us again, but I think we are in a stronger position than it may seem at first glance." Now it was Farley's turn to sigh. "It all depends on Mr. Benner."

Custer grinned at Farley. "You're right. They still have stock to unload and we're the only immediate game in town." His grin faded. "Benner. The key to this whole deal is a weak-minded spineless queer." Custer leaned back in his chair. It squeaked loudly in the otherwise silent room. "Maybe he needs a pep talk. Just to keep him focused."

"I think it will only make him more upset. He already knows what's at stake."

Farley sounded wise beyond his years and Custer appreciated it. The pair continued their discussion. They detailed options and reactions to every scenario they could think of. Some of the scenarios did not bode well for Benner. Although the distant future had not been discussed, both men knew that with Rollins no longer around, Benner's longevity was limited. By late afternoon the men had worked out plans for every conceivable situation they could come up with.

They picked up Benner, and the three went out to dinner. Although Benner was hardly in the mood, he did eventually eat. He was quiet and didn't seem to care that Custer and Farley were chatting away about anything from sports to the stock market. They still had time to kill so after the lengthy dinner, they moved to one of Rollins' bars and shot pool until it was time to meet the truck drivers and go to an old industrial complex about an hour away.

The group had made good time and arrived early. Now it was only a matter of waiting until over two hundred Asians, mostly women in their mid-teens to early twenties, were delivered. Benner, Farley, and Custer kept to themselves. The truckers, all smoking or chewing tobacco, leaned against the cars that brought them.

Exactly at ten o'clock, Benner's phone chirped. It was a text from his Asian supplier. **TOO MUCH GOING ON. NO DEAL.** Benner snorted and tossed the phone to Custer who stared at the text then swore loudly.

Farley gave Custer a quizzical look.

"No deal," Custer growled.

Farley nodded once and walked to where the truckers were gathered. He explained only what they needed to know and watched as the cars left. Once the vehicles were out of sight, Farley returned to Custer and Benner. He stood in silence as Benner ranted to Custer about how awful the day had been. When Benner stopped to pout, Farley muttered, "Plan B?"

Custer replied, "Plan B."

Benner looked at Custer with contempt. It was always business with him. He had no feelings for anything but his job. Benner hated the man. He began breathing heavily, preparing to lay a verbal assault on Custer. Turning his back to Farley, Benner stepped nearer, entering Custer's personal space. He was staring Custer eye to eye when Farley looped his garrote around Benner's neck and pulled. The razor wire sliced through skin and muscle, only slowing briefly to saw through the cartilaginous trachea and esophagus until the thin cable hit Benner's vertebrae.

Farley released his grip and both he and Custer stepped aside to let Benner fall over and bleed out. It was quick and silent. Once the heavy pulsing of blood had slowed to a thick trickle, Farley used his foot to roll Benner's body into a supine position. The back of his shirt was comparatively clean to the front. Using the shirt Farley wiped his hands and the garrote until they were passably clean.

Custer frisked the corpse removing Benner's phone and nothing else. He scrolled to the last text and using his own phone, Custer sent a message. AGREED. CHANGES IN LEADERSHIP. USE THIS NUMBER TO SET UP HOW WE CAN HELP YOU WITH YOUR CARGO. There was no reply. Custer removed the battery from Benner's phone and pocketed it along with the phone.

It was a good ploy. Custer would let them stew on their situation and realize they had no outlet for so many trafficked people. Custer was their only way out and they already had his deposit. He didn't tell Farley, but he would not have thought of handling things that way if it hadn't been for his suggestion of a Plan B.

The pair left Benner's body where it lay and returned to the car. Custer held the passenger door for Travis Farley on the off chance that there was still some blood trace on him. Even though he controlled a large portion of the local police, he wanted nothing of the sort in his car.

Custer closed the door and stood alone outside the car for a moment to relish the day. What started out badly had become a fortuitous chain of events. He was in charge now. He would get to live in the big mansion by the lake. Or at least once it was rebuilt. Custer came as close to smiling as he had in years. He climbed into the car, and the pair drove off.

Chapter 35

Saturday

Sadie didn't as much as wake up as she emerged from a heavy fog. She felt over-rested. She was in the most comfortable bed she could remember ever being in. It was like hers at home but felt newer, or at least unused.

Home. She was definitely not home. She rubbed her eyes and began to take in her surroundings.

"Gram? She's awake."

Sadie turned her head. Her neck ached. She blinked a few times to see a young woman she didn't immediately recognize hovering near her. The woman maintained a respectful distance. Sadie's Sig lay on a nightstand that screamed early nineteen seventies. The woman motioned to it. "I loaded it for you." There was an oddness about her statement. Like she was shamefully obligated to arm the weapon.

Sadie scanned the room as the mental jigsaw puzzle slowly came together. Family pictures, some trophies, more photos of friends adorned the walls and furniture tops in a room that looked like it had stopped in time. A varsity letter, slightly faded by age, thumbtacked to the wall caught her attention. She had done the same thing with her letter.

Closing her eyes, Sadie replayed what she remembered. The fire, the gunshots, the escape through the forest, and the chase. Dad. Dad had been shot. She bolted upright and instantly regretted it. In a loud, painful grunt, she gurgled, "Where's my father?" Shards of pain reverberated from her upper back.

The woman gently but forcefully assisted Sadie in laying down. "He's down the hall. He made it through the night but still has a slight fever. Nothing like it was earlier though which means he is probably doing better."

"*Probably?*"

"Yes, probably," came a strong voice from outside the open door. An older woman followed the voice. Sadie recognized her as one of the vets that helped them. "Your father had a dirty wound. We cleaned it but there was a little infection prior to your arrival at my doorstep." The woman beamed at Sadie. "I am very confident that he will *probably* be fine." She held a small glass of water. "Drink this and if you don't puke it back up, we can proceed to something stronger like tea or ginger ale. And then I will take you to see your dad."

Sadie didn't want to wait, but she was thirsty and she was not at all anxious to feel the pain in her back again. She winced as she took the glass.

"You also had been shot but you had a vest on. That probably saved your life. The bullet broke two ribs. One isn't so bad but the other required a small plate. You now have a piece of titanium in your back that was designed to splice a cat femur."

Sadie chugged the glass of cool water. She handed the empty glass back as a wave of panic hit her. "What day is it?"

Dr. Barbara Detweiler smiled. "It's Saturday, my dear. A glorious Saturday."

A tidal wave of panic slammed into Sadie. She gasped and flung the covers off her. She struggled against the pain to get out of the bed.

Dr. Detweiler quickly placed a firm hand on her preventing Sadie from getting to her feet. "Just what do you think you're doing?" scolded the vet.

"I need a phone! My phone, all the phones! I need to get to the car." Stiff and weakened from the previous day, Sadie flailed against the older woman and started to reach for her pistol.

"Hold on!" Maggie interjected. "I will get your phone. You stay put."

Sadie relented. Her upper back hurt like hell. "Get them all. And the batteries, too." She let the bed absorb her again, ignoring the vet's angry gaze. Refusing to make eye contact and with the weight of the world on her shoulders again, she pouted, "I'm sorry. We… I…" She pursed her lips and composed herself. "I'm just sorry."

Barbara Detweiler smiled warmly. "I have a feeling that you have been through quite a lot in the past few days. Although I would love to hear about it, I also have a feeling its best I don't know." She gently caressed Sadie's hair. The woman had a kind, maternal air about her that Sadie needed. "How's your stomach? The water hit the spot? At least temporarily?"

"Yeah," Sadie mumbled. "It's fine. Could I use your bathroom?"

Dr. Detweiler assisted Sadie out of bed. She walked her to the bathroom and once Sadie had finished, since she was already up, the vet took her to another room where she eased the door open allowing Sadie to see Brian. Otto was asleep on a cot next to Brian's bed. Barbara and Sadie approached Brian. He was asleep. His breathing was regular and strong, and his color looked good. He was not sweating. He looked comfortable. Barbara checked his temperature and seemed pleased. She led Sadie out and closed the door.

"He's stable. We'll see what happens when he wakes up, but for now, he looks good, hon. Real good." She took the opportunity to quickly check Sadie's sutures while the teen was out of bed, then guided her back to her room.

Although hungry and weak, Sadie felt good standing up. She slowly paced the room to get the blood flowing and stretch out her legs. She was very hungry. "May I get something to eat?"

"Not yet." The vet smiled. "Baby steps. When Maggie comes back, I'll get you some toast and ginger ale. If you keep that down, then we'll talk about breakfast."

Sadie and Barbara heard the entry door creak open and then closed. Maggie's footfalls grew louder until she arrived in the bedroom clutching what comprised of three cell phones. Sadie anxiously accepted them and began putting hers together. She turned it on and while she waited for it to load, she turned the burner phone on. That one didn't need as much time to fire up and Sadie pressed redial.

While her phone began to chirp repeatedly indicating multiple text alerts and voice mails, the call on the burner phone went right to voice mail. There was no greeting, just a tone. Sadie spoke in a guttural voice, "We completed our job on time. If he dies, you die. If Hannah dies, you die." Sadie ended the call.

Seeing the shocked expressions on Barbara and Maggie, she immediately wished she hadn't called Mike in front of them. Sadie fumbled for something to say before giving a simple shrug of her shoulders which in turn sent a bolt of pain through her.

Barbara nudged her granddaughter. "Let's give her some space." Turning to Sadie, Barbara whispered, "Hon, I'll bring that toast and ginger ale up in five minutes."

Sadie nodded then turned her attention to her phone. There were texts from her grandmother, drunken rants probably, so Sadie didn't even open them; texts from her sister but the time line was skewed since Sadie had just turned her phone on, myriad texts, Snapchats, and Instagrams from over a dozen friends wondering where she was and why she wasn't in school, and two texts from Mom.

The last texts caused Sadie's heart to skip a beat. She stared at them afraid to open either one as if they might bite her. She slid her finger over the name and opened the first one. It read: HANNAH AND SADIE, I LOVE YOU GIRLS MORE THAN ANYTHING BUT YOUR FATHER AND I HAVE GROWN APART. I HAVE MET SOMEONE ELSE AND AM GOING AWAY WITH HIM. I WILL SEND FOR YOU ONCE WE GET SETTLED. DON'T TRY TO FIND ME, I WILL CONTACT YOU. LOVE, MOM.

Again, Sadie found herself staring at the phone, afraid to swipe the next text and afraid not to. She held her breath and slowly moved her finger when the phone vibrated. Sadie almost dropped it. It was an incoming call from Hannah. Sadie stared at the screen, desperate to hear her sister's voice. She let the call go to voice mail until she fully digested the texts from Mom's phone.

Another call came in. This one on the burner phone. Sadie dropped her phone and grabbed the other. Rage coursed through her as she answered. "Who is in my house?"

Unfazed, Mike's smooth voice replied, "Well, well, Sadie. We haven't spoken yet. How are you?"

"Who is using my mother's phone?"

"Kid, you must always assume that your phone is being monitored. Okay? This one is probably safe, but we don't know for sure so let's think about our words before we blurt them out. That being said, I'm sure I don't know, but I might assume that your mother is using your mother's phone. Who else would it be?"

Sadie boiled inside. Mike knew damned well that Mom was dead.

Mike continued carefully choosing his words. "So, is your father well? I have the impression that maybe he is under the weather."

"If he dies, you die."

"I see. Very well, then. He fulfilled his obligation." Mike was silent for a beat. "And then some." *It sounded like the bastard was smiling*! "Lots of pieces are falling together. I haven't slept much but what a fascinating night I've had. Of course, that is all I can say but I am very pleased with him. And you too, of course. Quite pleased indeed. Have you heard from your sister?"

Sadie wasn't sure how to answer. She had listened when Dad spoke with this guy, and he often seemed guarded as if to try not to divulge any information that Mike could use in the future. Or maybe Sadie had just seen too many movies. She was too furious to concentrate right now. Her anger at Mike made her want to scream at him but she also craved any information on her sister that he could provide. Mike read her lack of response.

"I see. Well, let me assure you that Hannah is just fine. She had a little run-in two days ago, but it was handled efficiently. She is in her dorm room right now studying for her upcoming finals. My time is up. Keep me posted how your father is feeling. I hope it's not the flu. That can be so nasty."

Sadie felt her face flush. "The flu? You asshole! If he dies, you die. I will gut you like a pig. I...." She realized the call had ended. Sadie slammed the phone onto the bed. The motion caused her stitches to pull, and pain radiated throughout her back. She was so angry that she was trembling.

She had to calm down. *Nobody thinks clearly when they are emotional.* Dad must have told her that a hundred times over the years. He was referring to some situation in sports or school, but it applied equally in this case too. Sadie paced around the room like a caged animal. She took deep breaths, and eventually her mind began to narrow its focus. Mike was not an immediate threat. The texts from Mom were. If Hannah came home…. Sadie couldn't imagine talking her way out of five dead bodies lying in the house, one of them Mom's. And the dogs. The dogs had been on their own for days. She wished Dad would wake up. She kept pacing until a knock on the door broke her thoughts.

Barbara eased the door open. "Everything okay?" She was smiling so radiantly it practically made her glow.

"I don't know yet."

"Here. See what this does for you." The vet handed her a small plate with a single piece of buttered toast on it. In her other hand she held a glass of ginger ale with some ice cubes clinking.

"Thank you." Sadie was very hungry. She ate the toast and downed half of the ginger ale until she was warned to slow down.

Sadie sipped the rest of the drink as Barbara beamed. "The local news is going nuts over what appears to be a gangland attack. They figure a small army killed a local man and his bodyguards last night." Barbara rocked on her heels. She was acting like a little kid anticipating a big gift. "And that local man deserved exactly what he got!" The doctor looked like she wanted to hug Sadie but then turned and left the room. As she walked out, she started singing the mantra from The Wizard of Oz, "Ding dong, the witch is dead."

Chapter 36

"I don't know, Hannah. She was just gone. No note, nothing."

Sadie had read the texts. All of them. The ones from Mom, at least from her phone, were about beginning her new life with her boyfriend, although she never mentioned his name. She said they were going to tour the country to get a feel for where they wanted to settle down. Once they found a place, she'd lawyer up and push the divorce through and get custody of her girls.

As if. Mom didn't stand a chance getting custody because neither she nor Hannah would leave Dad to go live with an alcoholic in some unknown town. *Aside from the fact that you are dead.* Sadie's thoughts were still diluted by emotion.

"She didn't say where she was going?" Hannah grilled her sister again.

"What part of 'I don't know' are you having trouble with?"

Hannah sighed. "What's Dad doing?"

"Cartwheels." The sarcasm was uncalled for. Hannah was clearly upset. Sadie took a gentler approach. "You know they haven't been getting along for a long time. I think this was inevitable. He actually seemed relieved."

"I'm coming home. I have to pack all my stuff, but I'll be home for dinner."

"Why?"

"Huh?"

"Why, Hannah? What will you accomplish by being here and not studying? You have finals coming up. There is nothing you can do. The only difference is that now instead of Mom being too drunk to leave the couch to see us, she will now be too drunk to leave someone else's couch. She's been gone for years, only now her body went with her." It was harsh but true. Sadie felt weird saying it. She didn't like talking that way about Mom, but it was the truth. The weirdness dissipated. It was cathartic to finally admit that Mom only cared about her box of wine. "She's happy now. No more yelling at Dad for everything. She can drink as much as she wants with this new guy without us making comments. Good for her to finally take initiative for something."

Hannah was quiet. "You're right. Nothing's really changed. It's still just you, me, and Dad. Only thing different is that we can sit on the couch."

"Not for long. I think Dad wants to throw it out or ceremonially burn it."

"Where is he? He hasn't answered his phone either."

"He's out talking to a lawyer," Sadie lied.

"On a Saturday?"

"I guess so."

Hannah snorted. "Well, tell him to answer his damn phone."

"Okay, sis. Go study."

"I'm still their favorite," Hannah jabbed.

"Bite me." Sadie ended the call relieved that she had bought some time. Finals would be over in a week, and Hannah would be coming home. A week for Dad to fully recover, get him home, and completely clean the house and patch bullet holes all by herself while going to school. No problem.

School. She had missed four days of school. Friends were wondering where she was. She needed to tell them something too. She would stick with the lie. Parents had huge fight. Mom left with boyfriend. Her friends would want to come over to console her. She would tell them she went to central Pennsylvania to be with her paternal grandparents. Hmm. She wanted to think about that one. Lying was so much harder than the truth. The truth was not an option. She couldn't forget anything in her story. She needed a note-pad to jot some details. Smelling eggs and bacon cooking, Sadie decided to begin her search for paper in the kitchen but first she needed to check on Dad again.

Brian was still in the same position as he was last time Sadie saw him. Dr. Otto Detweiler was watching a morning news show when Sadie entered the room. He assured her that Brian was fine. The two were silent for a couple minutes. Otto had turned his attention back to the TV. The weekly business report was being shown with a chart of fluctuating oil prices.

Staring absently at the screen, Otto blurted out, "They found several bodies in that fire."

Sadie swallowed hard. The Detweilers knew. They had to. She and Dad had a no witness policy with Jarrod being the sole exception. Sadie didn't want to think about possibly having to eliminate the Detweilers after they had saved her father's life and probably hers as well. Neither she nor her father were that cold. She pushed the thought from her mind. "Oh, yeah?"

Otto whispered, "Yeah." He stared at the screen some more. He wasn't focused on the screen, though; it was just something to stare at. "One of them was Cooper Rollins."

Sadie tried not to react. She strained to come up with a non-incriminating reply. "You knew him?" She thought her voice sounded nervous. She cleared her throat and realized it only made her sound more uncomfortable.

"You could say that. I guess some of the bodies were pretty badly burned but somehow, he and two others were recognizable. At least facially." Otto continued to stare at the screen but still not really seeing it. "I hope he suffered. I hope he felt the pain of being burned alive and I hope it took hours for him to die." He turned to Sadie, tears streaking his cheeks. His eyes burned into hers. She wanted to look away but held his gaze. "Did he? Did he suffer?"

Shit. Sadie's heart was racing. "I... I wouldn't know."

Otto faced Sadie. His eyes burned into hers as if hurt by her lie. "No. I suppose you wouldn't know about it. You show up shot and wreaking of smoke and accelerant. Oh, and the gun. Every teenaged girl needs a silenced pistol." His eyes were watery but cold as steel.

Sadie stared him down. Jaw clenched, unflinching.

Otto softened. "Coincidence I guess." They locked eyes again. Sadie didn't budge. Otto stood, felt Brian's forehead and seemed content with the result. He lifted the covers and checked Brian's bandage. Otto even smelled it. Satisfied his patient was stable, he turned his attention back to Sadie. "Follow me."

Otto brushed by Sadie and walked into the room she had slept in. She followed and found him holding a framed photo of a family reunion. His hands trembled slightly. He pointed to a girl adorned in red, white, and blue clothes. She had ribbons in her hair that were equally patriotic.

"All of Barb's family came in for the Bicentennial. We went to Philadelphia then to Washington then back here. It was a week-long circuit. That's Colleen. Our daughter." Otto placed the photo on the dresser. "Colleen was smart. She was so smart. Number one in her class as a junior in high school. She earned varsity letters in field hockey, basketball, and softball. She had so many friends."

The room went silent save for Otto's heavier-than-normal breaths. He lovingly caressed the varsity letters and various awards that adorned the wall. He sighed and fought back tears. "She was always invited to any social outing and one day she met a guy at a party. Tony." Otto's tone grew harsher. "Tony was the anti-Colleen. He rode a motorcycle, smoked, and drank. He hated school and he hated the crowd that Colleen ran with. And for some unknown reason, Colleen was attracted to this guy."

Sadie listened. She knew girls like Colleen. Hell, she was like Colleen although she had excelled more in soccer than her other sporting endeavors. Sadie was very popular, invited to everything, and was in the National Honor Society. She doubted Colleen had ever assassinated anyone but that notwithstanding the similarities were pretty consistent.

"Soon," Otto continued, "Colleen began coming home later and later. And drunk or high. Her grades slipped quickly, and she quit sports. She was obsessed with Tony and his lifestyle. We tried to intervene, but the more Barb and I pushed to separate them, the more Colleen pushed back. She began missing school. Eventually, she graduated but barely.

"The summer after high school was a constant battle. Colleen would be gone for days on end. We tried threatening her, we tried counseling, we tried everything until one day she was gone." Otto's voice was trembling. He had to take a moment to compose himself. "Just gone," he whispered.

Sadie knew kids who also lived the lifestyle that Otto was describing. She kept a polite distance from those kids. Sadie never understood the glory in getting drunk and puking and the stoners, well, they were so clueless most of the time that she was repulsed by them. Why would a person do that to themselves? She would never understand. Of course, her mother had gone down that path, too. She hadn't gotten drunk to the point of puking but she'd spent a lot of time passed out on the couch. Sadie had no desire to ever try alcohol or anything else.

Otto continued, his voice strong again. "After that summer, she was gone. Colleen just left. Occasionally we'd get a call from the police saying they found her passed out somewhere and to come get her. She would stay home for a few days or even a couple weeks, say all the right things and act as if she wanted to get her life back together, but it was always the same. We would wake up one morning and she would be gone.

"Then, one day about twenty years ago, Colleen showed up looking for help. She was about seven months pregnant and going through withdrawal. She stayed with us until she gave birth to Maggie. She didn't know who the father was and about a month after Maggie was born Colleen left again. That was the last time we saw her alive."

Sadie stood quietly as Otto composed himself again.

"Colleen Marie Detweiler was found dead in the streets of a heroin overdose. She had been cast out from the brothel she was living in when she had become too unattractive and was no longer of value." Otto had given up fighting the tears and was now crying freely. "The person who owned that brothel and kept her supplied with drugs was *Doctor Cooper Rollins*." Otto snarled when he spoke the name.

"Rollins had cops and politicians on his payroll. They had coupons to his brothels. And of course, no charges were ever brought against *Doctor Cooper Rollins*." Again, the snarling emphasis on every syllable.

Otto turned and faced Sadie. He raised his voice and grasped her by the shoulders. "Please tell me he suffered!" Otto collapsed to his knees and wept loudly.

Over the convulsing sobs, Sadie heard footfalls approaching the room. The door burst open and both Maggie and Barbara rushed in. They dropped to the floor and embraced Otto, crying with him. Sadie stepped backward. She eased herself from the room to allow the family some privacy.

She got it now. Sadie understood the family's reaction to the news of the fire at the Rollins estate. There would have to be another exception to the no-witness policy. These people would take the Turner's secret to their grave with the satisfaction that Doctor Cooper Rollins got what he deserved.

Suddenly Sadie had to be with her own family. She needed to see her father. Speed walking down the hall, Sadie felt a lump in her throat. She entered the room and sat on the edge of the bed where her father lay. She took his hand in hers and waited. She waited until the Detweilers got their emotions under control. She waited until they left Colleen's room. And she waited for her dad to wake up.

Chapter 37

Breakfast, which had actually turned into brunch as it was so late, started out somber but soon the mood elevated. Barbara occasionally hummed or sang "Ding dong the witch is dead," which perked things up. She seemed happy. After they ate, Sadie attempted to help clean up but was told it was safest for her to stay upstairs just in case some more people stopped by looking for the assassins.

Sadie borrowed a laptop and went online to retrieve what homework she could and to email her teachers. The story was that her parents had a major blow-out and Sadie had gone to central Pennsylvania to stay with her grandparents. She hoped to be back soon. She made notes of what she told the teachers and her friends. As long as Hannah didn't get wind of the story, it would work.

Sadie had immersed herself in her schoolwork all day and the time had surprisingly passed quickly. After dinner, Barbara checked Sadie's sutures and then put a makeshift plastic cover on her wound so Sadie could shower. She was given a set of Maggie's pajamas and had planned to retire early to Colleen's room to finish reading and then go to sleep.

Otto had gone to Brian's room directly after dinner. Sadie was in the shower as Otto was checking Brian's wound. Otto had just replaced the sheets when in a croaking voice, Brian whispered, "He suffered."

Otto froze. A smile grew over his lips, and he called for Barbara to bring some ice chips. He didn't need to explain why. She would know.

When Sadie came out of the bathroom, all three Detweilers were standing by Brian's bed. Brian was sleeping again, but Barbara excitedly informed Sadie that her father had used a bed pan, had some ice chips and a few swallows of water, and smiled when he was told his little girl was safe and sound.

Sadie stayed with her father until well past eleven that night. He had slept the entire time. Barbara had come and gone until finally telling Sadie to go to bed, insisting that Brian would be okay. Reluctantly, Sadie did as she was told.

Chapter 38

Sunday

Brian woke at the crack of dawn, per usual. His tongue felt like it had been adhered to the roof of his mouth for days. He was thirsty, hungry, and had to pee. And the side of his abdomen was sore. A minor headache topped off the list of what he considered fairly insignificant discomforts.

His eyes adjusted to the light, and he saw a man snoring in a recliner not far from his bed. Brian tried to mentally retrace his path to his current location, but he could only remember being in a fire in the woods.

Brian regarded the sleeping man. He didn't know why but Brian felt safe. He felt that Sadie was safe too but had no basis for this and decided he needed verification. He also really needed a bathroom.

Slowly, Brian eased himself to a sitting position. His side hurt badly, but it wasn't the same degree of pain he had remembered feeling when in the woods. The bed creaked loudly as Brian shifted his weight and the sleeping man snorted and opened his eyes.

"Hey, whoa. Slow down, buddy." The sleeping man was now wide awake and out of his chair. "Where are you going?"

The mental cobwebs were clearing rapidly, but Brian still didn't recognize the man, yet he felt that he wasn't a threat. "I want to see my daughter and find a bathroom."

"I can help with both of those, but you need to go slow. I don't want you undoing all my work." The man smiled warmly.

He grabbed the bed pan and offered it to Brian. "Let's use this for now." Addressing the scowl on Brian's face, the man replied, "You didn't mind using it last night."

Brian couldn't remember, but he really had to go. Reluctantly, he used the bed pan. The man introduced himself as Otto Detweiler then after insisting that Brian promise to stay put, he left the room to get Barbara. Brian heard a knock on a nearby door followed by hushed voices and within a minute Otto and his wife had returned.

Otto and Barbara had Brian standing and walking a few stiff-legged steps when Sadie appeared. The Detweilers flanked their patient as he and his daughter embraced in a tear-filled reunion. Sadie assured Brian that he was in good hands, and she explained what had transpired since their arrival.

Barbara left the room to start breakfast. Maggie joined her. Sadie and Otto stayed with Brian flanking him closely as he continued to walk around the room and stretch his legs. Brian was stiff and sore, but it felt so good to be up and moving. The trio traversed the hallway several times as the aromas of toast, coffee, and ham wafted through the house.

Brian wanted to try going down the stairs, but both of his spotters disagreed. Otto wanted him to eat and get some strength back. Sadie mentioned that someone had stopped by the previous day looking for them. Should someone else stop in again, Brian was hardly in the condition to run away to safety. Brian agreed and made several more laps of the hallway before Sadie left to get him something to eat.

Sadie returned with scrambled eggs, buttered toast with the crust removed, and ginger ale. She explained that Barbara said Brian could only have foods that were easily digested with nothing that might pass through the stomach intact. That meant no orange juice due to the pulp, no grains or nuts, no corn, nothing with a skin like an apple. Sadie told her father that he would have to eat like that for at least six weeks.

Brian rolled his eyes but was still all smiles. He was so hungry that he really didn't care about restrictions. After a few bites, he asked for pepper and was denied. Again, he offered no argument and continued to eat.

After breakfast, the Detweilers came up to Brian's room and the group began to discuss the Turners' exodus. Brian was anxious to get home. So was Sadie. They had a mess to fix before Hannah arrived for winter break. Sadie had to get caught up on schoolwork and convince her friends that she was anywhere but Kentucky over the past week. Brian could deal with inconvenienced clients, but his mother-in-law was going to cause problems. He mused about shooting her and throwing her body in the river but that was hardly practical.

The Detweilers wanted Brian to stay put. While Rollins' men coming around again was a concern, they felt they would be able to handle them again. They were much more concerned about Brian. He had a small part of his intestine repaired and was far from being out of the woods. The incision looked fine now but until his intestine was healed, he was vulnerable to having a piece of digested food get caught in the repair and causing an infection. He could not go to a hospital as it would be quite obvious to even a neophyte doctor that the wound was from a bullet.

The Detweilers suggested Sadie go alone but Brian vehemently disagreed. They offered for one of them to travel with the Turners but that too was shot down. Neither Brian nor Sadie wanted the Detweilers to know their names, let alone where they lived. Plus, knowing about the carnage that lay in their kitchen and living room, there was no way anyone was going to enter the house with Brian and Sadie.

After a lengthy debate, both parties reluctantly agreed on Wednesday morning for the Turners' departure. That gave Brian about two and a half days to convalesce. Barbara immediately began a list of banned foods while the others brainstormed on how to get them and the Firebird out of Kentucky. It took most of the morning, but a plan was soon developed. Brian returned to his bed for a rest while Otto, Maggie, and Sadie went to work.

Chapter 39

Tuesday

Brian had done exceedingly well since his surgery. He could walk and sit upright easily enough but getting into the upright position still caused him great pain. Barbara had given him some pain pills, but he wasn't too eager to use them. He wanted his senses as sharp as they could be. He also had a cane if needed but that too was only a last resort.

Brian's diet was greatly restricted. No meat at all for two weeks and then it was only tiny portions. His only protein would come from eggs, milk, and creamy peanut butter. Salads, along with every other vegetable, were banned. Brian found himself craving greens, so Barbara relented by going to the store and buying him stage one baby food. Brian was not happy about it but decided pureed green beans were better than nothing. It wasn't just the baby food he had to endure. Sadie couldn't resist making comments about her father having to eat baby food for the next eight weeks.

With Sadie and Maggie's help, Otto removed the divider in their horse trailer. It would be horribly tight but with the divider gone the Firebird fit inside the trailer. They put the car in neutral and with Sadie sitting inside, Otto and Maggie pushed it into the trailer for a trial fitting. It worked. The only problem was that the Pontiac's doors could not open once the car was inside. Sadie felt claustrophobic but she would have to deal with it.

It was agreed that the Turners would ride inside the Firebird to avoid detection. It would be a very long, cramped ride with no breaks. Food and water was

packed into the car as was a bucket should they need to relieve themselves. Neither Turner was thrilled about that prospect as the car had limited room and maneuvering was nearly impossible. They didn't have much choice though so again, they just had to deal with the possibility of an uncomfortable moment.

Shortly after sunset Barbara gave Brian and Sadie someconvenience items including flashlights, followed by a teary-eyed hug. The Turners climbed into the Firebird and with Sadie behind the wheel, they backed it slowly into the confines of the modified horse trailer.

Otto, Barbara, and Maggie packed bales of straw around the car so it was invisible to prying eyes. It was pitch black inside the Pontiac. Brian and Sadie heard muffled voices from the Detweilers followed by a short period of silence then the muffled rumble of the truck motor. There was some low-level white noise as the trailer rocked over the roads but other than that the silence was deafening.

Brian closed his eyes and replayed the week's events. Not only had his little girl killed people, she didn't seem to be fazed by it. At least toward the end she wasn't. He hashed out each situation in his mind's eye. *What is the body count?* He didn't know anymore.

And what did this do to her? She changed, she *had* to have changed. Should he get a shrink for her to talk to? How would that go? There had to be limits to the doctor-patient confidentiality thing. If there were limitations, he didn't know what they were. He couldn't imagine *that* discussion. Sadie probably would resist going. No, this was something he'd created, and he would have to handle. He sighed.

"You okay?" Sadie's voice boomed in the darkness. "Wow!" She toned her volume down a little. "This is quite the sound chamber." In a loud whisper she reiterated her question. "You okay?"

"Yeah, fine," Brian replied.

Sadie could tell her father was preoccupied. "How's your stomach?"

"It's all good."

"Good."

"How's your back?"

"Fine."

"Good."

There was a lingering silence. Brian wanted to ask how his little girl felt but he had no idea how to broach the subject. They had always been open with each other. He had a fantastic relationship with both of his kids. *Why is this so damned hard?* He closed his eyes. Frustrated that the words were failing to come, he clicked on his flashlight and eyed Sadie.

Sadie's expression tore at Brian. She was sixteen, on her way to womanhood, but in her eyes, he saw a glint of an insecure child. He reached for her and gave her a hug. She lunged toward him, and they squeezed each other tightly. Brian felt a knot in his throat but this time he didn't hold back. He let the tears come as he held his daughter. She clung to her father and sobbed along with him.

The Turners held each other tightly. The sounds of sniffs broke the monotony of the white noise coming from the trailer tires but other than that they were silent until Sadie started to giggle. Brian pulled back and looked quizzically at her.

Sadie wiped her eyes and smiled. "Some rough and tough assassins we are."

Brian smiled back. "Yeah, I guess professional killers probably don't cry much."

They both laughed at themselves.

Brian couldn't imagine what psychological impact the previous week had on his daughter. She was strong, resilient, and tough. He had to rely on that. Any issues would be addressed as they arrived. He felt their bond was stronger now than ever.

The laughter slowed to a few giggles. Both Turners sighed simultaneously. The apple didn't fall far from the tree. Sadie had mannerisms that were distinctly his. He was happy about that, and it made him warm inside. They shared a few more giggles before reality finally set in.

Brian pursed his lips. "We're not out of the woods yet," he said reluctantly.

"Yeah, we have a mess to clean up at home." Sadie's words drifted. Part of that mess was her mother.

"That and retaliation. They found us before, they could find us again."

Sadie hadn't thought of that, but it had been weighing on Brian. She clicked on her flashlight and pulled her Sig from under the seat. Brian retrieved his pistol as well. Both Turners checked their weapons and made sure their clips were filled. They would probably spend the rest of their lives looking over their shoulders.

After checking their guns, the Turners shut off their flashlights. Total darkness returned to the car along with the silence. It didn't feel awkward this time. They hadn't really discussed anything, but they were good. The gentle sway of the trailer and low rumble of the tires soon lulled Brian and Sadie to sleep.

They woke up when the trailer stopped moving. They could hear the muffled sound of the truck doors closing followed by the trailer ramp being lowered. Both Brian and Sadie clutched their weapons. The trailer rocked as straw bales were being removed. Shortly, Maggie's smiling face appeared through the swirls of dust on the windshield as more bales were removed from the car.

Maggie gestured for them to be patient as she and her grandfather cleared the path. Once all of the straw was removed, she gestured again, and Sadie started the Firebird. She eased it slowly from the trailer then shut off the motor.

Brian gingerly climbed from the car and stretched his legs.

Sadie followed. Noting the glow on the eastern horizon she asked, "Where are we?"

"Maryland."

Otto Detweiler smiled. He had driven all night. He looked exhausted but he was happy. "Let me take a look at your incisions." He checked Brian first. All looked well. Otto put a fresh bandage on.

Sadie was helping Maggie load the straw back into the trailer. When she finished, Otto checked her stitches as well. They, too, looked fine. He put a new dressing on her shoulder then packed up his med kit.

Otto shook Brian's hand. "You've got our phone number in case something goes wrong with your wounds."

"Yes. Thank you for all you did for us." Brian gripped Otto's hand firmly to emphasize his sincerity. "You saved our lives."

"Believe me, we are the ones in debt to you. What you did…." Otto trailed off then smiled. "I mean for what we suspect you may have allegedly done, we are grateful. Justice has finally been served."

Neither Turner commented on that.

Hugs and a few more handshakes were exchanged before Sadie fired up the Firebird. Brian eased himself into the passenger seat. The Detweilers and Turners waved again before departing in opposite directions on their respective long drives home.

Chapter 40

Wednesday

Sadie drove all but thirty minutes of the drive back to Dunning, PA. Brian had taken a turn at the wheel but half an hour into the drive his side began to get sore, and he relinquished the driving back to Sadie. They had stopped for breakfast and lunch, which delayed their arrival and subsequently postponed their having to deal with the mess at home. Still, they had a job to do before Hannah came home and the over-six-hour drive gave them time to mentally prepare for the task.

The Turners rumbled down familiar tree lined roads until they finally approached the driveway to home. From the road, the house looked as inviting as home always did except for an unfamiliar vehicle sitting in the driveway.

Sadie slowed the Firebird for a second before Brian told her to keep moving. They drove another half mile then Sadie pulled onto a dirt road and parked. Both just sat, staring at nothing, until Sadie asked, "What do we do?"

Brian didn't have an answer. He had let his guard down during the drive home. His mind was honing on the situation at hand now, and he began thinking aloud. "Unknown car in the drive. Why?"

Sadie shrugged. "Police?"

"I don't think so. If police were on to us, I would think they would be stealthier. They would have warrants and be sitting inside waiting for us. They wouldn't park outside for us to see. Or they would have gotten us by now before we even made it home. No. I am betting it's not police."

"Retaliation?" Sadie grimaced as she uttered the word.

"Again, think how we did our job. We parked and snuck over to Rollins. We certainly didn't advertise our arrival. Whoever owns that car wants us to know they are there." Brian rubbed his head. "But why?"

Sadie's posture shrank when she made the next guess. "Gram?" she asked hesitantly.

Brian was horrified at the notion. He'd have to kill the drunken hag and whoever brought her to the house, or she'd have him locked away for life. Shooting his mother-in-law was not entirely an unpleasant thought but the ensuing snowball of lies and cover-ups would be impossible to manage. "I hope not. If it is her, she'd have cops and EMTs and the National Guard there by now."

"Unless she just arrived."

Brian slumped and it hurt his abdomen.

The pair sat in silence contemplating their next move. Several long minutes passed until Sadie viewed the situation from a different angle. "Okay, so three," she paused looking for the right word, "groups know about us, right?"

Brian wasn't sure what she meant and responded with a quizzical expression.

Sadie continued, "The Rollins group. They know about us because they tried to kill us before we left and well, we did the job."

Brian remained silent, wondering where this was going.

"The police know about us, at least in Kentucky, because the fire company had to put the flames out and it was all over the news." Sadie was still putting pieces together as she spoke. "And we can presume that both of them, if they were waiting for us, would not advertise it. They would want to surprise us, right?"

Brian conceded a nod. They had just gone over this.

Sadie wagged a finger as her thoughts came together. It was a nerdy trait that Brian's father did and occasionally Brian caught himself doing. Evidently, he had passed the quirky gesture on to his daughter. She turned and stared hard at her father. "The third group that knows about us is Mike."

Brian straightened his posture. She was right. He had never thought about Mike. "Mike. But why would he be here?" Brian rubbed his chin while he contemplated this idea. The only explanation he could think of was one that he didn't like at all. He was tired. Sadie was tired. The previous week and a half had been brutal. The ordeal had exhausted them, both physically and emotionally. "To tie up loose ends?"

Sadie began to speak but Brian cut her off. "He struck me as a man of his word. I can't explain why, he just did."

"Who else would it be?" Sadie asked.

"I don't know." A wave of panic suddenly flashed through Brian. What if it *was* his mother-in-law? *No, she'd have called the police and then texted him death threats by now.* "But again, *why* would Mike be here?"

Sadie didn't have an answer. "We did what he told us to. Hannah's safe. We talked to her. She's fine. Clueless as to what went down. He kept his word." She looked at her dad for confirmation. "Right?"

"Yeah, that's what I thought." Brian rubbed his temples. "He knows us, but we don't know him. All contact has been through burner phones, right?" He didn't wait for a reply. "Even if we wanted to go to the police, what do we say? 'Some guy we never met told us to kill somebody else we never met. Go get him.' Yeah, we'd be locked up so fast it'd make our head spin. Mike's safe from us… I think."

Sadie nodded. "But does he think he's safe?"

Brian let out a frustrated sigh. "I don't know."

The Turners sat in silence for several minutes until Sadie said, "Well, let's go find out." She put her hand on the keys and glanced at her father before she turned the ignition. Brian nodded and Sadie fired up the old Pontiac.

When they pulled into the driveway, they caught a glimpse of something that was even more confounding. The Turners owned a little less than ten acres. They had close to an acre of it fenced in as their backyard. It was fenced to keep their dogs safely on their property. Over the growl of the Firebird, Brian and Sadie could hear Arfy, one of their two remaining huskies, barking incessantly.

Sadie shut off the engine. Guns at the ready, she and her father climbed out of the Firebird. The younger of the two dogs, Murphy, was wrestling with a woman in the grass. She was giggling hysterically as the dog tugged on anything he could grab. She would try to grab him, and he would escape only to playfully attack again. It was the same style of rough-house that Brian and the girls did with the dog. Murphy took off running and King Arfer approached the woman playfully. She lunged at him, and he ran away barking happily.

"Well, it's about time." A second woman called to Brian and Sadie. She was descending the steps from their deck. "I was beginning to wonder if you two decided to just stay down in Kentucky." She looked at the dogs and smiled. "Their great. Not much in the way of protection but they are fun to play with."

Her smile was disarming at first, but Brian and Sadie trusted no one. "Keep your hands where I can see them," Brian ordered.

The young woman continued smiling. She raised her hands to chest level, palms facing the Turners. "Good call but I could be a distraction. Maybe I have a sniper in the trees across the street."

"Why would you do that?" Brian fired back. She had mentioned Kentucky. The logic he and Sadie had discussed in the car still applied. He didn't believe she was a cop and if she were with Rollins' group, the Turners would be either subdued or dead by now. "We can't implicate Mike in anything. You'd have no reason to kill us."

"Very good, Mr. Turner." The woman seemed genuinely impressed. "You guys are thinking. Excellent deduction." Not the least bit bothered by the Sig Sauers pointed in her direction, the woman held out her right hand. "My name is Erin. That's my sister, Sydney, playing with your dogs."

Neither Turner shook Erin's hand.

Erin understood and was not offended by the Turner's caution. "Why don't you come in so we can talk?"

Sadie opened the gate and entered the backyard. Brian followed. Both kept their guns trained on Erin. The dogs were too engrossed in playing with Sydney to notice that the Turners had returned. The Turners kept some distance between themselves and Erin as they followed her up the steps, onto the deck, and through the back door into their kitchen.

The smell of fresh paint mingled with bleach and Pine-Sol lingered in the air. The kitchen was spotless. The walls were spotless. No bullet holes. No blood. Erin beamed as she watched Brian and Sadie take it all in. Brian slowly eased to a vantage point where he could see the living room. Spotless. He knew bullets had hit the oak doors, but they looked good as new. The couch was even clean.

"Believe it or not, the couch was the hardest to do." Erin reminded Brian of a real estate agent showing off a renovated home. "We finally found one that matched and bought it. The floors posed a challenge as well, but eventually they sanded up nicely and we put three coats of poly on them."

Brian marveled at the oak floors. They really did look nice. Even nicer than the day he installed them. There were no dings where he had used the fireplace poker on the man from Kentucky. Like the kitchen, the walls were patched and painted. The house looked just the way it was supposed to.

"Where's Mom?" Sadie asked.

Erin replied flatly, "She's on the road with her lover."

"So, you sent the texts," said Brian.

"And I will be sending out two more then they will stop. You'll never hear from her again."

Sadie and Brian were silent.

"It's the way it has to be," Erin added.

"What about her car?" Brian asked.

"She took it with her as well as cleaning out your bank account."

Brian frowned.

"I got you covered on that, too, but you should probably cancel Lisa's credit cards. At least the ones held jointly." Erin moved into the kitchen. "Let's sit and chat for a minute. I can clarify some things for you."

"Where's Suzie?" Sadie asked.

"We buried her near the field. That way her spirit can watch rabbits and deer."

It was almost a touching gesture.

Erin motioned toward the kitchen table and slid out a chair. She sat and patiently waited for the Turners to join her.

Sadie took a chair with her back to the wall and a view of the deck and foyer. Brian took a chair, the one Lisa often used for dinner, that allowed him views of what would be obscured from Sadie's position. Between the two of them, they could see any possible threat. This did not go unnoticed by Erin who smiled approvingly. Neither Turner acknowledged the smile. Both Brian and Sadie looked past Erin's comforting gestures for any sign of trouble. She didn't seem to be an imminent threat. However, Brian and Sadie felt they were in the presence of a viper whose demeanor could change in an instant. The pistols remained pointed at Erin.

"Mike, as you know him, was quite pleased with how things turned out. You satisfied your debt to him along with some unanticipated bonuses. The men who visited you before your trip? They were tipped off by someone in Mike's organization. He had suspected somebody had been double crossing him but that pretty much confirmed it. Fortunately, the two of you handled that.

"There is a gentleman by the name of Dalton Custer who worked security for Mr. Rollins. He was the one who sent the men. He was also the one who sent a man to Hannah's college."

Brian bristled. "A man? Singular? There were four and I thought they came from Mike."

"Yes, those four did come from Mike. You lost your bracelet, so he was going to kill your daughter. That was an unfortunate misunderstanding. However, it also showed the resilience that you both have. Very impressive. And the bodies have yet to be found," Erin said approvingly. "But Custer sent a man to get Hannah. After you explained the bracelet to Mike, he sent us to watch over Hannah. She is safe and never knew exactly what was going on. As far as she knows, an escaped mental patient was stalking her. That is it. He has been captured and returned to the hospital."

"What really happened to him?" Sadie inquired.

"He won't ever be a threat again," Erin replied.

Brian and Sadie got the gist of what she was saying.

"So, you got the job done in Kentucky. In the process you managed to take out yet another of Mike's people. However, this person was not supposed to be in Kentucky. In fact, he should have been elsewhere with Mike. It turned out that this person was the one supplying Rollins with information about Mike. This person was the rat." Erin smirked. "Your kill-everything-that-moves approach worked out in everyone's favor. It saved Mike a lot of money."

Fully aware of two guns pointed at her, Erin slowly stood and keeping her hands where they could be seen, moved to the kitchen counter and retrieved a cardboard box. She returned to the table and placed it between the Turners. Neither moved to open it so Erin opened the flaps to reveal its contents. She backed away as the Turners gazed into the box.

Money. Stacks and stacks of money. Neither had seen that much cash at one time although in Brian's pot dealing days, he had seen quite a bit. It was nothing like what lay in front of them though. Brian moved away from it and Sadie followed his lead. "What's that?" he asked cautiously.

"It's from Mike. It is a bonus for how things turned out. He knew you wouldn't be able to collect life insurance on Lisa and he felt somewhat responsible because it was a breech on his end that led to her death and a whole lot of hassle for you. But mostly he was happy to have found the rat."

Brian eyed Erin. "How much is in there?"

"Two hundred fifty thousand."

Sadie gasped.

Brian was shaking his head. "No. No more favors. He can keep his money. We are square."

"It's not a favor. It's what he feels is right. No strings attached," Erin insisted.

Sadie poked through the box. She began removing stacks to count them, but Brian gently put his hand over hers. He shook his head, and Sadie gave him a pouting look. Brian explained, "Don't even touch it. We aren't accepting it."

With maternal tone, Erin added, "Never count money where someone can see you. It's there, believe me." She grinned impishly, "Besides, who in their right mind would cheat an assassin?"

Sadie smiled back but only until Brian growled at her, "Put that money right out of your head." He turned to Erin, "We are *not* assassins."

Erin raised a skeptical eyebrow. "Oh, really?"

Brian did nothing to conceal his ire. "Really."

"You and Sadie worked well together. Mike would like to have the option to use you again." Erin leaned toward the Turners like a salesperson closing a deal and flashed a knowing smile. "It pays extremely well."

"Until someone puts a bullet in your head," Brian sneered.

"You have shown an aptitude for eliminating contingencies," Erin retorted quickly.

"How often would there be," Sadie searched for the right wording, "work? I mean would it affect school?"

Brian's initial expression of shock quickly morphed into un-adulterated anger. He glared at Sadie. "Are you serious? We're lucky to be breathing after what we went through! No!"

In a low voice Erin said, "Syd and I get about three jobs a year. Sometimes four, sometimes two. It pretty much averages three a year. We started with only one though. I'm sure…"

"This is a retainer, isn't it?" Brian interrupted angrily. He shoved the box of money back at Erin.

"No. It's all yours," Erin replied.

"Bullshit!" Brian sprang from his chair. He stood too quick-ly, and pain flashed from his wound. Instinctively he placed his hand over his incision and fought to breathe through the daggers. Brian's pain quickly subsided to a dull ache just as Sydney and the dogs entered the room. Brian moved his gun toward her, but he was slow and realized if she had wanted him dead, he would be by now.

Sydney acted as if she didn't even notice a pistol pointed at her. "Hi, I'm Sydney." The young woman extended her hand, but Brian didn't accept. Nodding toward Brian's side she comment-ed, "Looks like you may not have come out unscathed. Painful?" She brushed past Brian and picked up the dogs' water bowl. She emptied it in the sink, wiped it clean with a paper towel, and filled it with fresh cold water. She set the bowl on the floor and went into the pantry to toss the paper towel into the trash as if she were part of the family. She then washed her hands, took a pitcher of iced tea from the refrigerator, and a glass from the cupboard. "Anyone else care for a drink?"

Brian ignored the fact that a stranger had made herself so comfortable in his house and sulked away from the table.

Erin steered the conversation back to the money. "Look, I understand your suspicion. Mike uses Favors more than I would and honestly, most fail. But even a failure sends a message. I don't know how long he held a marker on you, but he often finds the older ones where people have more to lose than when they made the pact. I get the bitterness, but this is a bonus. Honestly, there are no strings attached other than a request to keep an open mind."

Brian's face grew red as he searched for the right words. He even debated shooting both women, but that kind of thinking had to stop. It was Sadie that injected the logic that began to calm her father. "Dad, we could use the money, at least some of it, to install a top-of-the-line security system. With cameras and computers that we could access from our phones. You know, just in case."

Erin pointed at Brian. She was about to speak when she noticed his expression. He was thinking about what Sadie said. She muttered, "Makes sense. Maybe part of that security could be another dog. One that's more protective than a Siberian Husky is. German Shepherds are great. Rots are nice too." She scratched King Arfer's neck and smiled at Brian.

"You could get one of each," Sydney suggested.

"Four dogs!" Sadie smiled.

Brian glared at both in response. He turned back to Erin. "No strings attached?"

"None whatsoever," she affirmed.

Overwhelmed, Brian stared at the box. *It would go a long way for psychotherapy*, he mused. The security system was a plus, too. And still, for some unknown reason, he couldn't shake the notion that Mike was good to his word. He hated to think he trusted the man, but no other word came to mind. Trust. Mike was going to have Hannah killed and yet Brian still trusted him. Maybe it was because Mike *did* do exactly what he said he would do.

Sydney broke the silence. "Well, now that you're finally back, we have to collect our things and go." Not waiting for a response, she left the room and went upstairs. She and Erin had used Brian and Lisa's room as their guest room until Brian and Sadie returned.

Brian collapsed into a chair and weighed his options. At least what few options he had. Keep the money, bolster his home security and use it for Sadie's future, Hannah's too for that matter, or refuse the money and go it alone without Mike. Mike. Brian was treating that bastard like an older brother looking out for his younger sibling. *Shit*. Brian sat staring at the box.

"I'm going upstairs to pack up too," Erin said. She paused at the foyer. "I can't take the box back, Brian. It's up to you to decide what to do with it, but I have to leave it here."

If Brian heard her, it didn't register. He said nothing.

Sadie and the dogs followed Erin. She watched the two pack their small bags. After a minute, Sadie whispered, "It doesn't bother you? What you do for a job, I mean. Does it ever upset you?"

"Nope." Sydney's reply was curt and with no explanation.

Erin gave her sister a sideways glance then elaborated. "No, we sleep just fine. There are too many people on this planet and most of them are assholes. We deal in assholes. The people we take care of are the worst. They are people who quite simply just need to be removed. Most of the time they don't even know it's coming. Once in a while a target might beg, but that is just weak and makes the job that much easier. I won't go so far as to say it is fun, but we have no remorse."

With an impish grin, Sydney added, "Plus, it pays well."

Sadie nodded pensively then turned her attention to her mother's closet. The closet that was normally packed with rumpled clothes, laundry tubs full of folded clothing that had never been put away, and more shoes than could be easily counted, was practically empty. "I guess Mom took all her stuff with her."

"I don't blame her," Erin said. "A person needs clothes."

The sisters wasted no time once they were packed. They left a phone number if either Turner had questions. They said their goodbyes to Brian, Sadie, and each dog, then they were gone.

Eventually, Brian left the kitchen and the box of money. Followed by Sadie, he went into the garage where Lisa's car was conspicuously absent. The Turner's stared blankly at the space for a moment before Brian pressed the wall mounted door opener. Sadie walked out, started the Firebird, and backed the car into Lisa's spot. They closed the door and began unloading the weapons from the old Pontiac. Neither spoke. Deep in thought, they moved robotically as they cleaned out the car.

Chapter 41

The Day Before Christmas

Brian was in his office. It was five-thirty in the morning. He had been up for forty-five minutes, but his routine was now slightly altered. Each morning he had to get dressed quickly and get into the kitchen to let Snookie and Abby out of their crates. The young German Shepard puppies were being groomed into a routine. Murphy and King Arfer would also get up with Brian, but they often went back to bed after their morning business. Neither of the older dogs were particularly interested in mentoring the puppies nor dealing with their endless supply of energy.

Far too young to be on their own, Snookie and Abby were put on leashes and taken outside. Brian excitedly praised them for doing their business in the grass then brought them in for breakfast, which they ate in their crates so the older dogs wouldn't get to it. While the puppies ate, Brian brewed a pot of coffee and turned on his computer. He had the routine timed such that the coffee was done about the same time the pups were done eating. He took them back outside then he brought them into the office with him, closing the door so the pups were semi-supervised. This way he could have his coffee while he checked his email.

There were some more charges on his credit card held jointly with Lisa. Erin had managed to create a trail of hotel and food bills that wove through New York, Vermont, then Canada until Brian had cancelled Lisa's card. Brian hoped these would be the last of the charges. Over three thousand dollars had been racked up on Lisa's card. Brian was annoyed by it but on the other hand he had the funds to pay for it and it showed activity that could be traced. It also meshed with the story that Lisa had left with her boyfriend. It was the foundation of a solid alibi.

Hannah had arrived home for winter break two days after Erin and Sydney had left. It had been awkward at first, but eventually the Turners realized they did not miss Lisa. The holidays often brought out the worst in her, but this year there would be no tension, no walking on eggshells, and no unprovoked, alcohol-fueled rants. Brian's parents had come up the day before like they always did, and thus far the holiday was peaceful and quiet save for the puppies getting into mischief.

As Erin had promised, there had been a few rambling texts from Lisa's phone. She even included a picture of a sunset from Ontario on the last text before Brian cancelled the phone service. The cancelation prompted several violent texts and two calls from his perpetually drunk mother-in-law, which Brian endured.

Being a ridiculously early riser, Brian was afforded a few uninterrupted hours to think or read or do whatever he wanted. He had come to enjoy the daily alone-time. This particular morning, he was creating a framework for increased income for Lionel Breckenridge. He also padded some invoices for his carpentry business in order to absorb the huge sum of money from Mike. Fifty thousand of the cash disappeared into Brian's secret vault in his shop. One never knew when that might be needed.

He clicked on the print icon and while the printer began churning out invoices for Breckenridge's handy man service, Brian shifted his attention to another computer with another monitor. It was the new one that handled the monitors of the security system.

The system had cost over seventeen thousand dollars, but he knew of every movement on his property, inside and out. He felt a little creepy checking the cameras that showed his parents and daughters as they slept, but he didn't linger. Brian replayed the past twelve hours and saw that Hannah indeed was home before ten and that a very large whitetail buck had passed through the front flower beds an hour before he had taken the pups outside. There were a few distant heat signatures of cats and an owl but other than that it had been a quiet night.

Brian went back to the falsified invoices and made deposit slips, all payments in cash. He would stop at the bank before they closed early for Christmas Eve.

The Firebird was being tuned up and when it was done, Brian would probably keep it at home instead of at the rental home in Easton. He wasn't sure if there would be retribution from whomever had taken over Rollins' operation, but he figured he would be prepared as best he could.

He also planned to begin martial arts training. He had taken some karate in his dealing days. Hannah and Sadie both were junior black belts but that was when they were about ten years old. Maybe he and Sadie could join together. He thought he'd like to try the Israeli style, Krav Maga. The more Brian thought about it, the more he liked the idea and would insist that Sadie find time to do this with him.

His reasoning was twofold. One, they would learn fighting skills that since he felt they needed to look over their shoulders, could save their lives. Two, it would get him back in shape and he knew there would be a renewed level of confidence once he gained experience.

Brian also realized that he had the feeling of being un-average again. He couldn't deny that he enjoyed the feeling, either. He had a secret identity. Not one to be particularly proud of but he felt, well, bad ass. BA as his girls would call it. It was the same as what he had tried to convey to Sadie when he was justifying keeping his aliases and their investments.

Brian gathered the newly printed paperwork for Breckenridge and put it all in a file marked Donahue Job. There was no significance to the name thus it wouldn't stand out to anyone poking through his files. He stored it amongst the normal business files and sipped his coffee.

The pups were running amok in Brian's office. They were sliding on the oak floors and tumbling over each other. Brian donned a pair of leather gloves for protection against needle-like puppy teeth and knelt in the center of the room. The little ones charged him, and he fought them off with a gentle force. The battle lasted less than ten minutes before the puppies collapsed for a recharging nap.

Brian returned to his chair, sipped his lukewarm coffee, and contemplated another issue. Sadie.

Sadie had told her friends, teachers, and coaches that she had been with her grandparents while Brian and Lisa had been fighting. She said her mother had left and she confided in texts to just enough of her friends to ignite the gossip. Soon the whole school knew of the break-up of Sadie's parents. It was a small community, so nobody was surprised when they heard Brian and his alcoholic wife had parted company. Except for Carla Gibbons and her brat, the community liked Brian and felt he was much better off without Lisa. The school considered Sadie's absence to be excused and she was able to make up her work and what exams she had missed with no penalty. Sadie met twice with the school guidance counselor, and both times she said she felt better about her parents' separation.

It was how Sadie was outside of school that had Brian wondering what was going on. She was fine. Perfectly freaking normal. No nightmares, no breakdowns, no remorse. Did she compartmentalize the days in Kentucky? The shootings and subsequent disposal of bodies in Gettysburg? What about the gun fight at home? Did she just forget about everything like water under the bridge? He doubted it but she really did seem, well, unfazed. Normal.

Up to the previous evening, Brian couldn't say what she was thinking. Brian's parents were inside helping Hannah with making dinner. Sadie had joined her father outside. They were stacking firewood on the deck when she asked about generating a second ID, just in case. She wanted to be a Breckenridge, too. She also pointed out that she was sixteen and now was the time to do it. She could do the same as he did and get two drivers licenses.

Sadie had another suggestion. She wanted to use some of the money from Mike to purchase two Sig Sauer P227s like the silenced ones they had used on their trip through Kentucky. She said she wanted to practice, and it would be safer to use legitimate guns rather than ones that were silenced or had their serial numbers removed.

Brian mentioned Krav Maga, and Sadie was excited to try it.

At least now Brian thought he knew what Sadie was thinking. She was thinking to be prepared if there was retribution. He didn't disagree. Best to be prepared. At least that was what he told himself. She also could have been thinking that maybe she would want to do another job for Mike. On one level, that idea bothered Brian but on another level, a thought that really bothered him as a person and especially as a father, he didn't disagree with the idea of doing another job either.

✶✶✶✶✶

Dalton Custer was feeling pretty good about himself. He had spent the time since Rollins had been murdered learning the business that he had inherited. The money in human trafficking was astounding. Custer had known Rollins and Benner were making money but he had no idea of just how much. It was mind boggling.

Custer had initially planned to seek vengeance for the attack on Rollins however as things settled into place, he began to realize that the assailants had done him a large favor. Custer had inherited the business and the power that came with running it. He was wary of letting it get to him but being in control was intoxicating. It felt good. He would eventually have to go after Rollins' killers to look good to his subordinates, but at the moment Custer was in no hurry. He told Farley that revenge was best served cold and that bought him some time.

He had a lot to handle after the demise of Cooper Rollins, but with Travis Farley's help, Custer had restored order to the system Rollins had in place. It was now back to business as usual and Custer had some time to get his thoughts in order.

Farley was a good man. Smart enough to handle things but not so smart that he would become a threat to Custer. He was not as cut-throat as Custer was, but the men and women in Rollins', now Custer's, operation respected him. And Custer trusted Farley as much as he would trust anyone. He still kept checks on the man, but for the most part Travis Farley had proven to Custer that he was trustworthy. Farley was now handling some of the same responsibilities that Custer had done for Rollins. Custer still had his pulse on security, but Farley was being looped in more and more as time went by. That was one good thing that seemed settled.

Benner had handled the accounting for Rollins. Since Custer had eliminated Benner, he was now handling the books. That was a problem. Custer could indeed do it on a temporary basis but he needed someone with an accounting background. He had put the word out and was in the process of vetting two people. In the meantime, Custer had everyone paid who needed to be, the money was rolling in, and both bookkeeping candidates seemed promising. That was another good thing.

Lastly, Dalton Custer had hired an architect and approved plans for a new lakeside house to be built on the site where Rollins' home was. The architect had a weakness for women and was kept happy with a steady stream of prostitutes. In exchange, he really pushed the job along, bypassing permits and paying a little extra to get top priority from the contractors. The blackened husk of Rollins' house had been demolished and hauled away. The burnt trees were cleared and the site was ready for construction. The foundation would be started between Christmas and New Year's Day.

The new house would be a fortress with bulletproof glass, a bi-level basement, and bulletproof walls. It would be fire retardant and have a state of the art fire suppression system. It would be a bunker fit for a world leader. That was another very good thing.

Custer was feeling pretty good with himself and decided he would treat himself to a long Christmas holiday. He called Madame Carter and requested a girl for three days. She always fulfilled his requests, and she often had the girls do a little something unexpected or a variant that Custer often appreciated. That was why Madame Sheila Carter was so damned good at her job. Today would be no exception.

He was still poring over the business records when Custer heard the chime indicating a vehicle was approaching. The tires crunched down the gravel drive of The Wet Garage. The repair shop was closed for the season. Thus, Custer was confident that the car was driven by the girl he had ordered. Still, he pushed away from the desk, grabbed his gun, and went to the window to check.

A clean but older Subaru parked by the primary boathouse. Custer watched as a leggy blonde dressed in an evening gown emerged from the car. *Nice.* Then, to Custer's surprise, the passenger door opened and another tall blonde in an evening gown got out. *Two? She sent two whores? That hag knows how to please her customers!* Custer allowed himself a rare smile. Madame Carter was something else. He had not expected two girls. But why not? He was Dalton Custer and right now he was the king of everything.

The women approached the building appearing somewhat nervous and Custer, with pistol in hand, opened the door. The women stopped. One said, "Hello, we heard you needed some company for the holiday." Simple as it was, it was what they needed to say to verify who they were. Custer nodded and stepped aside allowing them in.

The women entered the apartment. No pictures, few furnishings. A small kitchen, bathroom, a living area with a sofa bed, and the office. Even the few windows were small. They smiled at Custer.

Custer pointed to a corner of the living room. "Put your shit over there," he said in a gruff voice.

"Okay," the first woman replied, still smiling warmly. She held out her hand in a businesslike manner. "My name's…"

"I don't give a damn what your name is," Custer snarled. "I don't want to get to know you. I do not care who you are or what daddy-issues drove you to being whores. You are here to pleasure me for the next three days. That is all that matters. I have to finish some work then we can get started. While I'm doing that, take off your clothes and make me some lunch. I want you two to take your time and treat me the way a man of my position deserves to be treated." Custer returned to the office and firmly closed the door.

The women stood silent for a moment absorbing Custer's brusque rudeness. The first woman slowly turned to the other. "He wants us to take our time and treat him the way he deserves to be treated."

Sydney smiled at Erin, her eyes sparkling through the colored contact lenses. She opened her overnight bag and reached past the silenced Heckler and Koch VP9SK and handed Erin a Taser. She retrieved another for herself. She readied a packet of zip-ties and two Gerber fixed-blade hunting knives designed for skinning game. "We can do that."

ABOUT THE AUTHOR

Steve Badman lives with his wife, their kids, and their dogs in a bucolic section of Pennsylvania's Lehigh Valley. His family, including the dogs, enjoys skiing, kayaking, and hiking. He and his daughters compete in several long and muddy Obstacle Course Races during the warmer months – Mrs. Badman thinks they are crazy for participating in such endeavors, but no official diagnosis has been forthcoming.

After attending East Stroudsburg University, the author spent a lifetime in residential construction as a self-employed carpenter and general contractor. This experience afforded him the opportunity to witness many types of people, learn and appreciate their passions and quirks, and apply those traits to the characters that he writes about.

His other passions include home brewing beer and Philadelphia Eagles football. His family has held season tickets for the Eagles for 27 years and counting. The combination of rabid Philly sports fans and beer also provides an opportunity to witness a wide variety of interesting behaviors applicable to fictional character development – some may call it people watching, but he insists it's research for his next story.

If you would like to discuss future books, beer, or trash talk Eagles rivals, he may be contacted at stevelbadman@gmail.com.

A NOTE FROM IMZADI PUBLISHING

We hope you have enjoyed *The Favor* by Steve Badman.
You, the reader, are the backbone of the publishing industry; without you our industry simply would not exist. As such we depend upon you and your feedback.

Please take a few moments to leave a book rating and review for the book you have just read. It is not necessary to write a lengthy review, a few words will do. Reviews are remarkably difficult to obtain and we are incredibly grateful for every single one.

Happy reading!

Printed in the USA
CPSIA information can be obtained
at www.ICGtesting.com
CBHW061909060824
12799CB00007B/123